DANGEROUS CURVES

A HENSON SERIES NOVEL

DARA GIRARD

ILORI
Press Books, LLC

ISBN 13: 978-1949764192

DANGEROUS CURVES

Published by ILORI Press Books

ILORI PRESS BOOKS, LLC

PO Box #10332

Silver Spring, MD 20914

www.iloripressbooks.com

BOOKS BY DARA GIRARD

The Black Stockings Society

Power Play

A Gentleman's Offer

Body Chemistry

Round the Clock

Return of the Black Stockings Society

Playing for Keeps

After Hours

A Private Affair

Just One Look

Private Lessons

Henson Series

Table for Two

Familiar Stranger

Gaining Interest

Careless Rapture

Dangerous Curves

Duvall Sisters

The Glass Slipper Project

Taming Mariella

A Reluctant Hero

The Clifton Sisters

The Sapphire Pendant

The Amber Stone

The Emerald Ring

It Happened One Wedding

Unexpected Pleasure

Midnight Promise

Sweet Temptation

Always and Forever

Truly Yours

Novels

Illusive Flame

Honest Betrayal

The Daughters of Winston Barnett

Remember My Name

Dear Reader,

Kevin Jackson.

This playboy made his first appearance in my first published novel, *Table for Two*. Some of you already know that. But did you know that in my original version, he was Cassie's love interest? Unfortunately, they had so much fun together, that the story went nowhere.

Enter Drake Henson and everything changed.

But I still thought about Kevin. He was a fun character and I wanted to give him his own story.

That's when Dominique Cartwright came on the scene and his story came alive.

Hope you enjoy.

Dara

CHAPTER ONE

e woke up to the sight of rage. A quiet, simmering rage, reflected in the amber gaze of the last man Kevin Jackson ever wanted to see.

"I'm doing my best not to kill you," Drake Henson said, his island lilt coating his words.

"Steady mate," another voice said. Kevin looked to the side and saw Henson's brother-in-law, Clay Jarrett. He was a large, grim man, dressed in a brown leather bomber jacket and faded jeans. The sight of him chilled Kevin even more. Jarrett was never one to smile much, but his expression looked grimmer than usual. Henson, on the other hand, looked furious. As if Jarret's steady warning was the only thing keeping him from wrapping his hands around Kevin's neck.

Kevin swallowed, frantically looking around the room. A room that was clearly not his own. A room with cream colored walls, stark white tile floors, a bed with coarse sheets and a large window that didn't offer him the splendid view of trees and the lake that complemented his Maryland estate, but instead offered him the sight of another large building and a parking lot.

Where the hell was he? What was going on? And why were Henson and Jarrett looking at him like that? What were they doing there anyway? He had to be trapped in some sort of nightmare.

The last thing he remembered was taking Cassie and Marcus for a drive...

He sat up quickly, then winced as pain shot through his head, up his left side and down his right leg. He gritted his teeth and swallowed hard as his stomach roiled. He gripped his bedsheets in a fist, determined not to be sick. Slowly, the pain released him from its vise and he took a deep breath before feeling strong enough to meet Henson's gaze. "What happened?" he asked, surprised by how hoarse his voice sounded. It didn't feel sore, but the force of his voice was nearly gone, leaving it a husky whisper. "Where's Cassie? Marcus? What are you doing here?"

The angry amber gaze narrowed a fraction, clear against his brown skin. "You don't remember?"

"Remember what?"

"You son of a—"

Jarrett rested a hand on Henson's shoulder. "It's expected."

Kevin shifted his gaze to him. "What's expected?"

Henson hung his head in defeat and swore. "I don't believe this."

Kevin looked at the two men with growing alarm and frustration. "What's going on?"

Henson lifted his gaze and pinned him with a look of disgust. "That's what I plan to find out." He headed for the door.

"Wait! What...Where are you going?" Kevin pushed his

sheets back. It was just like the bastard to leave without explaining anything. He swung his legs over the side of the bed. "Henson! Where's Cassie? Marcus?" He surged to his feet just as Henson walked out of the room, but his right leg gave way. He would have crashed to the floor if Jarrett hadn't moved fast and caught him.

"You need to stay still and keep calm," he said in a low voice.

"Keep calm and carry on? Is that what you Brits say?" Kevin said, trying to cover his embarrassment as Jarrett helped him back in bed.

Jarrett wisely ignored the barb, keeping his gaze lowered.

Kevin looked down at his leg and saw some bandages, but nothing serious. He looked at Jarrett. "How can I stay still and be calm when I don't know what's going on? What's wrong with my leg and where are Cassie and Marcus?"

Jarrett folded his arms and lifted his gaze, careful to keep his expression neutral. "The police are investigating the accident. You were involved in a single car collision."

"What?" he said, his voice barely a squeak. An accident? He didn't remember any accident. Police? The police had gotten involved? Why? His mind started to spin as he looked at the grim look on Jarrett's face and remembered the rage he'd seen in Henson's eyes. Fear knotted inside him. "Cassie and Marcus..." he said, then stopped. He took a deep breath, his heart racing. "Tell me they're all right. Tell me they're not..." He let the word fall away. He wouldn't say it because it couldn't be true. They couldn't be dead.

Jarrett let his hands fall to his hips and released a heavy sigh. "If they'd died, do you think I'd be talking to you like this?"

"How are they?"

"Not good. Marcus has a broken arm, major bruises and won't speak, but he'll recover."

Kevin swallowed, his chest hurting in anticipation of the response to his next question. "And Cassie?"

Jarrett glanced out the window, as if looking at Kevin had become too hard. "We don't know."

"What do you mean, 'we don't know?'"

Jarrett shot him an ugly, dark glance. "Just what I said. She's in a coma. The way the car hit the tree, she received most of the impact. We don't know if she'll make it or not. The doctors haven't made any promises because they're afraid to. So she might leave this hospital with us or..." He ran a hand down his face. "Are you sure you don't remember anything?"

A coma? Cassie was in a coma and she might not survive? Because of him? How could that be? He was a great driver.

"Well?" Jarrett urged him.

Kevin searched his mind, wishing he had something to say. Something helpful to tell him, but his mind was blank. This was worse than a nightmare. "No, I don't."

Jarrett nodded, resigned. "Fine."

"I want to."

"I know." Jarrett turned towards the door.

"I have to see her."

Jarrett shook his head. "You know Drake will never let that happen."

"Please." He wasn't a man to beg, but he felt himself growing desperate. "Just once. I need to see her."

Jarrett sighed. "There's nothing to see except tubes and hospital monitors and—"

"I don't care."

He shook his head. "It's not a good idea."

Kevin bit his lip. "How much do you want?"

"You know it's not about money."

"I don't know what happened."

Jarrett hesitated, then shook his head again. "No."

Kevin sensed the reason for his hesitation and felt his anger grow. Henson stood in the way. "She's your sister."

"She's his wife."

"Just five minutes."

"Not yet."

Kevin sighed, admitting defeat. He knew it was too soon to ask for favors. When he was stronger, maybe they'd let him. And maybe not. He noticed how Jarrett avoided his gaze and he felt his heart drop. He kept his feelings more guarded than Henson but Kevin knew the two men felt the same. They blamed him.

"Oh good. He said you were awake," a nurse said in an overly cheery voice, like a kindergarten teacher addressing a group of five-year-olds. Kevin didn't mind the voice, sensing it was for her benefit as much as his. She looked as if she'd worked a long shift, her scrubs were wrinkled and she had dark circles under her eyes. She had ruddy skin and hair that had been dyed too dark, which made her look older than what he guessed to be her forty-some years. He knew women, loved women of all shapes and sizes and, although he knew his day had been bad, she looked as if her day had been worse and that one wrong look would make her collapse. So he smiled at her.

It did the trick. She smiled back, her shoulders straightened a little and the heaviness of her face seemed to lift.

"I'll see you later," Jarrett said.

Kevin watched him walk out the door, a part of him wanting to call him back, to give him answers to questions he couldn't put into words. His mind was a collection of images and thoughts that didn't make sense. It didn't offer him anything about how the accident happened or explained why Cassie was in a coma or why Marcus wouldn't speak.

Kevin leaned his head back on his pillow, fighting against tears as he kept his smile in place while the nurse checked his vitals and asked him questions. His heart was beating so hard it hurt. If Cassie didn't make it... no, he wouldn't even think about it. She was his heart, and if anything happened to her, Henson wouldn't have to worry about killing him.

CHAPTER TWO

A WEEK BEFORE

Kevin Jackson looked at his menu with careful consideration. He had a choice between vanilla or chocolate. He let his gaze do a slow inventory of the cool peaches and cream in ice pick high heels and a shimmering blue dress, and the ruby-lipped mocha delight wearing a leopard print dress, pressed up against him. They really made the choice difficult. Tonight's party had been a hit just as the one two weeks ago had been. Around him he heard the low hum of voices, rock music and the clinking of glasses. Since the party was a success, his only concern tonight was which one of his visual delights he would sleep with first.

"You have a guest at the door," his assistant, Adrian Ferguson, said. He was a fastidious man with a waxed mustache, slicked back brown hair and dark framed glasses.

Kevin made an absent gesture with his hand as he watched the rise and fall of the blonde's chest; her body made her blue dress resemble waves. He wasn't a breast man—he liked a woman's entire package, not just parts of her—but she could turn him into one. "Then let them in."

"She won't come in. It's Mrs. Henson."

Kevin felt his heart leap then twist with an odd pain. He scowled. "How many times have I told you not to call her that? Her name's Cassie."

"I know her name is Cassie," his assistant said without apology. "I also know it's Mrs. Henson. Just a friendly reminder."

"Of what?"

"That she's married."

Kevin shot Ferguson a glance, then headed for the door with an eagerness he'd never admit to. He opened the door surprised by the cool breeze of the spring evening, and how beautiful Cassie looked as she stood on his doorstep. A yellow cotton dress complemented her chestnut skin, caressing the curves of her full figure. She wore her hair swept back in a bun and her brown eyes shone bright behind her glasses. She reminded him of spring--fresh, lush and inviting. "Hello," he said, careful to hide the extent of his joy at seeing her.

"I can't stay."

He felt his mood dim then glanced at the dark BMW parked several yards behind her. "Is your husband in the car?"

"Yes."

He couldn't help a grin. "Good." He pulled her forward, dipped her as if they'd just finished a dance then kissed her fully on the mouth. Kevin straightened and waved at her husband. Henson didn't wave back.

"You are a devil," Cassie said with a laugh.

"I try," he said, his grin widening at the sound of her laughter. "I kind of like it. Want to try it again?"

She held him back. "No."

"Just—"

"Kevin, behave yourself."

"I don't want to behave myself." He winked. "Then again, if I'm bad you can punish me and—"

"How about I punish you?" Henson said in a soft challenge.

Kevin looked up at him, hiding his surprise. He hadn't heard him approach. Drake Henson was a tall man with more gray than black in his hair and had all the sophisticated polish of a rusty car. Although he was a successful restaurateur of The Blue Mango and The Red Hut, known for Caribbean and American dishes, he had no flair or style. Yet, he'd been able to steal Cassie away from him. After so many years, Kevin had been forced to admit defeat, but he still liked to remind Henson that he'd once been in the running and that he'd known Cassie a lot longer. "I see your sense of humor hasn't improved."

"Fortunately, my sense of timing has."

"I've always found that people are extra protective of things they're afraid to lose."

Henson's eyes narrowed. "And some people overestimate their ability to take what isn't theirs."

"And yet I still make you nervous."

Henson shook his head. "I'm not nervous. Everyone knows that real women play with boys, but they marry men."

Kevin smiled even though they both knew Henson had won that round.

"It's so nice to see that you two play so well together," Cassie said in a dry tone. "Drake, I'll be right there." She looped her arm through Kevin's and started to walk inside.

"Where are you going?" Henson asked.

"I need to talk to him alone."

His eyebrows shot up. "Inside?"

"Yes."

"You have five minutes."

Kevin flashed a sly grin. "That will be enough time."

Henson made a move towards him, but Cassie grabbed his arm. "Stop it."

"Let him go," Kevin said. "I like seeing him nervous."

When Henson's gaze darkened, Cassie took his hand and led him back to the car. She whispered something into his ear that made Henson send Kevin a quick look before his mouth softened into a triumphant smile. Kevin didn't need any words to know what the casual, intimate scene meant. Cassie belonged to Henson and nothing was going to change that. Henson had won and he'd lost.

Kevin turned away. He didn't care. He could get any woman he wanted. He had two waiting for him. He just didn't like being second best. He tapped the tip of his shoe into the ground, knowing he'd get it re-polished later, and listened to the croaking of a frog somewhere off in the distant trees. Moments later, Cassie's scent drifted towards him and he felt the light touch of her fingers on his arm. He shouldn't let her touch him, not when he was like this, but he couldn't help himself. She would probably playfully scold him or treat him like a kid brother. He didn't mind. At times he was. *Real women play with boys, but they marry men.* Damn, Henson had hit a soft spot, but he didn't want to think about it. Right now he had Cassie and that was all that mattered.

But she surprised him when she said, "We can't be friends anymore, can we?"

He turned to her, shocked. "What do you mean?"

"I mean." She looked away. "You and Drake have never

liked each other, but it seems to have gotten worse. I always feel as though there's something else going on."

"It's nothing," he said quickly, perhaps too quickly. But he didn't want to lose her friendship. She didn't know how much it meant to him. "Hey, it's my fault," he said placing a hand on his chest, ready to take blame. "I won't provoke him anymore."

She looked at him in a way that made him uneasy, as though she could read him, then she smiled. "Good, because Marcus wants you at his birthday party."

"What?" *Why would a five-year-old want him at his party?*

"There will be four other boys and his cousin and you only have to make an appearance."

"I'll just send him something. Tell me what he wants and I'll—"

"He wants you to come." She opened her handbag. "He made you this," she said, then slipped a colored macaroni bracelet onto his wrist. Kevin looked down at the childish art project, oddly touched. "Why?"

"I don't know. For some reason he seems to like you." She winked at him. "He has his mother's good taste. He also drew this for you." She handed him a picture of a car. "It's his new passion."

Kevin grinned. "That's my boy." His grin widened as a thought came to him. "I know a way to make this birthday one he'll never forget..."

CHAPTER THREE

Drake paced up and down the hospital corridor, trying to keep a hold on his temper.

"Sit down," his sister Jackie said when he passed her for the third time. "You'll make people nervous."

He opened his mouth to reply and tell her that he really didn't care when he saw Clay come out of Jackson's room. He approached him. "What's he doing now?"

"Flirting with a nurse."

"Did he say anything more?" Jackie asked when she saw her brother's jaw tense. She knew mentioning that Kevin was flirting with a nurse while Cassie lay in a coma would send her brother's temper over the edge. She had to keep things calm.

"Nothing," Clay said and she could hear the note of regret in her husband's voice. "He really doesn't remember anything."

"Do you believe him?"

"I don't think he'd lie about something like this. He seemed genuinely shocked." Clay rubbed his chin.

Jackie noticed the motion and sensed his hesitation. He

worked as a private investigator and she could almost see his mind trying to puzzle something out. "What is it?"

"He wants to see her."

Drake folded his arms. "That's not going to happen."

Clay nodded. "All right then, we just have to give it time."

"You two should go," Drake said, shifting his hands to his hips in a classic power pose, making it clear that his statement wasn't a suggestion. "There's nothing more we can do right now."

Jackie shook her head. "We can't leave you here alone."

"I'll be fine."

"The kids—"

"Are with Miss Quinn. Do you think I don't know how to take care of my family?"

Jackie looked at him for a moment, not ashamed by the sudden tears that sprung to her eyes. "That's not fair."

Drake rubbed the back of his neck, contrite. If Cassie were here, he knew she'd scold him for being too abrupt. He softened his tone. "I just don't need you to worry about me. I'm all right."

"But—"

"I raised you and Eric after our parents died, remember? I can handle a crisis. I take care of my family and—"

Clay rested a hand on his shoulders. "Nobody doubts that, mate. We just don't want you to forget that you're not alone now."

Jackie poked him in the chest with her finger. "And you never have to remind me how much you sacrificed for us."

"It wasn't a sacrifice."

"Yes, it was," she said, knowing her brother was being brave, hiding his fear. He'd let his anger show, but not his sense of helplessness and despair. He'd done the same when he'd taken care of them after they'd emigrated to America from Jamaica and their parents' deaths, forcing them to survive harsh winters and grinding hunger.

Drake took a deep breath. He tweaked Jackie's chin. "Sorry, Pest."

She made a face, making him smile. "Remember to eat something."

"I will." His phone buzzed. He took it out of his pocket and stared at the screen.

"Who's it from?" Clay asked.

"Eric."

"Talk to him," Jackie said.

"We'll catch you up later," Clay added, then they left.

Drake watched them leave, then looked down at his brother's text again. It was simple, brief and clear. Just a question mark.

The question mark should have been replicated and filled the screen. There were so many questions and so few answers. He didn't know what to tell him. And right now talking about Cassie hurt too much.

He remembered receiving the call, arriving at the hospital to the sound of his son's screams—from terror or pain or both he didn't know, but the sound still echoed in his ears, ripping his heart in two. He also remembered his wife's silence. How she didn't respond to anything and that silence tore at him as much as his son's cries. He remembered bloody clothes—a tiny shoe, blue jeans ripped away with scissors—and rapid-fire questions he could barely answer. Yes, he knew the driver. He was taking them out for Marcus's birthday. No, Jackson wasn't known for speeding. No, he didn't know where they were heading.

He hadn't slept. He couldn't sleep. He was afraid to close his eyes.

His phone rang. He glanced at the number. Eric again. His brother wouldn't stop until he got a response. If he didn't get a response, he'd show up at the hospital and then his house. He could be relentless. Drake took a deep breath and answered.

CHAPTER FOUR

She was devout, he'd give her that. She'd been to the church every Sunday without fail for more than a year, staying late in the pews and staring at the pulpit as if she expected the resurrection to come. At first, Pastor Desmond Redding of the Jordan Lake Methodist Church had felt a little uneasy about her, something didn't sit right with him. The woman who sat in the middle pew, with her hands gripped together and her head bowed in prayer, was in her late twenties, not pretty but average. Clean. Yes, that's what first came to his mind.

Everything about her was clean, from her flat brown hair, her coat, her shoes, her face and her hands. Clean, as if a speck of dirt would be repelled by her from sheer will. Clean, pure, wholesome features with skin the color of a wheat field. She looked as if she'd been transplanted to the city from a farm down south. Wide innocent eyes that followed him...maybe that's what made him feel so uneasy. She seemed to be very watchful. Watching, observing every movement around her.

But she was a child of God and obviously wanted to serve Him, so Pastor Redding would not judge her seemingly strange ways. She rarely met his eyes when he spoke to her. If he caught her looking, she'd glance away like a frightened child. She clapped to the songs, but she never sang. Didn't open her mouth once; he doubted she even hummed, but she kept rhythm almost mechanically.

"We're going to have to tell her to leave soon," Michael Leland, his music minister said. He was a thickly built man with a great baritone voice. Every holiday he'd have the congregation in tears with his rendition of "Amazing Grace."

Pastor Redding turned to him. "Let her finish her prayer."

"She needs it," Michael's wife, Patricia, said. She was as thickly built as her husband, with a soft voice and curly black hair she pulled back into pigtails. "Heard that the family she works for is in terrible trouble."

Pastor Redding frowned. "Trouble?"

"Yes, she's a nanny and the mother of the family she works for was in a horrible accident. Left in a coma. And the boy was hurt too."

He looked at the young woman again, feeling guilty for his uncharitable thoughts. "She must be praying for them. Such vigilant prayers," he said, offering up a prayer of his own. She clearly had a good heart. "Come, let's leave her for a moment." He ushered the other two out of the main chapel.

Alone in her pew, Ruth Quinn didn't hear the others leave. She was too focused on her prayers to be aware of anything around her. She gripped her hands together even tighter, desperate for God to hear her. Another week had passed and there had been no word of improvement. Cassie Henson hadn't opened her eyes in nearly two months. She couldn't believe it had been that long. She'd only had the job for five months before the accident.

Her heart pounded. She may not make it. May not wake up at all. Ruth closed her eyes and thought of Drake and his three children and said the fervent, diligent prayer of a woman of faith. "Thank you, God. Thank you, God."

CHAPTER FIVE

"Dominique, do you have anything to add?"

Dominique Cartwright looked at her father as he sat at the head of the conference table in the headquarters of Cartwright Cars and smiled. She knew her reaction would set him off balance and she was right when she saw his eyes narrow, but the men around him seemed to relax. She was the only woman in the room, except for Margot Bobkins, who didn't count because she was too old to be considered a woman and too stupid to be considered a threat. The only true threat was her father, Abraham Cartwright, a big, honey-colored man with exquisite taste in clothes. For ten years she'd helped him run Cartwright Cars while the men around him had helped his ego.

Her father had a studio voice, tinged with the sweet taste of his Trinidadian background, that could make bad news sound like you'd just won the lottery. That voice didn't work today. She'd been passed over for a promotion and it hurt like hell, but she'd never let him know it.

Giving the senior director position to Chester Lawson was

an excellent move to any outsider, and if she'd been one of them, she would have agreed. He was a tall, brown-skinned man who wore a trim goatee that gave him the appearance of a chin he didn't have. She'd championed him when he was brought on board because her father had been hard on him, and she had trained him. Trained him to step into the very position that should have been hers. However, she hadn't been the only person hoping for a promotion. Her soon to be ex-boyfriend, Berton LaSalle, looked dumbstruck. But then her father sent him a look that said 'Don't worry, I'm prepping you for an even higher position' and Berton quickly schooled his features. It was a silent exchange in the secret language of men, but she understood it.

She'd been around those secret exchanges for years. Her father wanted to marry her off; Berton wanted to be vice president. She was the ticket. Of course, after last night she knew that wouldn't happen, but she'd deal with that later. Right now she was tired of being moved around like a chess piece. She wanted to be a player, but as she looked around at the group of men, she finally realized it wouldn't be here.

"Congratulations," she said, offering her hand to Chester, who for a moment looked as if he'd suffered a case of heartburn as he reached his hand to hers. "You'll do an excellent job."

He shook her hand, visibly relaxed, and the atmosphere lost its chilly air. Her father nodded, looking pleased. She knew the gesture would please him. He'd raised her not to display hysterics, pout, or disagree. She was trained to be the good daughter and stay obedient. She nodded back while adjusting her necklace, and discreetly gave him the finger.

MOMENTS LATER, Abraham looked down at the letter of resignation his daughter had set on his desk. He stared at it as if she'd placed a rotten fish in front of him. "What am I supposed to do with this?"

Dominique rested her hip against his large custom-designed chrome desk, glancing at the enormous, sleek airbrushed painting of a Lamborghini on his side wall. She toyed with her necklace and said in a bored tone, "Do you need me to write out instructions?"

He shoved the letter towards her. "Let's pretend this didn't happen."

She slowly slid it back without looking at him. "You know what to do."

He grinned as if expecting an insult. "Aren't you going to suggest where I should put it?"

"No. I don't care what you do. I'm finished working here." Dominique wanted to shout and say *'How could you do this to me after all I've done? I've given you ten years of my life and you still treat me as if I don't matter!* But she kept her expression controlled and instead looked at the series of awards and photos of him with satisfied celebrities and other high profile customers that lined his wall.

"You can't quit. You love this company as much as I do."

"I'll give you two weeks."

"Next meeting we'll—"

She pinned him with a dark look. "Dad, it's over."

"You're upset. Go home and cry, then come back tomorrow."

You think I'll shed tears for you? She folded her arms and took a deep breath; he was trying to make her angry and it was working. She couldn't let him have the upper hand. "I don't have to give you two weeks. I can leave right now."

"You can't quit."

"Watch me."

Her father's face fell as if he were suddenly heartbroken. "Are you really going to leave me because of Chester?"

"This isn't about Chester."

"What about the lawsuit? You know that's given us bad press."

Yes, the Kevin Jackson lawsuit was a problem, but she wasn't going to let her father pull her back in because she was worried about it. When she'd heard about the accident, she'd immediately found out all she could—even anonymously sending flowers to the woman left in a coma. But there wasn't enough evidence that their company was at fault. Kevin Jackson was just a rich man with a grudge who refused to take responsibility for his own recklessness. "You've been sued before. And the press isn't bad enough to destroy you. The lawyers will come to a deal and make him go away."

Abraham held out his hands in a beseeching gesture. "You are my most valued worker. I have so much I have planned for you. I just need you to be a little more patient."

She turned to the door. "Goodbye."

"What will you do?" he called after her.

She stopped. She didn't know, but that didn't matter. She could bluff. She turned back to him with her head high. "I have lots of plans and—"

"I'll tell you what you'll do," he interrupted as if she hadn't started speaking. It was something he did often. "You'll leave with my money, invest in a company that will burst into flames, lose your money and then come back to me, begging for your job back."

Dominique gritted her teeth. Her father would never let her forget that one mistake. That one careless risk she'd taken in her early twenties, desperate to get out from under his rule. She was older and wiser now. When she left, she wasn't coming back. "Not this time."

"You're not getting my money."

"I don't need your money."

He stared at her for a long moment, then his mouth spread into a grin, and suddenly he started to laugh. He tapped the side of his nose, then pointed at her. "You get me good."

She blinked at him, confused by his strange behavior. "What?"

"I know what you're up to. You don't need Daddy's money anymore. You plan to marry it instead. Clever girl." He glanced at her hand. "I don't see a ring yet, but when you get it, let me know. Your mother and I will throw you a grand wedding and I'll be so proud to walk my little girl down the aisle...why you scrunch up your face like that?"

"I was never your little girl."

"That's true. You were such a small baby your mother and I never thought," he gestured to her figure, "you'd fill out so much. But you're still my darling daughter and—"

"You know you make my stomach turn when you try to be sentimental. Goodbye, Dad." She left his office before he could say another word. He'd soon find out that she wasn't marrying Berton or ever seeing him again, but the timing wasn't right to tell him so. She cleared out her office and dumped everything in her car trunk. She slammed the hood shut, remembering last night...

The night was supposed to be special. She'd dressed with extra care for her date with Berton, wearing her favorite wine-colored satin dress and matching high heels. She'd gone to his place because he worked late and they'd drive to the concert together from there. She was surprised to see an unfamiliar red

Mercedes in the driveway, but hadn't thought much about it. The evening was bright and warm, echoing with the sound of crickets. She knocked on the door. Berton took a while to answer and when he saw her his eyes widened. "Dominique! What are you doing here?"

She looked over his state of undress. He wore just a towel around his waist. Did she catch him getting ready to go in to the shower? She glanced at her watch. "The concert."

"It's tonight?"

"Yes. We still have time."

He sent a furtive glance over his shoulder. "I don't think I can make it."

"I don't mind waiting. Aren't you going to let me in?"

"This isn't—"

Dominique paused when she saw a lady's handbag resting on the table near his couch. A red and gold clutch with tiny green accents. "You have company."

"A business associate."

She glanced down the hall and saw high heels and a skirt laying on the floor. "And you decided to get undressed?"

He shook his head, looking both embarrassed and remorseful. "Look, Dominique, it's not what you think."

Dominique smiled, although her heart cracked. He'd completely fooled her. She'd let herself believe that he cared. Her boyfriend of nearly six months had blandly handsome features, a great dark body and a sharp mind. *Did you really think he'd stay true to you?* her mind echoed. *Why would he be loyal to someone like you? He probably only dated you because you were the boss's daughter. He wouldn't have looked at you twice without that asset.* She'd believed him when he said she was like no one he'd ever met before. That she made him laugh and that he loved being with her. All lies.

"Let me guess," she said, pleased that her voice didn't betray her. "Business got too hot and you both got naked."

"We can discuss this later."

"There's nothing to discuss." She turned.

"Wait!"

She kept walking to her car.

He ran behind her, holding on tight to his towel. "This has never happened before."

She opened her car door and got into the driver's seat. "You can stop lying to me," she said through the open door.

"It's true. Besides, how long do you expect me to wait?"

She glanced back at the house. "Obviously the wait is over."

"I would have preferred it to be you, but—"

"I know," she said in a tone of pity. "I'm such a prude, making you wait when you want it so bad." She put on her seatbelt. "Dad's going to love this."

"No need to tell him."

"I don't plan to, so don't worry."

Berton looked relieved as he leaned against the car hood. "I'm sorry. I met her at a bar and one thing led to another."

"I see."

"I know you're angry and you have every right to be, but it was a moment of weakness."

"I forgive you."

"Good."

"But it's over."

"How can you forgive me, then break up with me?"

"Then how about you break up with me?"

"I don't want to break up. We aren't allowing this relationship to progress naturally. If you'd let us take this to the next level."

"I'm not going to sleep with you."

"You have some issues. If it's your weight…"

Dominique wagged a finger. "Careful."

"I'm just letting you know that I don't mind."

That's when she wished she'd slapped him. Or slammed his fingers inside the car door frame. That he could look at her, cheat on her, and make her feel ashamed because she wasn't skinny. Try to make her feel that his behavior was her fault. She'd wasted half a year on him, but she wouldn't waste any more. She was through with men for now.

But convincing her mother of that proved to be difficult. She met her mother in the sunroom of their family home, after her mother's manicurist had gone. The scent of acetone filled the air. Her mother sat like a queen, her nails and toenails painted a shocking blue. Blondish red streaks in her hair caught the light, her trim, ginger-colored figure encased in dark trousers and a green blouse.

"I heard you quit," Carla Cartwright said, watching her daughter take a cube of melon from the fruit plate sitting in the middle of the table. "That wasn't a wise move."

Dominique swallowed. "I had to." She sat down and grabbed another. "I can't play his games anymore."

Her mother shrugged, inspecting her manicure. "After you marry Berton, you may change your mind."

"I'm not marrying Berton."

Her mother paused. "Why not?"

"I saw him with someone else."

She looked at her, startled. "So what? You and I both know that's not a reason not to marry him. He's attractive and ambitious--"

"Then he can marry someone else."

Carla stared at her daughter for a long moment, then

shrugged again and inspected her pedicure. "Never mind. You were better than he was anyway."

"I know."

Carla pointed at Dominique with pride. "You're angry, but not upset. That's a good sign. Men are never worth your tears."

Dominique could only nod, feeling the anger in her heart grow. He'd made her cry, that's what bothered her the most.

"What are you going to do now?"

"I'm going to take a break for a while."

"That's good. Let your father feel how hard it is without you, then go back."

Dominique shook her head. "I'm not going back."

"You have to if you plan to run the company one day."

"I don't care about it anymore."

Carla's voice hardened. "I didn't raise you to be a quitter. You have time on your side. You just have to be patient. Your father won't live forever and that business is ours. We let him think he owns the kingdom, but we're the key to its survival."

Dominique sighed. That story had been told to her all of her life, but now the dream felt empty.

"It's been an upsetting day for you," Carla said in an indulgent tone. "You need to relax." She clapped her hands together and smiled. "Let's go to Portugal and—"

Dominique opened her mouth to protest. She wanted to be alone to think things through. It wasn't like her to make rash decisions and she knew there would be a consequence. But instead of telling her mother this, the phone rang. Her mother picked up, then swore. She nodded in response to the voice on the other end. "Yes, yes. Okay, good. We'll be right there." She hung up.

Dominique leaned forward, concerned. "What is it?"

"It's your sister. She's in the hospital."

REVENGE. That's the word that whispered in her ear as she looked at her sister, who lay pale-faced and weak in her bed after attempting to overdose on painkillers. Yes...Dominique wanted revenge. Revenge against men who thought that their power meant they could get away with anything. Revenge against men who lied and cheated and broke promises. Revenge against a patriarchal system that rewarded them.

She'd never tell anyone how she'd cried that night after finding out the truth about Berton—more from humiliation than heartbreak. She'd gone through a carton of ice cream and deleted all of his images and messages from her phone, angered by all the wasted hours. She'd played it cool with her mother, but inside she burned. She hated men. They were liars and losers, heartbreakers and cowards. She didn't need them and never would.

Her father saw a dutiful daughter to clean up his messes, her boyfriend saw her as something to get his leg over while he tried to climb the corporate ladder.

Revenge would be sweet and she was strong enough to fight and patient enough to get it. There was nothing she could do to Berton or her father, but she could make Kevin Jackson pay for what he had done to her sister. Although she was only four years older, Dominique felt as if many more years separated them.

Her mind still buzzed with rage at the story her sister had told them. It had been reckless of her sister to go to Kevin Jackson to try to persuade him to drop the lawsuit, but Gloria didn't always think things through. She could be flighty, but she had a good heart.

Initially Kevin had promised he would listen, but instead

he'd seduced her, convincing her that their relationship was something real, toying with her heart until he captured it before tossing her aside and continuing with the suit anyway. She'd never seen her sister fall so hard for someone. Gloria had always had crushes and there were plenty of men in line to adore her. She had their mother's trim figure and complexion and their father's impeccable taste in clothes. She wore her hair in intricate braids that passed her shoulders. Dominique hadn't even known her sister was in a serious relationship until now.

Gloria wasn't one to settle down. At twenty-seven, she always said she wasn't ready. But somehow Kevin Jackson had convinced her to keep their relationship a secret and had broken her heart in the process. He'd used her little sister and she wouldn't let him get away with that. Her plan wasn't clear yet, but she needed to take action. She would not let her sister be a victim to a heartless playboy. She'd make sure his playing days were over.

CHAPTER SIX

*A*braham Cartwright smiled as he glanced out the car window while his driver made his way through the DC traffic. He was so pleased by the phone call he'd just received that he started whistling a song his grandfather used to sing when he was working on an engine. He saw a tour bus stop and unload a group of tourists dressed for summer instead of spring, and watched a pigeon swoop down and grab a potato chip someone had dropped on the sidewalk. With Dominique on board, things would be okay. She was his secret weapon, even though he'd never let her know that. She wasn't an arrogant woman, but he didn't want her to know how much he depended on her. She was smart. Smarter than him in many ways, but not about people. He always had her in the dark and that's where he planned to keep her.

He pulled out his phone and dialed. "Good job," he said when the other line connected. "Everything's set. She's out for revenge."

Berton laughed a little uneasy. "I feel sorry for Jackson then."

Abraham paused. "You sound a little sorry for her."

"You didn't see her face. It was...I didn't think I'd feel so bad."

"Get over it. She will. She always has."

"But—"

"But what?" Abraham said in a sharp tone. He didn't take well to people challenging him. "Are you questioning my strategy?"

"It's nothing," Berton said, stumbling over his words. "I wasn't sure it would work."

"I told you how to leave enough clues to make sure she followed your crumbs. You made sure you got caught, right?"

"Yes, even though I thought it was a bit extreme to—"

"Nothing's too extreme when it comes to my daughter. I know how women think. Especially her. She thinks she's her own woman, but she's been dancing to my tune a long time."

"It's still a risk. Kevin Jackson's got a reputation with the ladies."

"Exactly the kind of reputation Dominique can't stand. I raised her. I know her weaknesses, I made sure she had them. There's a reason you'd think she was born with her legs glued shut. No man's gotten close and no man will. Trust me, Kevin Jackson will not be a problem."

"And you think Dominique can make sure he's not dangerous to us?"

"If Dominique does exactly what I expect her to do, I can guarantee it."

~

Carla Cartwright sat at the oak dinner table, the scent of lemon drizzled asparagus scenting the air. It was a smaller room than their second dining room meant to host guests. She looked at her husband with shrewd interest rather than affection. He was still a handsome man; many women thought so. She'd transformed him from a lowly laborer to a respected business owner. At times, she knew she needed to remind him where he truly belonged. Dominique should have been promoted; it had been their agreement. He didn't look concerned and that bothered her. When he wasn't uneasy, he was dangerous. She traced her finger along the base of her wine glass, keeping her gaze on his face. "What are you up to?"

"Why should I be up to anything?" he asked, sawing through his steak like a lumberjack.

Carla pursed her lips in distaste. The meat had been baked to perfection, but her husband had yet to develop the swift clean motion necessary to cut and enjoy it. Instead he attacked it with his utensils as if it were still alive. She held out her hand. He wisely handed her his plate.

"Don't play coy with me," she said, expertly slicing through the meat and creating edible morsels. "Dominique should have gotten the position."

"I didn't want to look like I was playing favorites."

"When has that ever bothered you before?"

"I have something better in store for her."

Carla handed him the plate, unable to stop a smile. "My god, you even look good when you lie."

He looked at her surprised. "Why would you think I'm lying?"

"Because I've lived with you long enough." His business and drive had been his mistress their entire marriage. "Just understand one thing."

"What is that?"

"If you break my daughter's heart, I will destroy you."

"Does she have a heart to break?"

Carla took a sip of wine. "What does that mean?"

"Now who's being coy?"

"Dominique is a very good daughter."

"Yes, you raised her well. I love you my darling, but we both know I could get more heat from an icebox. And any man who tries to get close to Dominique will find out the same."

Carla straightened her knife and glanced at her manicure. "Don't talk as if I raised her alone," she said softly before lifting her gaze to his.

"No. We both used her for our purposes." He winked at her. "You used her to get me."

She touched his leg with her foot. "It was an accident."

"A very convenient one."

She couldn't help a light laugh. "You did the right thing by marrying me. Fate is a funny thing."

His eyes darkened when she placed her foot on his lap. "Yes, but you can't replicate it. Dominique isn't like you."

Carla met his heated gaze, knowing tonight they'd share a bed, but not secrets, but she still couldn't help her question. "What are you up to?"

He rested his hand on her foot, cupping her heel in his hand. "Patience, my dear. The fun has just begun."

Dominique still didn't have a definite plan of action as she drove past the private lake and row of trees on Kevin Jackson's Maryland estate. She would initially play it by ear and get to know him a little first before she enacted a solid plan. She'd done some research online, but most of the information she found was positive, along with the many pictures of him.

She parked and was halfway to the front door when it opened.

"It's about time you got here," a man with slicked back, black hair said. "I wasn't sure what I was going to do." He glanced at his watch. "There's still enough time for me to give you the particulars before you start. I'm Ferguson, by the way."

Dominique stared at the man and waved her hands, knowing he'd mistaken her for someone else. Although she'd arrived at Kevin Jackson's without a plan, she knew this wasn't it. "No, wait, I—"

"You can ask questions later. Follow me," he said, walking past her.

"But—" She stopped. He was already around the corner and out of hearing. She reluctantly followed him.

"I was afraid it was going to rain today," he said, obviously continuing a conversation he thought she'd been part of. "But we got lucky." He stopped in a courtyard bracketed by two three-car garages. "You drive stick of course? Of course you do," he said, shaking his head. "The agency knows what we like. It's just that the last driver lied. Nearly burned the clutch to the ground." He headed up a set of stairs that led to a walk-up above one garage. "You'll be staying here." He opened the door. "As you can see, it has everything you need." He headed back down the stairs and pushed a button, slowly revealing a Bentley. "You'll pick him up at the university today. The car will lead you."

A chauffeur? She was being hired as a driver? "I'm sorry, but—"

"I know I haven't given you a chance to change into your uniform, but it's been a busy day. Okay, that's a lie. It's always busy around here. Jackson's a man who likes to keep active, but he's also informal so he won't mind you showing up as you are." He measured her dark trousers and grey blouse. "What you're wearing is suitable enough." He handed her the keys.

Dominique gripped them as a devious idea formed in her mind. Being a driver for Kevin Jackson would be a great way to get close to him. This was an opportunity she couldn't pass up, and by the time they discovered her deception she'd be way ahead of them.

"Do you have any questions?"

Dominique glanced at the Bentley, then the man, and pasted on a smile. "No, you've been more than helpful."

THIS WAS the last place she thought she'd find a playboy like Kevin. A stuffy university didn't seem to suit his reputation. An off-campus frat house filled with coeds—yes. A distinguished university building with the sound of Beethoven coming from one room and the voice of a teacher discussing the virtue of symbolism in literature in another—no.

Dominique walked down the empty halls, briefly remembering her university days. She didn't remember much. She'd been too driven, too eager to prove herself to have much fun. Or any fun. She hadn't attended one extracurricular activity. No football or basketball games, concerts, or parties. She glanced out the window and saw a couple laying on the campus lawn, kissing. The man's hand sneaking up the girl's top. Dominique suppressed a grin. She certainly hadn't done that. Her routine had been simple—study, sleep and eat. The latter two being more debatable than the former. She'd followed her routine for four years and had her life planned out. That plan hadn't included Chester getting her promotion, Berton cheating on her, or Kevin Jackson.

Kevin Jackson. He was the reason she was here. The reason she'd briefly allowed herself to stroll down memory lane and recall how much she'd given up for a dream her father continued to hold out of reach. She stopped at the room number given to her and glanced at her watch. She was right on time. That should please him. Or annoy him. She didn't know what kind of man he was yet.

Dominique opened the large wooden door, then stopped. For some reason she'd expected a large lecture hall where she could hide in the back row, but instead it was a small room with chairs situated in a circle. That wasn't what shocked her the most. It was seeing Kevin.

He was magnificent, gorgeous, and completely naked.

CHAPTER SEVEN

"Oh, I'm sorry," she said, quickly leaving the room to the sound of laughter.

She sat in the hall, her face burning. An art class and he was clearly the model. She'd made an idiot of herself. Why couldn't she have just taken a seat and pretended it was no big deal? It wasn't as if she'd never seen a naked man before.

Okay, to be honest, she hadn't seen a naked man like that before. She'd seen naked men in paintings or as statues. If she was really honest, she'd admit to seeing one in a porn movie that had been as unimpressive as the storyline and another youthful mistake she'd made with a guy who liked to keep the lights off, but clearly couldn't find his way in the dark.

No, she'd never seen a naked man lying on his side in broad daylight as if he'd commanded the sun to touch his skin with reverence and grinned with the arrogance of a god. He was perfection. There was nothing wrong with him. She'd briefly heard a rumor that he'd been disfigured after the accident and although that had quickly been disputed, she couldn't believe how it had ever gotten started. He was beautifully made with hazelnut skin. More muscular than she'd imagined him to be, heralding a quiet strength that was both virile and sensual. She'd expected a more lithe, carefree figure considering his reputation. She'd expected him to be more boyish in physique. But from what she saw, he was pure male.

Dominique touched her cheeks and took a deep breath. She'd made a miscalculation, but she wouldn't again. She had to stay cool and focused. He was a player. She'd underestimated the type of playboy based on photos she'd seen of him partying, but now she'd gotten a fuller view. She briefly closed her eyes. No, fuller view wasn't the right word. A better perspective. Yes, that was it. She'd gotten a different perspective of him. Of course he was attractive; her sister wouldn't have fallen for him otherwise.

Dominique quickly rose to her feet when the door opened and students streamed out of the room. She tugged on her sleeves, smoothed down her hair and waited. Cool. She'd play it cool, she reminded herself as her heart raced. He was going to walk through those doors any minute and she had to make a good impression. She was just his driver. He couldn't suspect anything else. She could do this. She was a professional.

Kevin walked out of the room, now fully dressed, wearing dark trousers and a checkered shirt. He looked at her and she wished he hadn't. He sent her a brilliant, brown gaze filled with mischief and he flashed her a knee-melting grin. "Ready to go?"

She swallowed and forced herself to stare at his face and not dip lower. She didn't want to remember the sight of his bare chest, the shape of his legs, the size of his…"Yes, sir."

He nodded or winked, she wasn't quite sure what because it was fast, but she felt the impact. Warmth swept through her and she stood paralyzed a few moments as she watched him walk down the hall. It took her a moment to realize she hadn't moved and she raced to catch up with him.

"What's your name?" he asked.

"Dominique," she said, matching his gait. His pace was slower than she'd expected it to be, he didn't seem to be in a hurry.

"You don't have a last name?"

"Cartw--Carter," she said remembering her cover. She glanced at him to make sure her lie had gone over smoothly and again regretted meeting his eyes, but this time for a completely different reason. The look of mischief had disappeared, replaced with a look of such genuine interest that she stared at him for a second too long and stumbled over her own feet. She quickly caught herself and waved him off when he reach out to help her. "Don't worry I walk better than I drive." She paused. "No wait. I mean I drive better than I walk." She inwardly cringed. Now she sounded like an idiot on top of looking like a klutz.

A soft smile touched his mouth. "I know what you meant."

Damn his eyes. She couldn't stop looking at him. At them. They kept pulling her to him. He didn't have to be very charming with eyes like that. But she could see something else that surprised her.

She could see shadows in his eyes, as if he were in pain, but there was no visible sign of what had caused it. He didn't limp or use a cane or have any slow, awkward movements. For a brief moment she felt a little guilty about her deception, but then thought of her sister and knew that men could be clever actors. But the shadows seemed real and they bothered her.

No, she couldn't feel sorry for him. What she had to do was necessary. She'd find some dirt on him or find a weakness and use it and then leave. He was a player and she'd play his game.

"But are you sure?" he asked.

She glanced away, annoyed that her eyes kept being drawn to the shadows haunting his gaze. She didn't want to care. "Am I sure about what?"

"That your name is Carter. You sounded like you hesitated, or are you just flustered?" He shoved his hands in his pockets. "Was that your first live drawing class?"

Gorgeous and smart. That was going to be a problem. She kept her gaze straight ahead measuring their steps to the door. "Well, I—"

"Kevin!" a voice called.

They stopped and turned to see a woman racing down the hall. Dominique felt such gratitude for the interruption that she had to stop herself from running and giving the woman a hug.

The older woman stopped in front of them. Up close Dominique noticed the brunette wig, lack of eyebrows and the woman's puffy, round face, but the look of delight on her face made none of that important. "I'm so glad I got you before you left. You forgot your phone."

"Oh thanks, Elizabeth," Kevin said, taking the cell phone and putting it away. He squeezed his eyes shut and groaned as if in pain. "I'm dying."

"Why?"

He turned his cheek to her and tapped it. "Because I haven't been kissed by a beautiful woman today."

Elizabeth Kirkpatrick playfully hit him on the arm and giggled like a school girl. "You're such a flirt."

Kevin's face fell and he looked as pathetic as a puppy left out in the rain. "That means you won't kiss me?"

"If I were thirty years younger and not married—"

"You'd still be beautiful." He glanced down and picked up something off the ground Dominique couldn't see. "Wow, look at that. Someone dropped this," he said, handing it to the woman. "This must be your lucky day."

Elizabeth took the object from him, then stopped when she realized what it was. Dominique could understand the woman's disbelief. She leaned in closer just to make sure her eyes weren't deceiving her. When Elizabeth flipped it over she realized they weren't. He'd given her a hundred dollar bill. Her green eyes filled with tears. "Kevin, it's too much."

"It's nothing." Kevin looked at the floor as if he were searching for something. "I wonder if I can find some more."

She tugged on his sleeve. "No, don't."

He tapped his cheek again. "Can I get a kiss now?"

She kissed him, then held the money close to her chest. "This helps more than you know."

He squeezed her arm with affection. "Tell Jed I say hi."

She nodded, then turned and left.

Dominique watched her go, seeing Elizabeth wiping her eyes. When she turned, Kevin was halfway down the hall. She rushed to catch up with him. He didn't walk fast, but he didn't stand still long either. She couldn't believe what she'd just witnessed. Was he a magician? How had he managed to make that money appear out of nowhere? She hadn't seen him reach for his wallet and when he bent down she could have sworn there was nothing in his hand. She opened her mouth to ask him how he'd done it, but he spoke before she could.

"Yes," he said, "it's cancer."

Dominique paused. She'd been so busy focusing on the money she hadn't paid attention to the reason why he'd done it. She thought about the wig and the puffy face and the sudden tears and felt in awe of his compassion. How he'd told Elizabeth that she was beautiful and made it sound as if he meant it. "I'm sorry."

"Treatment seems to be working, but it's still hard."

Dominique nodded, not sure what to say. She didn't understand why he was sharing that with her. He spoke to her as if they were friends instead of employer and employee. She'd never seen a man of his status do that before. She was supposed to be part of the furniture—used and ignored. Maybe he was thinking aloud. She hadn't even known him an hour and he was already confusing her. Who was this man? Seeing him as a nude model, yes that made sense. Seeing him as a man who cared for a married woman with cancer? No, that was harder to swallow. But it didn't matter. She wouldn't be swayed. Hadn't Berton appeared to be one thing and then turned out to be another? Hadn't her father taught her what men were really like? Untrustworthy, ruthless, conniving...

Her thoughts faded when Kevin rushed forward and helped a woman struggling to open the main doors to the building while she pulled a luggage cart in one hand and held two bags in another. Kevin took one of the bags and the luggage cart.

Dominique, feeling that she should do something, took the other bag from her. "Let me help you," she said, her face reflecting in the woman's dark glasses. The woman was petite with corkscrew twists, making Dominique feel like a wide lumbering giant standing beside her.

The woman smiled in relief. "Thank you."

"It's not that sunny, Nora," Kevin said. "Are the sunglasses really necessary?"

Nora Winestone sighed. She worked for the chair of the department and had just finished a discussion about possible budget cuts. "Not now, Kevin." She smiled at Dominique. "My car's over there. I can take—"

"It can get dangerous if you stay longer," Kevin said.

She frowned. "Nothing's wrong."

"Then let me see your face."

She stopped and lifted up her sunglasses, revealing her brown eyes. "Feel better now?"

"The makeup looks good." He touched the side of her face, she winced. "But not good enough."

She set her glasses back. "I don't need a lecture."

"No, you need something else."

Nora sent him a hard look, then marched to her car. She opened the trunk and smiled at Dominique as if Kevin didn't exist. "Thanks for your help."

"You're welcome," Dominique said, putting the bags inside.

Kevin put the luggage cart inside. "You know I'm here if you need me."

Nora slammed the trunk closed. "I don't need you," she said, then got into her car and drove off.

Kevin watched her for a long moment, then spun on his heel and said, "I need something to drink."

Dominique nodded, expecting him to ask her to take him to a bar or liquor store but instead he turned to one of the buildings. Moments later he stood in front of a vending machine, gulping down a can of apple juice. He finished it and crushed the can in his fist as though it were tissue paper. The sound of aluminum being violently compressed in one swift grip startled her as much as if he'd taken the can and crushed it against his forehead. She cleared her throat. "Are you okay?"

"No." He threw the can in the garbage. "I'm angry."

Dominique bit her lip. It wasn't her business. She knew it

wasn't her business, she should stay out of it. But she couldn't help herself. He intrigued her. She followed him to the car and said, "Does her husband--?"

"No, it's her son. Eighteen and useless. There's nothing I hate more than a man who hurts women. But women..." His words fell away and he shook his head in frustration. "Just yesterday I was with a friend who's gotten her heart broken over a guy who promised her marriage after seducing her out of fifty thousand dollars and leaving her with a kid."

Dominique laughed with bitterness. "That's funny coming from you."

"Funny?"

Damn she'd revealed too much. She shrugged hoping to appear nonchalant. "I'm sure a man like you knows something about breaking promises."

"Me?" He shook his head. "I don't make promises. Women always know where they stand with me."

Was he really such a hypocrite? He could treat her sister the way he did and then say he hated men who mistreated women? Was this all for show? And why show this side to her? She was just a driver; she was surprised he was even talking to her. But his anger seemed—no, felt— genuine. And then there were those damn shadows in his eyes.

No. She had to focus. She looked down at the ground, watching her shoes pound across the asphalt. She had to block everything else out. The blue of the sky didn't matter, the sight of Elizabeth wearing the ill-fitted wig, Nora with her dark glasses, Kevin's impassioned speech. This impression of him was not the complete picture. There had to be a hidden side. A dark side that had hurt her sister and she'd find it.

She let out a yelp when he yanked her backwards. She turned to him, stunned.

The corner of his mouth kicked up in a grin. "You were about to walk into a car."

She turned and saw a black Lexus she was only feet away from smacking into. She rubbed her forehead, wanting to melt into a puddle. One moment he had her tripping over her feet, the next walking into cars. She had to get a grip. "Thank you, sir," she said straightening her back and holding her head high. She wouldn't cower, she was his driver, she had to earn his trust. "I'm sorry. I should be more attentive." She quickly walked to his car and opened the rear car door.

Kevin leaned against the door and studied her. "Nervous?"

Dominique glanced at a spot on the hood and rubbed her sleeve against it as if trying to clear a spot. She couldn't look at him yet. "Nervous?"

He nodded. "About me?"

"No, sir." She opened the car door even wider, still unable to meet his gaze, silently begging him to go in. "I know I will do a very good job."

He sat inside. "I like a woman with confidence."

"Yes," she said, then closed the door and got into the driver's seat.

"Nice to know I'm in good hands," Kevin said as she started the ignition.

For one wild, brief, dangerous moment Dominique thought about holding him in her hands. She thought about molding him, sculpting him, tasting him. She pushed the thought aside and gripped the steering wheel. Other women had fallen for his charm and she wasn't going to be one of them.

"I should probably fire you," he said.

Dominique felt a chill slide through her. One moment she felt safe and the next uneasy. He could unsettle her so easily.

"Why?" she asked, making sure to keep her tone neutral. She glanced at him through the rearview mirror. "What have I done?"

Kevin looked out the window, his tone bored. "Nothing, it's just a feeling."

Dominique searched her mind, trying to figure out where she'd gone wrong. How could he suspect anything? "I'm good at what I do. I know cars and—"

"What brought you to me?"

"The agency." At least that sounded legitimate. She'd figure out what to do when she dropped him home. So far her deception hadn't been revealed, Ferguson would have called him by now if it had.

"I mean, what made you want to be a driver?"

Dominique shifted lanes, wishing he'd drop the subject. Why did he have to be so chatty? Shouldn't he be on the phone talking dirty to one of his girlfriends? "It's a long, boring story."

He shrugged. "I like stories."

She had to change tactics, be a little defensive. "Do you have something against female drivers?"

He flashed a quick grin. "I'm not against female anything. No, it's just you."

"Me?"

"Yes."

"What's wrong with me?"

"I'm not sure yet, Ms. Carter. Is there anything you want to tell me?"

She resisted the urge to adjust that A/C or better yet, roll down the window and feel the air from outside. She needed something to cool her skin. She felt closed in and hot. His questions sounded innocuous, simple, but she knew they weren't. "I need this job."

"I like how you handle the car."

She gripped the steering wheel, waiting for a 'but'...

"My drivers follow strict rules," he continued.

"Okay," she said letting her grip relax. He was going to give her a chance.

"They work long hours."

"Okay."

"And must know how to be discreet."

"I'm very discreet."

Kevin leaned forward, resting his chin on the back of her chair. "I know," he said, close enough that she could feel his warm breath on her neck, and smell the heady scent of his cologne. "I can always tell when a woman's keeping secrets."

Dominique didn't reply and to her relief, he sat back and didn't ask any more questions. But she knew she had to come up with a new lie fast.

"Why haven't you returned any of my calls?" Ferguson demanded in a state of panic when Kevin got home.

Kevin pulled out his phone and saw the list of missed calls. "Sorry, I had it on silent. What's the problem?"

"At least you're safe and the car is safe, so that's something."

"Ferguson, what's wrong?"

Ferguson took off his glasses and rubbed his eyes then shoved them back on again. "I made a mistake."

Ferguson always rubbed his eyes when he was agitated. But

lots of things could agitate him. Rain on a day he'd hoped to be sunny. A house staff member with an unironed shirt. Kevin patted him on the back in reassurance. "Calm down. What mistake?"

"It's about the new driver."

Kevin folded his arms and tried not to smile. Ferguson was worried for no reason. "Don't worry, she's fine. I like her."

Ferguson shook his head. "That's not it."

Kevin let his hands fall to his hips. "What is it then?"

"She's not a driver."

"You're not making sense."

Ferguson rubbed his eyes again, but this time didn't return his glasses to his face. Instead he collapsed the frames and used them to tap his forehead. "You have every reason to fire me after this."

"I'm not going to fire you. Just tell me what's going on."

He shook his head and closed his eyes. "I should have—"

Kevin whacked him on the arm. "Pull yourself together."

Ferguson stared at him then nodded. "You're right." He put his glasses back in place. "It was a busy day and a lot was going on..."

Kevin silently groaned, knowing this was going to be a long story. He sighed and headed for the living room so he could sit down. His leg was already starting to hurt and he couldn't stand much longer. He settled into a chair as Ferguson continued his story. He'd learned to tune him out until he got to a point that mattered. He glanced at the ground and noticed a woman's earring lying next to a table leg. The maid service was getting sloppy. He hadn't had a party in two days; that should have been cleaned up by now.

"...After I showed her around..."

He wondered who the earring belonged to. He went

through a catalogue of prospects in his mind. He'd gotten good at matching women with their jewelry.

"… and saw her leave to pick you up, the driver from the agency arrived. He apologized for being late."

Kevin shifted his gaze from the earring to Ferguson. Now that was interesting. "She's not from the agency?"

"No."

Kevin nodded. "So that explains it," he muttered to himself.

"What?"

"Never mind. Who is she?"

Ferguson gripped his hands together, his voice rising in dismay. "That's where I messed up. To think I handed her the keys to the Bentley and—"

Kevin held up his hand. He wasn't in the mood for one of Ferguson's meltdowns. They didn't happen often, but when they did they were messy. "Tell me what went wrong."

"I didn't get all her particulars before sending her to you. I didn't want you waiting, so I gave her the go ahead. I thought I'd go through all the proper procedures when you got back."

Kevin nodded. "That's understandable."

"No, it's not. I even told the other man that I'd hired someone else just to save face. I'll get rid of her right away."

Kevin stood and picked up the earring. "No, don't do that."

Ferguson looked at him confused. "But we don't know who she is or why she's here."

Kevin tossed the earring to him. "Exactly."

Ferguson glanced down at the earring then up at Kevin, perplexed. "Do you want me to investigate?"

Kevin shook his head. "No, I want to see how far she'll go. And I don't plan to let her leave until I find out what she's really up to."

CHAPTER EIGHT

She was just his type, Kevin thought as stood at the arched window in the hallway and watched Dominique wash his BMW with careful consideration. Everybody knew Kevin Jackson liked his ladies and he was very shrewd in making sure he wasn't particular. He was an equal opportunity admirer of the female species. He liked ladies of all shapes and sizes, races and ages.

But he had a weakness for one specific type and now she worked for him. If it had been a couple of months prior he would have made a play for her, but those days were over.

He would have to be careful, but that didn't mean he couldn't enjoy the view.

She was beautifully proportioned with luscious curves. From their first meeting he knew there was more to her than what she seemed. She carried herself with a regal certainty he'd never seen in someone who'd been in service.

She had the bearings of a queen, someone used to being obeyed. Half the time he expected her to hand the keys to him and tell him where to take her. He wondered what she'd done before she'd shown up at his door. Was she running from someone? Hiding? Her missteps and awkwardness at their first meeting weren't her natural state. He could tell that she wasn't a woman who was shaken easily. She was a woman usually in command of herself. He'd learned to read people.

No, not just people—women. Women were his favorite subject and Dominique was a lesson he wanted to study. She was a strange contradiction. An attractive woman who didn't seem to know how attractive she was. A woman used to leading, taking a job that forced her to follow. She'd tried to trick him, but her attempt was sloppy, although he did enjoy the effort.

And then there was her voice. Yes, her voice was going to get him into trouble. It was smooth, deep and husky like a good bourbon. The kind of voice that could turn any word into a naughty invitation. Just hearing her say 'yes sir' made him want to hear her say 'yes' again. Over and over. Preferably in bed with her legs wrapped around him.

Right now he could picture her washing the car naked—soaping up the car and bending over the hood. Then he could picture her hosing it down. Then hosing herself. He couldn't help a grin. Ferguson would definitely scold him for his thoughts right now. He was supposed to be worried, instead he was turned on.

But right now his imagination was all that he had. There was still so much he couldn't share with anyone. If only Cassie...

His mood dimmed. Cassie was still in the hospital—still in a coma. The woman he didn't want to love anymore. He hadn't even known he had a type until he met her. She'd been the first and only woman who'd made him—Mister-can't-keep-still-Kevin—think of settling down. She'd completely shaken him like no other woman had.

He'd met her in a class he'd taken about social grace. A class he didn't need. He'd done it for fun to see what kind of people would show up. Cassie had been the instructor—Cassandra, her alter ego—a successful author and speaker. A woman who moved like a goddess. As Cassandra, her eyes weren't hidden by glasses and she commanded attention. But instead of being haughty or distant, she cared. When one of the students broke down after sharing one of her disastrous dates, Cassandra gave the young woman such a motivating speech about self-love that the other students burst into applause and at the end of the class the young woman had left the room beaming.

In that instant he'd lost his heart. She possessed a level of warmth and sweetness that had no guile. She didn't want something from him and that was rare in his life. She also didn't fall for his charm, seeing him as a friend instead of a man. It had bruised his ego at first, but he'd decided to be patient, sure that in time she'd see him as he wanted her to.

He'd been wrong. First there was her bastard ex-husband and then she had married Henson. Even after all these years, he couldn't say that man's name without a feeling of annoyance. He didn't know what she saw in him.

Real women play with boys, but they marry men. Henson's words burned at the very core of him. He wanted to forget them, but they kept coming back. He gripped his hand into a fist and pounded the wall. He was a man. A good man. A strong man. But nobody saw it. Nobody saw past his fun-loving ways. But what was wrong with having fun?

At least he still had Cassie as a friend and Henson couldn't do anything about it.

Except now. Now Henson was in control. He kept Cassie away from him and he couldn't blame him. It was his fault Cassie had gotten hurt, and Marcus too. If only he knew what had happened. It had to be the car. There had been skid marks so he'd lost control of the car and tried to brake. Something mechanical must have failed. The accident report had been inconclusive.

He'd taken Marcus and Cassie on a special ride for Marcus's fifth birthday in a specially designed custom car he'd ordered from Cartwright Cars. He'd used Marcus's drawing as inspiration for some of the details. He remembered the look on Marcus's face when Kevin sat him on his lap and let him handle the steering wheel before setting off on their journey. He remembered how the sun glinted against the chrome finish. He remembered feeling happy having Cassie by his side, feeling like the old days when she'd bitch about bad dates and he still thought he had a chance.

It was supposed to be memorable.

But he couldn't remember anything after that. Nothing had warned him of what loomed ahead of them. Now his mind filled with things he couldn't forget, like waking up in a hospital bed and Henson's look of rage. A rage that crept into Kevin's dreams, a rage he also felt because he felt helpless and hated the feeling.

He rested his forehead against the cool glass of the window and closed his eyes. He wished for a miracle. He didn't care if he never remembered if only Cassie would just wake up. He'd let her go, never see her again, if he had to. He'd surrender and let Henson win for good if she'd just be okay.

He opened his eyes and looked at Dominique again. He couldn't get too close. He could fantasize, but he'd keep his distance. He'd toy with her, find a way to draw her out, but he wouldn't go further than that. He'd learned to keep some things out of reach.

CHAPTER NINE

Seducing a rogue was supposed to be easy, but Kevin Jackson was proving to be anything but. She'd been his driver for over a week now and hadn't made any progress. She still couldn't believe her deception had held this long. The agency hadn't called and Ferguson agreed to pay her in cash. No questions asked. She found it strange, but didn't want to press her luck.

She'd dropped Kevin off at home that first day, certain it would be her last. His questions had unnerved her and she felt her time was short so she'd come up with a new scheme as she parked the car in front of his house. A crazy scheme now that she thought about it, but it had seemed like a good idea at the time.

She knew he was a man with a seemingly insatiable appetite for women, so she thought of exploiting that weakness. Since he wanted to know a reason why she wanted to work for him, she'd give him one.

She held the car door open for him, and then said in a rush, "I took this job because I wanted to get close to you."

Kevin stared up at her. "Why?" he asked, but she couldn't read his expression. He didn't look surprised or repulsed, not even really curious.

"What woman wouldn't?"

He smiled. "Do I look like I need to get my ego stroked?"

"No, but I do."

"Why?"

Dominique counted to three. The man was like a kid, why did he have to ask so many questions? Wasn't he supposed to feel proud? She searched her thoughts for a good lie, then decided it was better to tell him something true. "I caught the man I love with another woman."

Kevin slowly got out of the car. "How?"

She widened her eyes, amazed. Was he being dense or cruel? "What do you mean 'how?'"

"How did you catch him?"

She closed the car door. "Does it matter?"

"Do you think I'd ask if it didn't?" He touched her chin. "I need to know what kind of woman you are."

She cleared her throat. His touch was soft, tender, but his penetrating gaze held a lethal intensity. She had to remember not to underestimate him. "And how I found out will tell you that?"

He nodded.

She bit her lip. "It was by mistake. He was supposed to take me to a concert and he forgot. I showed up at his house and she was there."

Kevin frowned. "That's very sloppy."

Her brows shot up. "There's a clean way to find out your boyfriend's cheating?"

He rested against the car. "No, it was sloppy for him to get caught that way. Why didn't he pick you up at your house?"

"He thought it would be better for me to meet him since he gets home late and we'd then go to the concert from there."

He shifted his position again, making Dominique wonder why he didn't seem to keep still. "That still doesn't make sense."

"Does cheating ever make sense?" She waved the question away, remembering who she was talking to. "Never mind."

Kevin lifted a brow as if reading her thoughts. "I've never cheated on a woman. I've never had to and never will. I have my standards. What was his name?"

She hesitated then said, "Berton."

"Are you sure?"

"Of course I'm sure."

"And you loved him very much."

Not very much. She'd never loved a man very much, but it had hurt. "Yes."

Kevin absently rubbed his leg. "Until he hurt you and you want to use me to forget him?"

"Yes."

"I don't believe you," he said softly. So softly that at first she wasn't sure she'd heard correctly.

She blinked. "What?"

He shifted his weight again and looked up at a slowly moving patch of clouds. "I believe you're angry, but he's not the reason why you're here."

"You think I'm a liar?"

He turned to her. "No, I don't think you're telling me the truth."

"Isn't that the same thing?"

He grinned, then walked away.

He'd turned her down! A free invitation, carte blanche, and he'd walked away. Her face burned with anger and humiliation at the memory. The man with no scruples had turned his back on her and left her standing there like an idiot. Had she come on too strong? Not strong enough? Why didn't he completely believe her story? It was true, dammit! And wasn't a woman who'd been cheated on an ideal plaything for a man like him? A woman desperate and emotionally vulnerable was like a velvet cake to a sugar addict. Where had she gone wrong?

Five hours later, Dominique pulled up to the DC club and parked in front of the entrance, glad she'd quickly recovered from the incident. He hadn't brought it up again and she certainly wouldn't. She'd thought of leaving—her pride still bristled with outrage—and thinking of another plan, but this was the best way to get close to him. As his driver she could find out his habits and routines.

At least that was what she'd told her sister when Gloria had caught her packing. She'd hoped to get out of the family house without being spotted by anyone, but Gloria had returned from her yoga class early. Thankfully, she'd recovered quickly and spent only one night in the hospital. The family used their influence to avoid getting police or psychiatrists involved.

"What are you doing?" Gloria asked, coming into the bedroom.

Dominique took some shirts off their hangers and put them in her suitcase. She could lie, but then that would make her sister curious. "I'm going to get back at Kevin." She told her about the mistake and becoming his driver. "But don't tell Mom or Dad about this."

"What should I tell them?"

"I told Mom I needed space and she'll believe me and convince Dad. This shouldn't take too long."

Gloria sat down on the bed and stared at her, tears shining in her eyes. "I can't believe you're doing this for me." She jumped up and hugged her. "You're the best."

"No need to exaggerate," Dominique said, pleased. She loved helping her little sister; at least she appreciated what she did for her.

"Let me help you pack."

"I'm already done."

Gloria searched through the suitcase with a frown. "But there's nothing interesting in here." She opened Dominique's drawer and pulled out a cream blouse. "At least take this."

Dominique smiled at her sister's naiveté. "I'm supposed to be a driver, I can't go around wearing a three-hundred-dollar top."

"But you got it on sale."

"I know...for three hundred dollars."

Gloria frowned, still confused. "But don't those people wear sale items all the time?"

"Right," Dominique said, taking the blouse. She wouldn't wear it but she didn't want to explain why it was inappropriate either.

Gloria clapped her hands together. "Oh, and there's something else." She disappeared then came back moments later holding a gold chained necklace with a hanging pendant. "I was going to wait for your birthday, but since you're being so sweet I want to give this to you now. Turn around."

Dominique looked at the expensive gift in dismay. "But I can't wear--"

"You can wear it under your blouse," Gloria said, forcing her sister to turn. "It's to give you courage." She draped the necklace around Dominique's neck. "You'll need it against Kevin."

"But I—"

Gloria stood in front of her. "Listen to me. He's dangerous." Her eyes filled with tears again. "He hurt me more than any man ever has. Don't fall for his tricks."

Dominique affectionately patted her sister's cheek, a little surprised by her sister's changing emotions. That wasn't like her. "I don't plan to."

"You will if you're not careful." Gloria tapped the chain. "Keep this on at all times so you'll remember me. So that you'll remember what he did to me."

Her sister's words are what kept her going. That first day Dominique hadn't found out enough about Kevin that would be useful, but after a week she knew plenty.

She'd learned one major truth—Kevin Jackson took the word 'playboy' to its own dimension. She knew he lived off of inherited money from a lucrative export business his great-grandfather, a Haitian immigrant, had developed.

Twice she'd heard him mutter a sigh and say 'I hate these things' when he received a text, and then he would text for several minutes before he put his phone away. He hadn't gone back to the university and when she'd asked about his art class, he admitted that he'd done it one time as a favor to Elizabeth.

She didn't know a man who did nothing—he didn't seem to work or do anything with a purpose—could be so active. He went out partying nearly every night. If he wasn't hosting a party, he was going to one at a friends' home. If he wasn't at a friend's house, he was in an exclusive club. She'd pick him up at two or three in the morning. He also had the strange habit of wearing dark shades at night or early morning as the case may be.

He had the stamina of a college freshman although he was in his mid-thirties. No wonder he'd worn out his other drivers.

She wasn't sure she'd last much longer. Especially when he had his marathon nights where he'd go to three parties in one evening.

Tonight had been one of those nights. She could feel the drum beat of the music from inside the club, and saw the neon sign reflected in pink on the dark finish of the car. She looked up and saw Kevin emerge from the club. He seemed to have had too much to drink. He stumbled and caught himself against the hood of the car. Dominique opened the door for him, hoping he wouldn't be sick. She wasn't in the mood to clean up after him. Strangely, he didn't smell as if he'd had anything to drink.

Another thing that surprised her was how he always came home empty handed. For a man with his reputation, she'd expected to be driving him home with a female companion. She'd had images of him making out in the back seat, embracing a woman with long hair and a short skirt—make that two or three women. But that never happened. She'd see him with ladies—beautiful ladies and some not so beautiful—but he never took them home with him.

Dominique waited until he was settled in his seat with his seatbelt on before she closed the door and she got in the driver's seat. She glanced at him through the rearview mirror and saw him pop two white pills in his mouth. He washed them down with water. His hand shook and his mouth looked tight as if he were in pain. But maybe he just felt ill. She knew hard partying could have that effect. But she wasn't going to scold him. It served the bastard right. If he wanted to live recklessly then he'd have to deal with the consequences.

But as unfeeling as she wanted to be, she grew concerned when they arrived at his house and she saw his hand tremble as he gripped the side of the car door's frame to pull himself up to get out of the car. When he stumbled, she reached out and caught him. She buckled a bit under the force of his weight, but managed to keep him upright. She looked at him and mingled with the moonlight and porch light she saw beads of sweat drenching his skin.

"Maybe you should go to the hospital," she said.

"I'm fine," he said through clenched teeth. He straightened. "Sorry about that." He turned and headed for the front door.

She stared at him, alarmed, realizing he wasn't drunk, but in pain. "But I think—"

"I don't care, just open the door."

Fortunately, she didn't have to. Ferguson beat her to it. "I'll take it from here." He pulled Kevin inside and closed the door in her face.

Dominique stared at the door for a long moment, then sighed in frustration. She didn't care. She didn't want to care. What he was up to was none of her business. She'd stayed longer than she should have anyway. Maybe it was the aftereffects of some party drug. He was Ferguson's problem now. Not hers. He'd never be her problem. She should only think about what he'd done to her sister.

But as she lay in bed later that evening, she wondered about the tightness of his mouth, the labored breathing, the sweating and the little white pills. What could they mean? A playboy with a drug addiction wouldn't be anything new, but it might prove useful.

CHAPTER TEN

"How bad is it?" Ferguson asked, helping Kevin to a couch, knowing he wouldn't be able to make it to his bedroom even with the elevator.

Kevin collapsed onto the couch with a grimace. "I'll be okay in a minute."

"I shouldn't let you do this."

He closed his eyes and managed a weak smile. "You can't stop me."

"It's not going to make things better."

He didn't care. He had to dance, he had to party, he had to stop the thoughts that threatened to consume him. He had to keep busy, he had to keep smiling, he had to keep up appearances. It was the only way to survive.

Ferguson sighed at Kevin's silence. "You still don't want me to do something about Dominique?'

"No," he whispered, barely able to speak, the pain in his head gripping him.

"We'd better think of something soon because if she finds out that you can't—"

"I'll take care of it."

S HE COULDN'T BELIEVE he was the same man from three nights ago. Kevin looked bright, sexy and full of energy. Dominique watched him from a distance as he spoke to a hostess who helped him select items for lunch. The restaurant was designed for a casual dining experience with a buffet setting and expensive decorative accents like real crystal vases and real wood flooring. She'd chosen a table in the corner because he'd insisted she come inside with him. She wasn't going to eat anything here, although she wanted to. She'd never heard of this place and the options looked delicious, but the prices were out of her present budget. She had her savings, but had to prepare for when she looked for proper work and she didn't know how long that would take. Plus, she doubted he expected his driver to eat lunch with him. He didn't tell her he had a date, but she suspected that was the reason they were there. She glanced at her watch, wondering when the date would show up and what type she'd be. Likely a corporate attorney. Considering the neighborhood attracted more high-powered businesspeople, a party heiress likely wouldn't be in this part of the city.

And that could be a problem for her. She and Kevin didn't travel in the same circles, so she'd never worried about bumping into someone she knew. However, that was a possibility here in a place filled with executives, lawyers, investors and other professionals. Although she'd chosen a table that kept her out of view, she wasn't completely safe from someone making a connection with her and Kevin.

She saw Kevin thank the hostess and turn. Dominique

quickly looked away. She didn't want to be caught staring. She watched a car drive by and then a man on a bicycle.

She jumped when she heard a tray settle on the table. She turned to him and surged to her feet. "What are you doing? You can't sit here."

Kevin stared at her. "Why not?"

She couldn't have anyone see them together. Kevin turned heads and drew attention even when he wasn't trying. "Because..." She lowered her voice. "Because I'm your driver."

He sat down. "So what?"

She sent a panicked look to the door. "What are you going to do when your date shows up?"

"I don't have a date."

Then why are we here? "You're not supposed eat with your driver."

"Who says?"

Dominique scanned the room. She didn't recognize anyone and although two women had sent glances towards their table, their interest was fixed solely on Kevin and not her. "It's important to establish boundaries and distance and—"

"What's wrong with you?" he asked, spreading his napkin on his lap. "You want to sleep with me, but you don't want to eat with me?"

Dominique leaned forward and lowered her voice, hoping nobody had overheard him. "No, that's not—"

"Then stop talking and spoiling my appetite." He gestured to the tray filled with three full meals. "Choose what you want and eat up."

"But—"

"Want me to choose for you?" He set a plate of grilled chicken and broccoli in front of her. "There you go."

"But—"

"You don't want that? Okay—"

She grabbed his hand, stopping him from removing the plate. The colorful sight and aromatic smell made her mouth water and stomach grumble. "It's fine," she said, letting his hand go. She caught the quick satisfied grin on his face, but didn't care. She would eat, she just wouldn't eat with him. She eyed an empty table. "I just think you should be aware that—"

"I'm always aware of what I'm doing," he said, taking a plate of sliced turkey. "If I want to eat with you I will, if I don't, I won't. I don't need you to tell me about protocol."

Heat burned her cheeks. He was right. She had no right to lecture him. She'd forgotten that he was the employer and had the right to do whatever he pleased. His phone buzzed. He checked it, then muttered, "I really hate these meetings," then started texting. As usual it didn't take long before he looked satisfied and put the phone away. "All done. Just made five million."

Dominique blinked. "Five million?"

He nodded. "I like to keep my business meetings short."

"That was a business meeting?" she asked, surprised. The ones she'd known all her life were never like that.

"Yes, I like to keep them short. At least I'm not stuck in an office so I can't complain. But I have to keep track of the businesses I own or co-own." A slow smile spread over his face. "Did you think I just live off of my family's money?"

"It's none of my business," she said, heat burning her cheeks. She'd misjudged him again.

"Don't worry, you wouldn't know most of the businesses I'm connected to."

"Right," she said, feeling foolish. All this time she'd been with him and she still knew so little about him. She took a deep breath, then noticed a small piece of dried food still on his fork. She shouldn't make a big deal of it. It was a classy place and it appeared he'd been there before. It was none of her business. He probably wouldn't even notice. But as he put the fork to his mouth she cringed and grabbed his wrist. "No."

Kevin looked at her startled. "What now?"

Dominique couldn't hold his gaze so she waved to a waiter. "Excuse me, but we need new utensils." She snatched the one out of Kevin's hand. "This one is filthy. And can he please get a glass of water, not a glass of ice?" she said noticing Kevin's glass stacked with so many ice cubes she could barely see any liquid. "Thank you so much."

Once the waiter left, she hung her head, waiting for Kevin to berate her. She couldn't help herself; she didn't like when minor details were missed and... Why wasn't he saying anything? She slowly lifted her head. Kevin sat with his chin in his hands, a devilish grin on his face.

"What?"

His grin widened and his eyes lit with amusement. There were no shadows there, no hint of pain, just pure merriment. And for a moment she could picture him as a little boy, wrapping his mother around his finger.

But she wasn't his mother and she wouldn't fall for his charm. "What?" she asked again, wishing her skin didn't feel so warm, wishing she didn't feel a tingling in her stomach.

He lifted a brow. "Freeport or the Caymans?"

"I don't know what you mean."

"Where does your family vacation?"

"I don't know."

The waiter returned with the requested items.

"Maybe the South Seas, perhaps?"

Dominique thanked the waiter, then opened her mouth to

respond to Kevin's question, but someone interrupted her. "Dominique, is that you?" a female voice said.

Fear gripped her throat and knotted her insides. She knew that voice. She'd heard it for years. And the owner of that voice could ruin everything.

CHAPTER ELEVEN

The well-coiffured woman approached the table and squinted down at Dominique. She needed glasses, and had three pairs, but was too vain to wear them in public. "I knew it was you."

Dominique reluctantly stood and kissed both cheeks of one of her mother's friends, Mariah Copeland. "What a surprise," she said, after an introduction.

"I know," Mariah said, drawing out the last word. "Your mother told me what happened. Your father—"

"It's okay. I'd really prefer not to talk about it."

She patted Dominique's hand. "Of course, dear. But you had your mother worried. It's not like you to run off the way you did."

Dominique glanced at Kevin keenly aware of how he watched them. She didn't want to be rude, but she couldn't have Mariah rattling off about her family.

"Mom knows I need space."

Kevin stood. "Would you like to join us?" he said, grabbing another chair.

"Yes," Mariah said.

"No," Dominique said.

They both looked at her. "I mean...you seemed to be in a hurry and I would hate to keep you."

"Oh yes," Mariah said with a nod. "You're right. I do have an appointment with the contractor for our beach house. It's been a nightmare, but I won't bore you with the details. You already know. Remember that French chateau your father bought for your mother? The headaches you two had to deal with renovating it was heaven compared to what I'm going through, but I'm sure your mother will fill you in on all the details." She glanced at Dominique's plate. "I see you're watching your weight, which is always a good thing, but as I've told you a million times, big girls don't have to hide themselves in black. Wear what suits you not what's in fashion. The classics never let you down, but current trends..." She waved her hands as if dismissing a foul smell. "I mean, and I'm not being cruel because you know I love you, but my goodness what you're wearing looks like a uniform." She turned to Kevin. "Doesn't it?"

"Yes," Kevin said. "Probably because it is."

Dominique briefly closed her eyes. The end was near. He was going to tell her mother's dearest friend that she was his driver and Mariah would have a coronary.

Mariah looked confused. "It is?"

Kevin nodded. "It's my fault. She knows it turns me on." He winked at Dominique. "I love a woman in uniform."

Dominique looked at Mariah's shocked expression. "Ignore him."

"Other men like nurses or maids," Kevin continued. "But a woman who can handle a machine and make it hum and hug the road..." He let his words fall away.

Dominique shook her head. "He's just—"

Kevin pressed a finger to his lips. "But nobody's supposed to know about us yet."

Mariah's eyes widened. "It's because of your father, isn't it?"

Dominique jumped to her feet. "We'll talk later," she said, ushering her to the door. "You don't want to miss that appointment."

"Does your mother know?"

"There's really nothing going on, but I'll explain it later."

"My lips are sealed until then." She glanced back at Kevin. "Do you really know what you're doing? He looks like a heart-breaker."

"I'll be fine." To her relief, Mariah agreed with her and left. Dominique returned to the table, determined to ignore Kevin's smug grin.

"That was fun. Think we'll bump into anyone else you know?"

She focused on her meal.

"At least I know I was right about you." Kevin cut into his braised turkey breast. "I can smell money. I thought as much the first day we met. Let me guess. Daddy cut off all your accounts and credit to force you to 'rough it' for a while. Why is he punishing you?"

Dominique had to stop a smile. Of course! This was the perfect story and Mariah had sprinkled it with enough truth so she could use his assumption to her advantage. "I won't marry the man he wants me to."

Kevin paused. "The cheater?"

"Yes."

He nodded in approval. "Good girl."

"My mom's not happy about it either."

"She'll get over it. So is that why you lied about your name? You're afraid if you told me I'd know who your father was?"

You'll definitely know who he is. "Yes."

"I may not know him."

"You do."

"I mean personally."

You do. "Can we change the subject?"

"Sure. Do you like chocolate?"

"We probably should be getting back," Dominique said as they drifted in a hired boat along the Potomac. After lunch, he'd taken her to a chocolatier friend who'd shown her how to make a batch of truffles. Now, as the sun set, they sat on the deck of the small boat eating them. She didn't like to admit how much fun it was or how natural it felt to be around him.

"Why?" Kevin asked. He lay on a lounge chair with his head back and his eyes closed, looking like a man of leisure. "Do you have an appointment or something?"

"No, I just..." *I'm not used to wasting time. I'm not used to sitting around enjoying myself* she wanted to say, but knew he wouldn't understand that. She'd never done something like this before. Her time had always been spent figuring out a goal or executing a plan. "This really is too much."

"What's too much?"

"This day. The lunch, the chocolatier, the boat."

Kevin opened his eyes and sat up. "You don't like it?"

Dominique looked out at the water, feeling the soft touch of the sun on her face. She liked it too much. She liked him too much. That was the real trouble. He wasn't anything she'd imagined him to be. Her sister's story about him just didn't match. Or was it her? Was she not seeing the real him because she didn't want to? She'd prided herself on being able to read men, but now she wasn't so sure. "I didn't say that." She tapped her chest. "And you shouldn't ask me questions like that, I'm your driver."

"Why do you have to keep reminding me of your position?"

"Because..." She sighed. "It's just it's too much."

"No, it's not. You just don't know how to enjoy yourself."

"I shouldn't be here," she said more to herself than to him. "I'm your driver, for goodness sake. I should be on the shore waiting for you while you host several supermodels or something."

He shook his head. "I only do that on the ocean in perfect yachting weather."

She folded her arms. "You think I'm being funny."

"I think you don't know how to have fun and I'm trying to help you." He picked up a truffle and held it out to her. "Try to relax."

She reached for the truffle, but he moved it out of reach. "Just open your mouth," he said.

"You want to feed me like a child?"

"No, I just want to put something in your mouth." He suddenly frowned. "And that just sounded wrong. I'm usually smoother than that."

Dominique laughed. "It's good to see you off your game."

"And it's good to hear you laugh." He waved the truffle. "Come on, it's melting."

She shook her head. "It's embarrassing. I've never..."

His eyes widened with delight. "You've never had a man feed you before? I get to be the first?"

"No."

"No, I don't get to be the first or no you have been fed by a man before?"

She snatched the truffle out of his hand and popped it in her mouth. "Question answered."

Kevin sighed disappointed, then leaned back and closed his eyes.

Dominique looked at her watch. How long did he plan to stay here?

"I know what it's like to break away," he said. "To face a parent's disappointment. It's not easy. My Dad was a good man and I watched him work. That's all he ever did was work. I never once saw him smile. He worked day and night. I only remember him sitting behind his desk. Once I saw him standing and mistook him for the staff because I didn't recognize him. Work was his life and it sent him into an early grave. That won't be me."

"I like working. It's just..." She stopped, realizing she'd revealed too much. He was too easy to talk to.

"What?"

She stared at his profile. He still had his eyes closed and seemed nonchalant. They were talking to kill time and what he'd revealed about his father surprised her. Although his words sounded carefree, she sensed a hidden defiance and pain. She found she wanted to share with him, she felt he would understand. Besides, he probably wouldn't remember any of their conversation later. "My father doesn't care," she said, surprised how much that revelation hurt. "It's never enough. I'm never good enough."

"Did he say that?"

"He doesn't have to. Everything he does tells me so and then D—" She shook her head. "It's a boring story."

Kevin turned to her, his eyes dark and compelling. "I told you I like stories."

Dominique reached for another truffle and popped it in her mouth. She couldn't look at him. He had an uncanny ability to make her feel as if she were the only woman in the world, as if she mattered to him. That had to be his trick, the power of his dangerous charm. "I'll tell you another time."

"I've been waiting for you to make your next move," he said in a velvet tone.

Dominique felt goose bumps raise on her arms. "Move?"

"Didn't you want to sleep with me to annoy your father? Isn't that the real reason you came to me?"

"I'm sorry I said anything."

"Don't be. You're more honest than most and at least I know what you want. Nobody is nice to me for no reason."

That thought bothered her, but she pushed the idea away. "You made it very clear you weren't interested." She looked at him with chagrin. "I know when I'm beaten."

"I'd expected you to try harder."

"There's no point when I'm not your type."

His eyes held hers. "You're exactly my type."

Dominique felt a shiver race through her. She steeled herself against the feeling. She wouldn't allow herself to be affected; he was toying with her. None of what she was experiencing was real.

"You don't believe me," he said softly, his eyes darkening with an emotion she couldn't read.

"I didn't say that." *I can't believe you because I don't know what's going on. I hate myself for deceiving you when I know I shouldn't. I shouldn't be falling for your charm. I wish I'd never met you.* She didn't want him to care. She didn't want him to matter to her. She folded her arms, determined to build a wall between them. To keep her safe. "I'm not one of your damsels."

He frowned. "Damsels?"

"Yes, I don't think you even realize how many distressed females you have in your life."

He shrugged. "Not as many as you think. Besides, I like helping people."

"I don't need your help." She took a deep breath. She might as well get it over with. She'd stayed too long and she wasn't helping her sister or anyone. "The truth is--"

Kevin held up his hand. "I don't want to know."

Dominique blinked surprised. "What?"

"I just realized I don't want to know."

"But—"

"I don't care who your father is. I don't care about your past. I like having you around." His mouth curved into a smile. "Okay?"

She stared at him, stupefied. Was this a new game he was playing? What strategy was this? Why did his words make her heart pound with longing? "No, it's not okay. You have to know--"

He waved her away. "I don't care."

"But you should care. I—"

He pulled her into his arms and kissed her. He kissed away her questions, giving her answers she didn't know she sought. He kissed away her fears and her doubts and replaced them with a hunger that scared her. She'd fallen for Berton's deception. Hadn't he made her feel this way?

No, her body whispered. Berton had never held her this way. He'd never caressed her lips and cradled her body. He'd never made her feel as if her world was ending and beginning anew. In Kevin's arms she felt no shame. She didn't feel the need to suck in her stomach or worry that she wasn't slender, that she had rolls as well as curves. She didn't want to kiss him back, she didn't want to surrender to his chocolate gaze and sexy mouth, but like someone had bewitched her, her body responded to him. And her lips indulged in the warm, wet, sensual assault.

Kevin drew away and the abrupt distance stung like a Band-Aid being ripped from her skin. Dominique took a step back and opened her mouth to say something, even though she didn't know what to say.

He pressed a finger against her mouth. She expected his teasing grin to appear, but his expression remained serious, his eyes piercing. "Now listen to me closely," he said in a low voice. "I like you. More than I should and more than I want to, and I don't want you going anywhere. Okay? Don't open your mouth just nod your head. That's it. Thank you." He bit his lip.

She wished he wouldn't bite his lip because she didn't want to focus on his mouth. His beautiful mouth.

Kevin sighed and turned away with a look of regret. "And I made a mistake. I don't usually, but I just did." He turned to her, his gaze darkened. "I shouldn't have kissed you like that because now I want to do it again. Can I? No, you don't need to speak just nod your head...why are you shaking it?"

"Kevin, I—"

He covered her mouth, stopping her words with a kiss that sent her senses spinning. Her body refused to pull away. *He's the one,* her heart whispered. *No, he can't be,* her mind rebelled. *He's all wrong for you. This is just for fun. This won't last. It doesn't mean anything.*

Yes, he was beautiful to look at. No, beautiful was too soft a term...magnificent. Larger, more virile than she'd expected him to be. He was all man. A big, well-suited, confident sexy man with the power of an illusionist. He seemed one way, but she knew he was another. He was a riddle to her, but she didn't know why. He was dangerous, off limits in many ways. She couldn't be tangled up with him even in her dreams.

But she didn't care.

She'd have to tell him the truth and then he'd never speak to her again.

She still didn't care.

Dominique wrapped her arms around him and leaned into the kiss with more force than she'd meant to. They stumbled back. Kevin lost his balance and she landed heavily on him.

He swore. "I shouldn't have done that."

She scrambled off him, horrified. "I'm so sorry."

"No, it's not you," he said through a forced smile, but she noticed his hand gripping his thigh.

Her humiliation turned to fear. "I hurt you—"

Kevin kept his smile in place. "No, you didn't. I fell on my pride that's all."

"But your leg—"

"I'm fine. Really." He sat gingerly on the chair. "It's nothing."

But she knew by the tightness of his jaw and the shadows in his eyes that wasn't true.

Kevin walked—limped really, now that no one could see—into his house and closed the door behind him with more force than he meant to. He shouldn't have kissed her. Now he wanted her so much he ached. He leaned against the door for a moment, remembering the feel of her body against his. If she felt this good with her clothes on, how would she feel when they were naked? Her legs wrapped around him, her breasts pressed against his...He groaned.

"Get rid of her," Ferguson said.

Kevin lifted his head and glared at him. "No."

"I've seen that look before. You'll get into trouble. She's not worth it."

Kevin pushed himself from the door and headed to his bedroom.

"You can't be with her."

"I know that," Kevin said heading up the stairs.

"Take the elevator."

"I need the exercise."

Ferguson followed behind him. "You need a cold shower."

Kevin laughed. "Yes, that too."

"What is it with you and fat girls. She's not even pretty and--"

"Then why did I see you blush when she complimented your tie the other day?"

Ferguson rushed in front of him. "All right, I admit that she's attractive. I may even like her if given the chance, but I can't see you risk—"

"I'm not risking anything," Kevin said, pushing him aside. He was losing energy and his leg was really starting to ache. If he didn't get to the landing soon, he wouldn't make it.

"She can't find out about you. You can't trust her. She's like all the others. She's using you."

"No, she's not. She needs me."

"Are you sure it's not the other way around?"

Kevin paused for a second, gripping the railing. The thought frightened him. He'd made that mistake before, needing a woman more than he should have. And for a moment he felt the ache of that pain in his heart. A pain that rivaled the pain in his leg. A private misery that haunted him. He'd thought of bribing a nurse in order to see Cassie, but had changed his mind. He wasn't ready to see her yet. "I'm sure," he said, then continued up the stairs.

CHAPTER TWELVE

"Are you sure you weren't mistaken?" Dominique asked her sister later that evening as she sat in front of her TV, flipping through movies to stream while talking to Gloria on the phone. *Nobody is nice to me for no reason.* Kevin's words bothered her. They carried more weight and feeling than she wanted them to. He truly sounded like a man used to being used. And she hated being one of the users. But didn't she have a right? If he'd hurt her sister, he should be hurt as well. But something wasn't right. The Kevin she'd come to know over the last couple of weeks was nothing like the man her sister had described. And the shadows in his eyes were real. He couldn't fool her; something was wrong. And she wouldn't let herself think about the kiss, think about him telling her that he liked her. She couldn't think about how much she liked him too.

She needed more details.

"Positive," Gloria said in a pitiful voice. "He really hurt me. Don't you believe me?"

"No, it's not that, it's just...something doesn't feel right."

"You're falling for him, aren't you?"

Yes. Dominique silently admitted, but instead of feeling ashamed, she felt suspicious as a new question arose in her thoughts. *But why are you changing the subject?* That was a tactic their father had taught them: When you feel cornered, put the other person on the defensive. She decided to stay quiet and see if her sister would let anything slip.

"I knew you wouldn't believe me," Gloria continued. "Nobody would. Everybody likes Kevin."

Exactly. So why would he mistreat you? Why doesn't his reputation match what you've said? "That's not it," Dominique said, doing her best to sound affronted. "I just want to know more so that I can manipulate him better."

"Really?"

"Yes, really."

She paused. "You don't have to do this if you don't want to."

Dominique nodded, recognizing another manipulative tactic: Make the other person feel guilty. "I do. I won't let him get away with hurting you. I even tried seducing him." She squeezed her eyes shut, hoping her sister would take the bait.

"Oh my God, are you serious?"

"Yes."

"No, you didn't."

"Yes, I did. I wanted to hurt him, break his heart like he broke yours."

"That is so unlike you. I didn't realize you were so...so..."

"Committed?" Dominique finished for her.

"I was going to say crazy, but that's good too."

"You know I'd do anything for you."

Gloria fell silent, then said, "I didn't mean for you to embarrass yourself."

Dominique stiffened. "Embarrass myself?"

"You said you tried, but...it didn't work, did it? Forget I asked, we both know that's not your thing?"

"My thing?"

"You and guys," she clarified. "But it's really sweet you tried. Did you find out anything about him?"

Dominique paused, unnerved by her sister's words. That was interesting. What did she expect her to find? And why was she so confident that she hadn't been able to seduce Kevin? Wasn't Kevin a predator? Or did she think she wasn't a worthy prey?

Gloria's phone beeped. "Hold on, I've got another call."

Dominique sat back and waited for silence when her sister put her on hold. Instead she heard her father's voice come on the line. Her sister had accidentally put her on conference call. Dominique opened her mouth to let them know she was still there when her father said, "What has she told you?"

"I've got her on the other line right now," Gloria said. "She's working on it."

"Why the hell is it taking her so long?"

"She's close, Dad, she sounds like she has something on him."

"But she hasn't told you anything specific yet?"

"No, she's trying to seduce him." She giggled. "Poor Kevin. That would be funny to see. Maybe that's why it's taking her so long."

"Let her have her fun as long as she gets us what we want."

"I said you should have sent me."

"No, Dominique's the right choice. She can get men to talk. They trust her."

"And they don't trust me?" Gloria asked in a pouty tone.

Her father laughed. "The smart ones know better."

"I guess you're right. At first I wasn't sure about this, but I think it will do her good."

"Exactly. You and I are of the same mind. Your mother wouldn't understand. You're definitely your father's daughter. That's why you were always my favorite."

"Don't make me feel guilty. Dominique works hard."

"That's all she's good for. And you're her weak spot. Get her to tell you what she knows no matter how small. No detail is insignificant."

"I will. Bye."

"Bye." He hung up.

Dominique felt as if she couldn't breathe. Her sister and father had set this up? It was all a lie? Why? Why had Gloria made up a story about Kevin and why did they want her to take revenge on him? What information did they want? Why was Kevin seen as a threat?

"Dominique?" her sister said.

She couldn't speak.

"Dominique?" Gloria repeated. "Damn, I must have disconnected." She hung up and moments later the phone rang, but Dominique didn't answer right away. Should she play along and pretend she hadn't heard them? Confront her? She picked up.

"Sorry, sis, I—"

"You lied to me," Dominique said finally getting her voice back.

"What?"

"Kevin didn't hurt you, you and Dad made that up."

"Why...why would you think that?" Gloria asked, stumbling over the words.

"Because I just heard you."

Gloria swore. "It's not what you think."

Dominique briefly closed her eyes. Berton had said the same thing. The same lie. Were they all against her? "I trusted you."

"I was doing this for you. Dad told me that if you pulled this off he had a prime position he wanted to give you. One created especially for you."

He'd been using that carrot all her life. Dangling it in front of her, but always keeping it out of reach. But that wasn't what hurt. "You lied to me. I can take Dad, but not you. I believed you."

"Dad said it was important that you—"

"And you just do whatever Dad says, right?"

"I don't know what's going on, but Kevin makes Dad nervous and he asked me to help him."

Dominique jumped up and paced. "You're not sorry."

"What?"

Just like Berton, she wasn't going to say she was sorry. "Are you proud of yourself? Yes, I can get my big dumb sister to do whatever I ask her to."

"That's not true. I'm sorry--"

"Sorry that I overheard you."

"Will you just listen? I don't know what Dad has against Kevin Jackson, but I know it's huge. The guy isn't what he seems. I've never seen Dad so anxious about a lawsuit before. He didn't want to ask you personally. He thought you'd be more interested if you were doing it for me. This isn't personal. Dominique?"

"I'm still here," she said softly, glancing at the door.

"You want to save the company, right? I know you quit your job because you got upset, but it's important to us. To you. You've given it your life. All you have to do is get a little dirt on Kevin and Dad will let you come back without any drama. And he—"

Dominique blinked back tears of rage. Did her father really think he could use her like this without her finding out? "I'm not coming back."

"You don't mean that."

She switched her phone to the other ear. "I mean every word."

"What will you do?"

"Don't pretend to care."

"I do care."

"Kevin Jackson's lawsuit isn't big enough to destroy the company. That's just a lie Dad said to scare you."

"I am scared, Dominique. Kevin Jackson is dangerous to us for some reason. Please help. Just...it doesn't even have to be something big. Just—"

Dominique hung up. She couldn't take her sister's lies anymore. How long had she been blind? She knew her father favored Gloria, but that hadn't bothered her until now. That he could pass her over for a promotion, then use her sister to lie to her and go on a while goose chase... She felt gutted and humiliated. Her sister had giggled as if she'd expected her to fail with Kevin. Kevin Jackson would sleep with anyone, but would he really stoop so low to sleep with her? That stung. She'd never known that side to her. She'd taken pride in being the older sister who'd protected her baby sister from the big wide world, and in return her sister saw her as a dowdy bore who couldn't lead a thirsty horse to water.

She was glad she hadn't told them about Kevin's pills or even the kiss. She'd deceived him, but she wouldn't hurt him. Especially not for her father.

Waves of emotion struck her as if she'd been tossed in the

ocean during a storm. She felt consumed by humiliation, then rage, then sorrow, then pain. Is that what her sister really thought of her? Her sister's betrayal sliced to her core. Gloria had been her heart. The little sister she'd always stood up for. The one she'd cover for when Gloria swiped their mother's jewels or favorite perfume. Did she really think Dominique had no life except for the business? That she would coldly and callously hurt someone else for the sake of the company? Was that the reputation she'd created? Or the one their father had created for her?

She'd always suspected Gloria was her father's favorite, but to hear the words...all that she'd done had never meant anything to him. Never would.

'She's so busy looking at the details she misses the big picture' she'd once over heard her father say to a colleague about her and he'd been right. She shouldn't have been so reckless. She'd altered her entire life, moved out of the family home, and become a driver for the sake of her sister's honor.

Now she was left with nothing. She'd been a great, big fool.

But she wouldn't be a fool again.

She'd make this work in her favor. Her father wanted something and so far she hadn't given it to him and she was going to make sure that he didn't get it. Why was Kevin such an interesting target? She'd read the lawsuit and there wasn't anything there. Why the worry? What was his fear? Why had they wanted to use her?

She was glad she quit. She'd thought of becoming an industry expert, but didn't want to have anything to do with her past. She was leaving the business world behind, along with any ties to her family. At least she had a job. Not one she would have chosen, but it allowed her to make a decent income and gave her a place to stay while she thought of her next steps.

Dominique looked around the cramped quarters—the simple bed, the view overlooking the garage—with grim satisfaction. This was where she belonged. Out from under her manipulative family's rule. She would stop her foolhardy attempts with Kevin. He needed a driver and she'd be one of the best. Whatever information they wanted about him, they wouldn't get it from her.

But it did make her wonder what made her father nervous about him. Cartwright Cars's lawyers would deal with a lawsuit as they'd done plenty of times in the past. Something else was going on and she'd find out what.

She'd been her family's cleanup crew since she was a little girl. She'd been her parents' little accident and they'd never let her forget it. They'd gotten married because of her, although it had worked well for both of them. Both completely self interested-- his ability to make money matched her mother's looks. To her mother's annoyance, she took after her father. She had a heavy, stocky build, square jaw and serious nature.

"If I hadn't been there when you were born I wouldn't have thought you were mine," she liked to tell her. Fortunately, her second daughter suited her better, matching her in looks and temperament. And yet she still loved them. Although she was nothing like them, they were her family and had her devotion.

Not any more. She wasn't going to be used. She wasn't going to be passed over. She wasn't going to be hurt again. And she was going to uncover what her father feared most.

CHAPTER THIRTEEN

Jackie sat at her kitchen table, looking through the photographs taken of Cassie right after the accident. They were in a folder, and part of the investigation to be used in the lawsuit. It still felt surreal. She couldn't believe Cassie still hadn't woken from her coma, though at least Marcus had his cast off, but he still wasn't talking...

She thumbed through the pictures, then stopped when something caught her eye.

"Clay, come here," she called.

Clay got up from the couch in the living room and joined her. "What is it?" he asked, taking a seat beside her.

"I hope it's not what I think it is. Look at the pattern of the bruises taken of Cassie's back."

"What about them?"

"They look like something may have hit her in the back and ricocheted off..."

He took the photo from her. "Let me see them."

"I've seen this pattern before." She thought of her work

with HOPE Services. Some of her clients, many of whom had hard lives, had come to her with various wounds and bruises.

"It looks like something grazed her back," Clay said.

"When she was examined at the hospital, they would have just seen them as individual bruises, since she was pretty banged up, and no one thought to take a closer look. They certainly wouldn't have been looking to connect them." She paused, watching her husband's expression closely. "Is it what I think it could be?"

He swore. "Yes, it looks like a bullet grazed her back."

CHAPTER FOURTEEN

The day of reckoning arrived on the heels of a summer storm. The air outside the hospital was heavy with the scent of wet earth and pavement, but inside the air was as cold as the arctic. Dominique had never planned to meet the family connected to the accident. But when Kevin had given her instructions to drive him to the hospital, and since she hadn't told him about her family's connection to the case yet, she had to obey him. She didn't know what she was walking into or why they were going to the hospital. Kevin remained oddly subdued.

He'd briefly told her that a woman named Jackie had called him, but that's all she knew. At the hospital, he'd stopped at the nurse's station and told her to go ahead.

Dominique took a deep breath as she walked towards the three men in the waiting area outside of Cassie's room. One leaned against the wall, away from everyone else, the kind of man one wouldn't want to meet in a dark alley; another stood with his arms folded and his head hung down, as still as a rattler, his hair was full of grey but he didn't look that old; and lastly she saw another man seated, wearing gold-rimmed glasses. He was of a slighter build and lighter complexion and looked the most approachable of the bunch. Unfortunately, she knew he wasn't Cassie's husband and that's who Kevin wanted her to talk to. From her online research she'd been able to gather about Cassie's life, Dominique knew the quiet rattler was Cassie's husband, Drake Henson, a successful restaurateur. There had been plenty of photos of the couple at various events. But she didn't know the best way to approach him. She'd have to feign innocence.

She walked up to the man with the glasses, but halted when his eyes met hers and a chill went through her. He had assessing brown eyes that could make him just as dangerous as the other two. Perhaps she'd miscalculated, but she couldn't back down now. She had to play it cool and pretend not to know anything.

"Mr. Henson?"

He stood. "Yes?"

"I'm very sorry to bother you, but I was told to talk to you about Cassie—"

The man shook his head. "You shouldn't be talking to me." He gestured to the quiet man behind him who'd lifted his head. "You should talk to him."

That's what I was afraid of. She shifted her gaze to Drake and met his amber gaze. She wished she hadn't. For a brief unguarded moment his eyes reflected such anguish, she felt her own heart shatter. And she felt the impact of all that had happened. She'd sent flowers, but they'd been woefully inadequate. At first, she'd thought about the lawsuit as just a nuisance, but what if their company had been at fault? What if her father was hiding something crucial? Soon she felt hazy and light as horrible thoughts filled her mind...

"Give her some room," a voice said.

Dominique felt herself being placed in a chair.

"Who is she?" another voice said.

"I don't know."

"Don't hover over her like that," a female voice said.

Dominique looked up and saw a petite woman with big brown eyes looking down at her. "I'm sorry," she said embarrassed.

"Don't be," the woman said with a soft smile. "Are you a friend of Cassie's?"

"No, I—"

Dominique stopped when she felt the energy in the room change. All three men tensed and the woman sighed as if resigned. "This is not good," she said in a soft voice.

Dominique turned to see what had gotten their attention and she saw Kevin a few yards away. His carefree expression gone and for the first time she saw how alone he was.

"How is she?" he asked.

Drake took a menacing step forward. "What are you doing here?"

The big man rested a hand on his shoulder. "Careful, mate. This isn't the place."

Kevin held out his hands in surrender. "Look, I don't know—"

Drake moved too fast for the other man to stop him. He grabbed Kevin by the collar and shoved him against the wall. "You don't know anything because you don't care. Because you're too busy partying every night and living your life as if nothing happened. While every day I wake up to the reality that at any moment everything I've ever wanted could be taken from me." He shoved him again. "Maybe if I took you outside I could help you remember."

"Drake, not here," the woman said. "Let him go."

Dominique saw Drake's grip tighten and rushed forward. "He really doesn't know anything."

Drake shot her a glance. "Really?" He looked at Kevin in disgust. "Hiding behind a woman? Why am I not surprised?"

"I'm not a woman, I'm his driver." She realized the inanity of her statement when Drake frowned at her. "What I mean is, I work for him."

"Then if you want to take him home in one piece, remove him from my sight." He casually shoved Kevin away as if tossing out garbage.

Dominique swallowed, terrified, but Kevin stared at Drake's back, and when he spoke his tone was defiant. "I have to see her," he said.

No one spoke. Drake didn't turn.

"I don't know what happened," Kevin said. "I don't know how she got shot."

Drake spun around. "Who told you that?"

"I did," the woman said. "I thought he should know."

"Why?"

"It might help him remember something."

Drake gestured to Kevin as if he were a broken appliance. "As you can see it did nothing."

The man with the glasses, adjusted his frames. "Since he's here—"

"No."

"Just for—"

"I said no."

"It may be good," the big man said. "It could trigger a memory."

"It won't," Drake said.

"You don't know that."

"But I know him." He looked at Kevin. "And I know he's a guy who's never suffered a day in his life. No one has ever had to depend on him. He's never had to sacrifice, he's never had to struggle. He won't remember because that would take too much effort."

"Then let him see what he's done," the big man said.

Drake paused.

"Let him see what we see," he continued. "Let him see what we live with, let him remember that."

Drake sighed and nodded. "Fine."

He turned and walked to Cassie's room, and Kevin and Dominique followed.

ERIC AND CLAY watched them go. "I hope this is a good idea," Eric said.

"Kevin's driver can play referee," Jackie said.

"It's better than nothing," Clay said.

Eric sat down, leaned back in his chair and looked up at Clay. "Found out anything?"

"Not yet."

"He's working really hard," Jackie said. "But you can't expect it to be easier for him than it's been for the police."

Eric sent his sister an affectionate grin. "Relax, I'm not Drake, remember? I'm not in the mood for a fight."

Jackie sat down beside him. "I know and I can't blame Drake. I'm mad too, but I don't know who to be mad at."

"Whoever did this," Clay said.

Eric leaned forward, resting his arms on his knees. "You know the longer Cassie stays in—"

"She'll wake up," Clay said, stopping Eric from saying what he didn't want to hear. His sister was going to recover. She had to. She was the heart of their family and he felt as if it were slowly breaking apart.

CHAPTER FIFTEEN

braham pounded his fist on his office desk and glared at his youngest daughter. "You're just telling me this now?"

Gloria grimaced. She probably should have used tears when she'd told her father about her last conversation with Dominique. She hated making mistakes. Just once she wanted to be considered the clever one. "I knew you'd be mad."

"So you waited nearly two days to tell me that she found out the truth? You're lucky I..." He stopped and shook his head. "You've given her time to plan."

"Plan what?"

"Do you know what she could do to us?"

"No," Gloria said throwing up her hands, exasperated. "I don't know. I don't know anything. Why won't you tell me anything?"

"Because you make mistakes like this."

"She sounded too angry to think straight."

"Dominique thinks even sharper when she's angry."

"Don't worry," Gloria said with a smug grin. "Dominique won't be staying there long."

"Why do you say that?"

"I sent Kevin a text. Once he finds out she's a fraud, he'll fire her and then you won't have to worry anymore."

KEVIN READ the text with cool detachment. After seeing Cassie being attached to monitors and an array of tubes, he felt numb. He didn't have the energy to care about Dominique's identity or her true intentions. He looked at the back of her head as she maneuvered the car through traffic. At least one puzzle was solved.

She'd wanted to tell him the truth, but he'd stopped her. He now wondered how long she would stay. Had she gotten the information she wanted? Would he wake up one day and find her gone? Did he really care? He wanted to sleep with her, but that was it. It was a pleasure he knew he'd never have, so he wasn't too disappointed. He'd miss her, but not for long. He'd learned not to depend on anyone.

He put his phone away. "Have you heard about Cartwright Cars?"

"Yes," Dominique said. He noticed that she didn't stiffen or make any indication that the topic bothered her. Like any leader, she knew what emotions to conceal. She was a cool customer.

"Did you know I'm suing them?"

"Because of the accident? Yes, I heard about it."

He brushed fuzz from his trouser leg. "This new development should make them happy."

"Why?"

"They can't be blamed for the car being shot at."

"Are you thinking of withdrawing the lawsuit?"

"Do you think I should?"

"It's none of my business."

"I'm just asking for an opinion."

"No."

He paused. "No, you won't give me an opinion or no I shouldn't withdraw?"

"No, you shouldn't withdraw," she said in a fierce tone. "Don't do anything yet."

Kevin stared at her for a long moment, surprised by her answer. She didn't want him to stop the lawsuit? Wasn't that the reason she was here? What was going on in her head? One thing he did know was if Dominique or her family had anything to do with putting Cassie in the hospital, he'd give her more than a lawsuit to worry about. He'd make her regret the day they ever crossed paths.

CHAPTER SIXTEEN

Ruth Quinn wiped her hands after taking out the trash at the end of her day. The children were asleep in bed and she had a streaming series she wanted to get back to. She stopped when she saw a faint trail of smoke and turned the corner. She saw Drake leaning against the side of the house, a cigarette to his lips. It was dark, so she couldn't make him out. He was more of silhouette in the darkness, the tip of his cigarette glowing red. He was an extraordinary man. Tall, handsome and most of all, kind. One of the few people in her life who ever looked at her. Really looked at her.

His wife was nice, but he was wonderful. He had the most mesmerizing amber eyes and soft island accent that gave her goose bumps. He didn't have to look or acknowledge a nobody like her, but he did, always asking how she was. If she was happy. Even though she called him Mr. Henson, he was always Drake in her dreams.

She'd never thought her dreams would ever come true. She'd imagined being alone with him in the grand house. Of sharing a meal with him, of just being with him, and now she was. She was so close. She wanted to comfort him. To let him know that she was there to handle his sadness. She'd overheard him talking to his brother about Cassie being shot and heard the surprise and anguish in his tone and wanted to rush to him. To let him know that he wasn't alone, but instead she stared and loved him from a distance.

She must have sighed or made a noise because he suddenly turned to her. And the spell was broken.

"Is something wrong?" he asked in a sharp tone. He could be impatient, sometimes curt, but it never bothered her.

She quickly shook her head, realizing that he must think she had news from the hospital. Good news for her would be bad news for him, but she was prepared for when that moment came. Unfortunately that moment hadn't happened yet. "No, I was just taking the trash out and saw the smoke." She nodded to his cigarette.

He looked down at the cigarette with chagrin. "I know I shouldn't."

She took a tentative step forward. "You're under a lot of stress."

The corner of his mouth kicked up in a quick grin that lightened his eyes and made her pulse race. "Yes." He winked at her. "This will be our little secret."

She nodded, no longer able to speak. A secret. A secret between them and nobody else. Wasn't that a sign of intimacy? He was growing to trust her more and more. Soon his heart would follow.

CHAPTER SEVENTEEN

He wasn't the same man.

Dominique sat in Kevin's silver Jaguar outside the club, tapping her fingers on the steering wheel, waiting for Kevin to emerge. He partied harder than he had before and that bothered her. Something wasn't right.

The man who had walked into Cassie Henson's hospital room hadn't been the one who had come out. She wasn't quite sure who had. He didn't look shattered or devastated, just composed as if he'd gone to a museum—respectful but untouched. Dominique could tell that Drake had expected to see something more, they all had. But Kevin had left the hospital without giving them the satisfaction. She could see why Drake had such a violent dislike for him, if she hadn't known him, she'd feel the same. He came across as a cavalier playboy.

She didn't know what to make of any of it. The palpable pain that hovered in the waiting room wasn't just the Hensons; she could feel Kevin's pain too. Through his words of anger she could see the pain of Cassie's husband. His love for her. She didn't know a man could love a woman that much. If she hadn't seen it, she wouldn't have believed such devotion was possible. And the other two men cared for her too. She felt almost envious of the comatose woman.

No one would care for her like this. Her mother perhaps, but no man in her life ever had or would. But that hadn't been the greatest shock. In the hospital she had learned that Kevin loved Cassie too. Not as a friend. Not as a brother. As a man. How long have you loved her? she wanted to ask him, but kept her thoughts to herself. She'd also seen for the first time how much Kevin was an outsider. She'd seen the men close ranks. He wasn't part of them and they made that clear.

There were so many questions.

What was going on? How had Cassie gotten shot? Kevin cared about her too much to put her in harm's way. His lack of memory didn't seem fake. He desperately looked like he wanted to remember when Drake threw his accusations at him.

One thing was clear. Kevin partied to escape. But his way of coping was becoming dangerous. For the past five days he'd been out every night and she'd seen him popping his white pills with more frequency. She knew it wasn't her place to interfere, but that wouldn't stop her.

"What did you just say to me?" Kevin asked after a long moment of silence.

"I said no." Dominique turned on the windshield wipers when a leisurely drizzle began to fall. She could feel his angry gaze on the back of her neck, but kept her eyes on the road.

She sighed with regret. She'd hoped the rain would hold, it would make what she had to do easier.

"You don't say no to me."

"I'm not driving you to another club, another party, another concert or anything else that leaves you hung over and barely able to stand by the end of the evening."

"How I spend my time is none of your business."

"But you—"

"Just shut up and drive."

For a moment he reminded her of her cousin Pat who had a habit of making his staff quit within a week. But she wasn't going to be provoked. "That's exactly what I'm doing."

"Drive me where I tell you to go. That's your job."

"You can't keep this up. I'm not going to watch you kill yourself."

"I didn't realize you cared," he said in a sour tone.

"I saw what you've been taking. It's a strong pain medicine."

"And it does its job."

"What do you need it for?"

His tone turned to ice. "What part of 'pain' and 'medicine' confused you?"

"Why won't you admit it?"

He paused. "Admit what?"

She gripped the steering wheel, reminding herself she was in control no matter how angry he got, she had him hostage. "Admit that you were more hurt in the accident than you're willing to let on."

He didn't reply. She looked in the rearview mirror and saw him staring out the window.

"You need to stop feeling guilty about what happened and find out the truth."

He kept silent.

"Maybe Drake was right about you."

"What do you want, Ms. Cartwright?" he said in a bored tone.

For a moment she lost control of the wheel and nearly swerved into the car in the next lane. He knew who she was! How long had he known? When had he found out? "I want to find out why your friend was shot," she said, glad to keep the tremor of fear she felt out of her voice.

"Try again," he said softly. She'd never heard that tone before. It had a cold, ominous quality that let her know that she may be behind the wheel, but he was still the one in charge.

She couldn't panic. She couldn't start to wonder how much he knew or care. She had to stay focused and deliberate. She wouldn't apologize and wouldn't explain. "Your life could be in danger and I want to help you."

"Why should I want the help of someone who can't admit when they're wrong?"

"Wrong?"

"You expect me to accept the help of a cold hearted bitc— woman who deceives me?"

She swore. Wasn't that how she felt after the talk with her sister? She'd just wanted her to say she was sorry, but apologies meant weakness. She'd had that drilled into her. She couldn't back down, she could use his outrage as a weapon, she could manipulate him so easily... she looked up and her heart turned cold when she met his eyes in the rearview mirror. She could see him assessing her as much as she was assessing him. They were rivals now and if she wanted to help him, she'd have to try a new strategy.

She pounded the steering wheel and swore again. "I'm sorry."

"Because you got caught?"

"Because...because I shouldn't be here in the first place. Because..." She knew the moment would come and if she was going to help him he had to know the truth even if it made her look ridiculous. "I came for revenge."

"Because you wanted to find something on me so that I would stop the lawsuit?"

"No, because of my sister. She told me that you seduced her, and..." Dominique shook her head, ashamed. "Let's just say I fell for a lie and then uncovered the truth."

"How?"

"That's not the point."

"I want to know how."

"I knew something wasn't right about her story, so I called and accidentally overheard her talking to my father. I think he's hiding something and knows more about the accident than he's letting on."

"Why do you want to help me?"

"Because I want to find out the truth about your accident."

"Why should I trust you?"

"I have no reason to lie anymore. I no longer work with my father, nor am I on speaking terms with my family and we—"

He turned and his eyes flashed. "You're mistaken. There's no 'we.'"

"If you want to find out the truth you'll need me."

He tapped a lazy beat against the window.

"Drake was right about you."

Kevin laughed amused. "Is that supposed to hurt me?"

Yes, it was supposed to make you angry. She tried another tactic. "Partying won't solve anything."

"You don't know anything about me."

"I know that you love Cassie."

He fell silent.

She suppressed a grin. Bull's eye. She had him now. "And if you love her as much as I think you do, I can help you. We're dealing with life and death."

Kevin glared out the window. "Where the hell are you taking me?"

"To the place you don't remember."

HE'D BLAME her for the nightmares.

Kevin sat in his gazebo watching the moonlight slowly sweep across the hushed garden. He hadn't remembered anything from seeing the accident site. He hated her for taking him there. He wanted to shout at her and tell her that he'd tried. He wanted to tell her how in his dreams he'd begged for a memory to come. That although he'd been questioned by the police, his mind lay empty. He knew he was the only key, but that didn't help, it only made him feel more useless. But he didn't let her know this. Instead he answered her inane questions as they stood at the accident site as if they bored him.

She covered her irritation and frustration well. Ferguson was right. He should have fired her when he had the chance. Now he needed her. Or had that been her plan all along? Her interest seemed genuine, but a woman like Dominique wasn't easy to read. But he'd go along until he had more information.

"What do you want me to do?" he remembered asking her on their way back from the accident scene, trying not to sound as angry as he felt.

"You have to stop partying for one. Just for a month," she quickly added.

"I have one scheduled next week."

"Then that will be your last one for a while. And you have to cut down on the medicine, if you can't stop completely. Are they just for your leg?"

He made a noncommittal sound.

"Okay, then you need to be careful. I need you to be healthy, and it's going to take a lot of work."

He inwardly groaned. He hated being told what to do. "Fine, what else?"

"Who was that tall guy in the bomber jacket at the hospital?"

"Cassie's brother, Clay. Why?"

"What does he do?"

"Does it matter?"

"Yes."

"Why?"

Dominique sighed sounding annoyed. "Can't you just answer a simple question?"

"No, why does it matter?"

"I think he might know something he hasn't told you."

That insight had him hooked. He'd never noticed that. Could Clay be keeping something from him?

"I really want to hate that woman," he muttered to himself as he remembered their conversation.

"But you still want to sleep with her," a deep voice said.

Kevin jumped up and spun around to see Ferguson coming out of the shadows. "What are you doing?"

"Checking on you. I noticed you didn't go out tonight."

"How do you know?"

"It's only twelve, and you wouldn't be home yet if you'd been partying."

Kevin sat back down. He couldn't argue with that logic.

"Am I right?" Ferguson asked taking a seat.

"You know you are. I should be up in my room recovering from a night of bright lights, loud music and Pussy Galore."

"You could get slapped for a comment like that."

"I was referring to the Bond Girl."

"No, you weren't."

Kevin grinned. "You're right. I wasn't." His grin widened. "And I'm not afraid of punishment."

Ferguson stared at him for a long moment. "Is that why you're keeping Dominique?"

Kevin's grin faded.

"Do you want her that bad?"

Yes. He wanted to hate her but he couldn't. He wanted to stop thinking about her, but couldn't stop. "She's helping me find out what happened."

"Do you trust her?"

He didn't want to need Dominique, but if she could help him find out what happened to Cassie, then he was willing to do whatever it took. "No, but she's the best option I have."

CHAPTER EIGHTEEN

The birds were going to drive her crazy. Dominique chewed on a sugar biscuit trying not to let the sound of chirping birds—*what the hell were they anyway? They didn't look like lovebirds*—bother her. She and Kevin sat in Clay and Jackie's cozy kitchen as she tried to focus on the seemingly mismatched pair. Jackie was as small as her husband was large; she had quick sudden movements while he seemed more careful and methodical.

"I requested the police report and investigated the scene and still don't have anything to tell you," Clay said. "No mechanical car failure, no witnesses."

"But—" Dominique said.

"But?"

"You suspect something, right? I could tell by the way you looked in the hospital that something was on your mind."

"Of course finding the bruising from a bullet changed everything. The police are trying to find out who may have wanted to kill Cassie or..." He shifted his gaze to Kevin. "Or you."

Dominique noticed the subtle accusation in his gaze and sighed. "Kevin still doesn't remember anything so you can stop being angry. Tell us what you really think."

Jackie nudged her husband. "Go on."

"Did you pick anyone up?" Clay asked Kevin.

Kevin shook his head. "No. Why?"

"Because the way the bullet hit Cassie it seems that whoever fired the gun may have done so from the back seat."

Kevin swore. "That doesn't make sense. I wouldn't have picked someone up. Only Cassie and Marcus were in the car. Do I look like the type who'd pick up hitchhikers?"

"It may not have been a hitchhiker. Maybe somebody you knew."

"Or someone Cassie knew."

They all fell silent knowing they couldn't ask her.

"But she doesn't have enemies," Jackie said.

"Neither do I," Kevin said, his tone soft, but certain.

"Maybe an ex-girlfriend or a married lover—"

"I don't sleep with married women. Or women with boyfriends. I don't need the complications."

Dominique rubbed her temples, trying to find calm and ignore the incessant chirping of the birds. "None of this makes sense. It was a pretty bad crash. If someone had been in the car, I'd be surprised that person was able to walk away from it."

Clay studied her for a moment. "You're not just his driver are you, Ms. Carter? What's your involvement in this?"

"I'm—"

"She's helping me investigate," Kevin said, standing. "If you find out anything more, let me know."

"WHY DIDN'T you want me to tell them the truth?" Dominique asked Kevin in the car as they drove home.

"We will, but not yet."

"Why not?"

"Because I want to solve this before he does. I'm sick of being the last to know."

"But he could help us."

"He's given us enough to start with."

"And—"

"He still doesn't fully trust me. Do you think they'll be this open once they know who your father is? The less people know about your connection the better."

CLAY STARED at the bird cage as their birds, Laura and Howard, ate.

"What are you thinking?" Jackie asked him.

"I'm not sure yet."

"His driver's interesting."

Clay turned to look at her. "She's more than interesting."

"Are you going to tell Drake about this?"

"Do you think I should?"

"I don't know."

"That's okay."

"What?"

"It's okay that you don't know everything. I don't want this to obsess you. We may never find out what really happened. Can you live with that?"

"No."

"What?"

"I'm not burying another sister before I get justice," Clay

said, referring to his sister who'd been killed. "I'm going to find out who did this."

"You're not burying anyone. Cassie will live."

Clay returned his gaze to the birds who were no longer chirping, desperate to believe what his wife had said. His cell phone rang, waking him from his melancholy thoughts.

"Who the hell did your sister piss off?" Detective Nicolas Douglas said without preamble.

Clay couldn't help a smile. "I thought you didn't believe in hell."

"Do you want to hear what I have to say, smartass, or do you want to talk about your Jewish book of fairy tales?"

"What is it?" Clay said, not in the mood to get into a discussion about religion with him.

"The car was tampered with."

Clay hung his head. "Shit."

"No, that's not the bad part. It was tampered with *after* it was in police custody."

He straightened. "What?"

"Yeah, the accident deconstructionist noticed that there were brake marks before the crash, but records show the brake line had been cut. The car's been contaminated. Someone doesn't want us to know what really happened. Someone with connections."

"Or deep pockets."

Nicolas laughed without humor. "My innocent little choir boy, they're usually one and the same."

CHAPTER NINETEEN

Drake stared at the little face in the window, a painful twist in his heart. *Don't do this to me*, he silently begged his daughter, Ericka. For the past couple days she'd started to cry every time he left for work. She'd never done that before. Even after the accident she'd been fine, asking when Mommy would be home, but that was it.

The morning crying fits were something new and they bothered him. But he had to soldier through. Marcus was doing well with his therapy and although he still refused to speak, he went to school and didn't show any anxiety when driving in a car.

Drake backed out of the driveway, then glanced at the window again. That was a mistake.

He saw her mouth open in silent screams, tears streaming down her face. He swore, then sighed.

When he walked through the front door she rushed up to him, burying her head in his trouser leg.

"I'm sorry, Mr. Henson," Ruth said. "She usually calms down."

He looked down at her. "Ericka, shh, I'm here." He pried her from his leg and knelt to her level. "Now what's wrong?"

She stopped crying, but didn't speak, her eyes and nose red.

"You know Daddy has to go to work. I know Mommy," he took a deep breath and started again. "I know Mommy is usually here with you, but she's away right now getting better. You like Ms. Quinn, you have fun together and you can tell me all about it when I get back."

She stiffened her chin. "Not Mommy."

"I know she's not Mommy, but she's here to look after you like she always has, so be good."

Her eyes began to well with tears again.

"Ericka."

"Not Mommy, not Mommy!"

"Ericka, stop it," Ruth said.

Drake held up his hand. "This isn't like her."

"She's throwing a tantrum."

"She's—"

"She's nearly three."

"And she's frightened," Drake finished. " I wish I understood what she wanted." He lifted Ericka up in his arms and stood. "I'll take her today."

Ruth stared at him alarmed. "But she'll calm down once you're gone. She—"

"Put some of her things in a bag for me," he said, leaving no room for argument.

Moments later, he strapped Ericka into her car seat. "We're only doing this today," he told her.

Ericka smiled, now in a better mood, all trauma forgotten.

He got in the driver's seat, briefly wondering if he was making a mistake. Ruth was probably right, she'd likely calm down after a few minutes. But it still bothered him that the behavior had started at all. Ericka was a very genial child. She took to anyone. Even at six months, she would go to anyone who was kind to her. She'd never displayed this kind of tantrum before. At a stop sign, he opened his glove compartment and reached for his carton of cigarettes. He had one in his mouth and was about to light it when he remembered Ericka in the back seat. He looked at her in the rearview mirror. "Your mother would kill me."

She smiled, then giggled as if he'd said something funny.

He sighed and put the cigarette away. He'd have to wait.

"Hey, what's this?" his brother Eric asked when Drake walked into the office of his restaurant, The Blue Mango, carrying Ericka in his arms.

"She was upset," he said, setting her bag on an empty chair.

Eric took his niece and kissed her loudly on the cheek then gave her a raspberry on the neck, making her giggle. "How's my princess?"

She told him, but neither man could make out exactly what she was saying. He set her down on the ground and handed her her favorite toy—a plush dragon.

"She looks fine to me," Eric said.

"You should have seen her awhile ago. Miserable and crying."

"About what?"

Drake sat behind his desk and shrugged. "I don't know. She wouldn't stop crying until I took her. She's started doing that the last few days. Ruth says she stops when I leave, but it just was too much for me. I'll only do this for today."

But the next day was no better. He decided to try tough love and left her, but once he reached the office, he called her. She still sounded tearful.

"It's a stage she has to grow out of," Ruth said. "She really is fine when you're gone."

"Hmm."

But for the next two days the pattern continued and his instincts told him something wasn't right. So that evening he called his brother.

"I need you to see something. Come over early tomorrow for breakfast."

"Okay."

Drake half hoped that Ericka would be fine. Through breakfast she eat and smiled and talked animatedly with Eric, but the moment they both stood to leave, her face crumbled.

"She's fine after a while," Ruth quickly assured Eric when she saw him looking at Ericka with concern. "Trust me, she's all smiles and giggles in a couple of minutes."

They nodded then left.

"You see what I mean?" Drake said as they sat in Drake's car staring at the little girl crying in the window.

Eric frowned, then jumped out of the car.

"What are you doing?"

He jogged up the front steps. "Sorry, I can't watch that."

"Did you forget something?" Ruth asked when she opened the door.

"I'm taking Ericka with me."

"Some children have separation anxiety, and she'll grow out of it."

"Fine, I'm still taking her with me."

"I don't think you should. You and Drake, I mean Mr. Henson," she quickly corrected when she saw his eyes narrow. "Are spoiling her."

Eric adjusted his glasses and waited.

Ruth wisely surrendered and turned to get Ericka's things.

he little girl was going to ruin everything! Ruth watched Drake and Eric drive away with anger roiling within her. Why did she have to start acting up? She'd been so sweet and easy before. She spun from the window and started clearing the dishes in the sink, light bounced off the copper pots hanging above, polishing the bowl of oranges, mangoes and apples sitting on the island. She saw a list of items Cassie had planned to buy tacked on the fridge. She knew better than to throw it away, although there was no use for it.

She'd help Drake get over his grief when Cassie eventually passed on. She'd let the list stay and may laminate it and put it in a special place. She already knew what dress they should bury her in. She'd gone through her closet enough times to know every item. Cassie would be proud to know that she'd left her family in the right hands.

Ericka would just have to get use to the change. Was it so hard for a three-year-old to call her Mommy once in a while? She'd have to anyway. What was wrong with a little pretend now? She usually liked make-believe. But every time she tried, the stubborn child pulled in her lip and glared at her. When she did become a permanent member of the household she'd let that child know who was in charge.

For now, she had to assure Drake and Eric that nothing was wrong. Drake would be easier than Eric. Eric was an odd man to her, and she wasn't really sure whether he liked her or not. When he came over he was always cordial, but his dark gaze was unreadable. He was a strange man. She couldn't believe such a boring looking accountant had been able to land a beautiful woman like Adriana. Adriana may be difficult too, the change would be hard for her since she was Cassie's best friend, she'd give her space to mourn. Maybe in time they could be friends too. Her main focus would first be the children. Fortunately, the Henson's youngest, Julie was still a baby and she'd only known Ruth as a mother figure in her life. It would take a couple of months, but then Ericka would calm down, but she couldn't let the men get in her way of assimilating her to the way things would soon be.

Ruth changed Julie's dirty diaper and put her in her bouncing chair. Slowly a new plan formed in her mind.

Perhaps she should let Ericka sleep a little longer than usual. If she gave her a light sleep aid at night then she'd still be asleep when Drake left in the morning. The only reason she even ate with them was because Ericka was a notoriously early riser and would wake up at the lightest sound, unlike her brother who could sleep through a tornado.

Marcus may also be a problem, but not as much. He was a good kid, but she knew his silence hurt Drake and that in turn infuriated her. Drake was stressed and unhappy enough, it was selfish of his son to refuse to speak to him. She'd have to talk to him again. The psychiatrist wasn't making much progress, but she didn't trust them much anyway. They rarely healed anyone, just gave them prescriptions or addictive drugs and charged for sessions that ended up lasting for years. She should know. Her sister was one. A know-it-all who actually thought she needed help. She was saner than anyone she knew.

Ruth looked down at Julie in her bouncing chair, then at the spacious living room, imagining curling up with Drake on the sofa, listening to him talk about his restaurants, laughing with him in the kitchen as he did with Cassie. It seemed to be their favorite room in the house. Although cooking never really interested her, she'd started to read the food magazines they subscribed to. She wanted to be interested in whatever he was. She looked at Julie and tweaked her chin, making the baby smile. "Yes, darling, I've finally found the life I was born to live."

CHAPTER TWENTY-ONE

"And then they just stopped," Drake said. He sat with Eric and Clay in Eugene's' Bar. The atmosphere had a strange quiet although a game on the TV was in full swing. There was the low murmur of voices, the clink of glasses, ice hitting the side of a glass, too loud laughter from a group that was either drunk or trying to be. "She stopped crying."

"Really?"

"Yes, she's sleeping later so I don't see her in the morning and when I get home she's fine. Still a little sleepy from her nap."

"Nap?" Eric said.

Clay looked at him. "Why do you sound surprised? Isn't that a good thing?"

He adjusted his glasses. "It just doesn't sound like her. Ericka never napped before."

Drake grinned. "She didn't used to. I know Cassie tried begging her, but she'd just stare at her. But I guess things have changed. I'm glad she's not so unhappy."

Clay glanced at Eric, who didn't look convinced, but wisely kept his thoughts to himself. "I thought I should let you know that I spoke to Jackson."

Drake stiffened; Eric's gaze sharpened. "Did he remember anything?" he asked.

Clay shook his head. "I thought I should mention him because of his driver."

"Driver?" Eric said.

"Yes, they both came and spoke to Jackie and me."

"He brought his driver?" Eric repeated just to make sure.

"Yes. You met her."

"We did?"

"Yes, at the hospital." When both men looked blank he said, "Come on, she's not that easy to forget. She was in a uniform. You thought she was one of Jackson's ladies."

Drake continued to look blank, but Eric nodded in remembrance. "Oh, right. Her."

"Who?" Drake asked.

Eric look at his brother disappointed. "She spoke to you and nearly fainted."

Drake nodded and snapped his fingers. "Yes, I remember now."

"Doesn't she remind you of someone?" Clay said.

Eric looked away. "Nobody is like Cassie."

"I didn't say she was. But there are similarities."

"Does it matter?" Drake said, catching the eye of a waitress for a refill. "Jackson always has a woman around him."

"Not a woman like this."

"He's been partying as if nothing's happened."

"Maybe," Clay said, pensive.

Eric looked at him closely, recognizing the tone. "Do you think she knows something that could be useful to us?"

Clay took a long swallow of his drink then set it down. "I think she's hiding something and I plan to find out what." He stood. "Catch you up later."

Eric nodded, then waited until Clay was gone before he turned to his brother and said, "Where are they?"

"What?"

"The cigs. I know you started smoking again."

He shrugged.

"Where are they?"

"Do I look dumb enough to tell you?" Drake grinned, then took a swallow of his drink.

Eric adjusted his glasses. "Don't do this."

"I'm not doing anything."

"I'm not going to stand aside and watch you fall apart like Dad."

Drake held out his hands. "Who's falling apart?"

"You know every puff is like a death knell."

"You're getting poetic."

"Where are they?" He held out his hand. "Are they in your pocket? In the glove compartment?" He wiggled his fingers with impatience. "Give them to me."

"I'm not Dad."

"Then tell me where they are."

Drake took another swallow.

"What are you going to do if she doesn't wake up?" Eric said, not giving him a chance to respond. "Go through a pack a day? Two packs? I'm not going to let you—"

Drake slammed down his glass. "I told you I'm not Dad."

"Then stop reminding me of him."

Drake shook his head, angered that his brother would compare him to a man who had withered away after the death of their mother. A weak man who'd left them orphans in a foreign country. At times he wondered if they'd stayed in Jamaica, how would their life have been? What would his life have been like if he hadn't been orphaned at sixteen with two younger siblings to raise? But that was the past. He'd proven he was stronger than his father and he always would be. What was a smoke here and there? It had gotten him through tough times before. He picked up a cardboard coaster and turned it over to look at the writing on the back. "I'm not Dad. Besides, it's different now."

"What do you mean by that?"

He tossed the coaster down. "If anything happens to me—"

Eric grabbed his wrist, his gaze dark, his eyes hard. "I'm not raising your kids."

The corner of his mouth kicked up. "Jackie will."

"You son of a bitch."

He shrugged trying to show a nonchalance he didn't feel. "I'm being honest."

"I'll tell you what you're being—"

"I thought you already told me."

"Do you want Marcus to hate you as much as we hated Dad?"

Drake yanked his wrist free. "I told you I'm not him, but I understand him now more than I had before."

"You believe in loving your wife more than your children?"

Drake's eyes blazed. "Don't tell me how I feel."

"Then don't tell me crap about understanding a man who abandoned us."

"He didn't abandon us. He died."

"He willed himself to. And you're doing the same. Every time you inhale that smoke you're willing yourself away from us."

Drake finished his drink then set the glass down. "I'm not going anywhere."

"Then tell me where they are."

"I'll quit."

"I don't believe you."

"Too bad." Drake stood. "You'll have to."

CHAPTER TWENTY-TWO

Someone had to look out for the children. Clay and Jackie focused on the mystery surrounding the accident, Drake focused on Cassie's progress or lack there of, but Eric worried about the children. He'd lied to his brother by saying he wouldn't look after his kids. He'd make sure that his nieces and nephew didn't suffer as they had. There would be no roach-infested rooms or days without eating. They'd get the very best. But it wasn't the future that bothered him as much as the present. The fact that his nephew still wouldn't talk and now his niece sleeping late and taking naps when she never used to before bothered him. He wanted to shield them, protect them, but he didn't know how, or even what from. Life could be a cruel teacher that didn't care about age; it didn't soften its lessons to accommodate innocence.

But he'd do his best to focus on them and make sure they were okay. Drake was a good father, coping as best he could, but Eric knew they could do more. They had to plan for the worst. Perhaps it was the accountant in him, but he had to pay attention to the details.

"We need to prepare in case Cassie doesn't make it," he told his wife Adriana later that evening as they put the plates away after dinner.

"She will," Adriana said, closing a cupboard. Her purple-black hair fell to her shoulders in soft curls, her bright red, gauzy top warmed her dark coffee skin.

"But just in case she—"

Adriana left the kitchen.

Eric took a deep breath. He knew the topic would be hard —Cassie was her best friend--but he didn't expect it to start off this bad. He hung up the dishtowel, then followed her into the living room. "I need you to be rational about this."

Adriana flipped through a fashion magazine. "I am being rational. Cassie is going to recover and—"

"But what if she doesn't?"

"She will," Adriana said, ripping a perfume sample. "She has to." Adriana took a sniff of the scent, made a face, then tossed it aside. "She can't leave her three children. She's so happy and she has plans to—"

Eric sat in front of his wife, stunned. "Do you think Death cares? That doesn't matter."

Adriana snapped the magazine closed and glared at him. "Of course it matters. She's a fighter. She'll make it."

"She may not. No matter how much we want her to live—"

Adriana held up her hand. "Will you just shut up?"

"People die. I know." He touched his chest. "You think my mother wasn't a fighter? You think she wanted to leave us?"

"Cassie will live." She clapped her hands together as a thought struck her. "I know what we need. I think we should schedule dinner next Sunday."

"No."

"It's been a while and we haven't gathered as a family since—"

"No."

"Cassie would want it."

"Oh, and we're supposed to pretend she's not there? Where would you hold it?"

"Here, of course."

"You can't even cook." His wife owned three successful lingerie stores and had her own growing line, but she wasn't good in the kitchen. "Or perhaps we could just hire a chef and also hire someone to provide the laughter."

Adriana glared at him. "You're not being fair."

"And you're being unrealistic. How do you think Drake will feel?"

"He needs to know we're there to support him. It's important."

"Pretending isn't the way to get through this period."

"It's not pretending. It's a way to look out for each other."

"That's what I'm trying to do."

"You're doing it wrong."

He threw up his hands, exasperated. "Why am I the only one willing to talk about this? Willing to think about what will happen in case things don't work out the way we want?"

"Maybe because the rest of us don't have the cold accountant heart. If you loved her even half as much as I did, you wouldn't be able to imagine what you're saying."

His voice dropped and turned hard. "I love her—"

Adriana jumped to her feet. "No, you don't. You already have her halfway in the ground. Do you have her funeral planned out too? Do you have a grief counselor lined up for the children?"

Eric pinched the bridge of his nose then stood and reached for her hand. "Adriana, I just want—"

Adriana pulled her hand away. "You can think and plan all you want, just do it without me. And we're having a Sunday dinner." She turned and stormed down the hall.

Moments later, Eric heard the bedroom door slam and softly swore. Why was he the enemy? First Drake and now her. He grabbed a water pitcher and watered some of the many plants that filled their home. He dusted the leaves on their large kangaroo fern and checked the impressive succulent agave plant that would soon outgrow its pot. But once he was finished checking his plants, he still felt restless. He grabbed his keys and left. He was half a block away when someone grabbed his hand. He turned and saw his nine-year-old step-daughter, looking up at him with fear in her eyes. "Please don't go."

"I'm just going for a walk." He squeezed her hand when she looked uncertain. "I'm coming back."

She nodded and looked ahead. "Where were you going?"

"Nowhere. I just need to think. I don't want to talk, just walk. Okay?"

She nodded. After two short blocks, she said, "Can we talk now?"

Eric sighed, resigned. "Go ahead."

"Do you think Aunty Cassie is going to die?"

His throat constricted. "I don't know."

She squeezed his hand and smiled. "Don't worry, she won't."

"Why not?"

"Because we love her too much and when you love something it never dies."

He stared down at her in wonder. *God, had he ever been*

that innocent? Had he ever been so full of hope? Eric stopped and knelt in front of her. "Sometimes people die anyway, it's nobody's fault," he said, holding her gaze and keeping his voice solemn. He could have sugarcoated the truth, but he felt that would be unfair.

"But she can't." Nina's eyes filled with tears and her bottom lip trembled. "She can't leave us yet. Tell me she won't."

"I can't promise you that."

"If she does leave us, does that mean she doesn't love us as much as we love her? Maybe heaven's so beautiful she doesn't want to be with us anymore. But I know Marcus will be so sad and I'll..." She covered her eyes and burst into tears.

Eric drew her close and hugged her. "I don't know what will happen, but I don't want you to be afraid. We'll take care of you, Marcus, Ericka and Julie."

She lifted her head and sniffed. "Even if you and Mom get a divorce?"

Eric paused. He'd thought she was up in her room and hadn't heard them. "We're not getting a divorce. We're both very sad and that makes us angry."

Nina wiped her eyes with the back of her hand. "What Mom said was wrong. I know you love Aunty Cassie."

For the first time Eric had to swallow back tears, he hadn't realized how much his wife's words had hurt him. He stood and took Nina's hand. "Right now I think you're the only person who thinks so."

"I NEED you to listen to me," Eric said in the quiet darkness of their bedroom. "Nina overheard us tonight, so we have to be careful about what we say to each other."

"I don't regret a thing," Adriana said, keeping her back to him. "I meant what I said. I don't want to talk about Cassie dying."

"I know you're upset and that's fine, but don't ever..." He took a deep breath to cool his temper. It wasn't until this moment that he realized how angry he was. "Don't ever say, hint or imply that I don't love Cassie."

She turned to him. "But you—"

"I said listen."

She pulled up the sheets higher, lay back on her side, but remained silent.

"When Cassie came into my brother's life, I felt as if God, the Universe or whatever you want to call it, was making up for taking our parents away. As if some cosmic injustice had been rectified. She filled a hole in my heart that I didn't even know I had. She is not just my sister-in-law, she is my sister, my family," he said and his voice shook with feeling, but he didn't care. "And my family is my heart. Don't you forget that."

Adriana sat up and turned on the lights, then looked down at her husband as he squinted up at her against the glare. As she looked at him without his glasses, she saw that he looked a little more vulnerable, a little less austere and she saw the pain in his eyes. Pain she'd caused him. Sometimes she forgot how much he could feel. How much he did feel. He came across so rational and calculating, his words tearing her apart inside. Shining a light on all her fears that she wanted to hurt him, she wanted to shut him up, but she'd been unfair. "I'm sorry." She took his hand and held it in both of hers. "Truly sorry. You're right, I was upset and I..." She set his hand down and folded her arms. "It's just that sometimes you drive me crazy. You say things in such a cold, matter-of-fact way."

"That's the only way I can face this. I can't afford to feel anything. I must think about my brother and my nieces and nephew. I will make sure that this doesn't tear my family apart and I know that it can." He took a deep, steadying breath. "I need you by my side. I know it's not easy, but please...don't push me away. I can take Drake, but not you."

"I'm not strong enough, Eric. I'm sorry. I can't. Not yet. I can't think of Cassie dying. Please don't ask me to."

He lowered his gaze, resigned. "Okay."

"You're angry with me."

"I'm not angry."

"Disappointed, then."

He shook his head, wishing he could tell her that he felt alone. How glad he was that she wasn't in Cassie's place. "No, I'm not." He turned on his side. "We should get some sleep."

Adriana turned off the light with a feeling of guilt. It wasn't like Eric to ask her for much and she felt as if she'd failed him. She had her fears, but she knew he had his too. She rested her hand on his chest and whispered in his ear. "I'll try."

He fell onto his back and looked up at her. "What?"

"This is hard for me, but...I'll be by your side. I'll get angry and frustrated, but you'll never lose me."

Eric gathered her into his arms, his heart aching for his brother because he knew this moment, this feeling, this connection was what his brother missed most.

CHAPTER TWENTY-THREE

"You might as well tell me," Dominique said, taking a chair in her father's office.

Abraham leaned back in his chair, an amused smile toying with his lips. "It's about time you showed up."

"Stop stalling."

"I'm not doing anything except trying to have a nice conversation with my daughter."

"You spew so much bull I'm surprised you don't stink." She folded her arms. "Go on, spill it."

He lifted his brows. "What?"

"Whatever you're trying to hide."

He lifted his brows higher. "Who says I'm trying to hide anything?"

"You and Gloria succeeded in making a fool out of me once, I won't give you that opportunity a second time."

Abraham glanced at his watch. "If you want to have a family squabble, can we schedule it for after business hours?"

"Why does Kevin Jackson make you afraid?"

Abraham shifted his gaze to her. "Did you tell him about us?" His look turned to pity. "Did you pour your little broken heart out to him to try to get back at us?"

Dominique let her arms fall to her side and studied him. "Is that what you wanted?"

"Are you sleeping with him?"

She narrowed her eyes. "Watch yourself, Dad. You don't want me as an enemy."

Abraham leaned forward, clasping his hands together on the desk. "I have enemies who can slice you into bits, and others who have been eager for my bones since you were still in nappies. You don't scare me."

"I'll find out who does."

"Not if you want to protect your mother."

Dominique's confidence faltered. "Mom can take care of herself," she said, although the words sounded hollow.

"We're tightly linked, and if anything happens to me, she'll follow. And don't forget that you carry my name and my blood. Are you willing to destroy your life in the process?"

Dominique swallowed, but held his gaze. She couldn't turn away; that would be a sign of weakness he could use. "I won't carry your secrets."

"You say that now, but you don't even know what they are. We're of one blood, and the more you hurt me the more you hurt yourself." He sniffed. "I shouldn't be surprised. You don't like yourself very much, do you?"

"I'll find out what you're hiding and uncover every secret—"

"The crash wasn't an accident," he cut in, his tone flat.

She paused, fear creeping up her skin. "What? You wanted to kill Kevin?"

"No. My dear, the crash was perfect." Abraham flatted

his hands on the desk and leaned back. "Beautiful even. It was the victims who were all wrong. They got into the wrong car."

Victims? He'd meant someone else to get hurt? "Who should have gotten in the car? What are you talking about? An assassination attempt?"

Abraham adjusted his tie then smoothed it down. "It's best that you not know."

"How deep are you in it?"

"Deep enough."

She swore. Secrets. He was forcing her to keep secrets when she'd vowed not to. "Then why did you want me to go after Kevin?"

"To see what he knew."

Dominique crossed her legs, studying her father's expression. "You're lying to me, you could have told me this before."

"I wanted to make sure his memory was really gone."

"What do you think he knows?"

"Why did you lie to your sister?"

"I didn't lie," she replied before recognizing his trap. He was putting her on the defense. "Don't you—"

"You could have had him. Both of you discussing your father issues."

"Why Kevin?"

"I just wanted some dirt, some leverage that's all. To play a psychological game."

She felt her temper rise, then stopped as a thought hit her. *Father issues?* How had he known about that? She hadn't told anyone, unless. She swore. The SOB had bugged her. She looked down and thought of the necklace her sister had given her to wear. The one she *always* wore. She tore it off and hung it out to him. "Is this what I think it is?"

Her father's expression changed just enough for her to get the answer. "You bastard."

"If you knew who we were dealing with, you'd understand."

They'd used her to spy on Kevin, to record their conversations. *You were always able to get people to open up.* Fortunately, Kevin hadn't opened up enough.

"Walk away from this. I know I made you angry, but it's just your pride talking."

"I think—"

"You don't. That's your problem. Every thought in your head I put there. You're just a tool and if you try to fight me, you'll be a tool for my enemies. Go home and forget any of this happened. It was just mistaken identities that's all. Kevin got in the wrong car and I was trying to cover my tracks. That's all."

She didn't believe him. Although his words ripped at the very fabric of her soul, wounded her to the core. It would have hurt less if he'd called her stupid, incompetent. But a tool? A useless instrument? That gripped her heart in pain, but she wouldn't focus on his words. That's what he wanted. He wanted to hurt and distract her from the truth. No. He was still hiding something. She didn't believe it was that simple. The wrong car, she could believe. Then why not just settle? Why fight the lawsuit? Why try to get dirt on Kevin?

She drummed her fingers. No. She was asking the wrong questions. It wasn't about her father. It wasn't Kevin who made her father nervous, it was someone else. Someone who'd chosen the wrong victim. Someone who had the power to make her father sweat. That person was the one pulling the strings and she wouldn't be able to get all the answers until she found out who.

She stood. "We'll see."

"Don't be naïve. Do you really think I've gotten this far by being a choir boy?"

"No, I knew you were ruthless, manipulative and sometimes an ass, but I never thought you'd shake hands with a murderer."

Abraham shrugged unmoved by the accusation. "No one's died yet."

"Is your contact planning to keep it that way?"

"That's none of my business. Or yours." His tone deepened. "Remember what curiosity did to the cat." He pointed at her. "And you only have one life."

Dominique just blinked. She didn't nod in agreement or scowl in disgust. She gave him no indication of how his words affected her. Instead she stood and calmly walked out.

Abraham watched her go, then pounded the desk with his fist. Gloria had ruined it. The whole incident was supposed to be settled weeks ago. If he'd pressed Dominique harder, she would have reported back to him with some information he could use to blackmail Jackson. Soon after the accident, he'd tried to find a woman to get close to Jackson, but the man seemed to know who to confide in. He'd even had one skilled lady attend Kevin's party, wearing earrings with a recording device, certain he'd get some pillow talk he could use. But she'd ended up empty. That's when he'd thought of using Dominique.

Dominique had a different charm with men like Jackson. He'd wanted her to be angry at Kevin to see what she'd do. She didn't care how she betrayed him, only that she did. And it would have worked. Kevin had gotten close to her. Through the recordings he could hear Kevin trusting her, but now that was over.

He took a deep breath. He hadn't gotten this far by being swayed by his emotions. Dominique was angry, but that would blind her to the truth. She'd focus on him and miss the big picture, that was always her strongest flaw. A flaw that would work in his favor.

"I told you there was nothing to worry about," Abraham said to the third occupant of the room who'd been hiding in the closet.

"I don't remember you telling me that," the man said.

"You heard her and you've listened to the recordings. Jackson doesn't remember anything."

"Do you think she'll find out you lied about the car?"

"No. You can relax now."

"Then we have a new problem."

Abraham stood and poured himself a glass of water. "I don't see it."

"Because you don't want to. Make sure she doesn't keep digging."

He took a long swallow then set the glass down. "She won't find anything."

"Are you positive about that?"

"Yes."

"Then you don't know your daughter as well as you think."

CHAPTER TWENTY-FOUR

Rating lovers had become a favorite hobby of hers. She didn't have a sophisticated rating system. She preferred to focus on the basics. Overall performance. Endurance. Creativity. Her latest lover had a cumulative rating of negative three. Fortunately, that wasn't why she was with him.

Carla looked at Berton as he pulled on his trousers. Dominique's ex-boyfriend was well made in every department, but didn't know how to use his equipment to the fullest and she wasn't in the mood to teach him. So far her affair had proved useful, but not enough. She still didn't know what her husband was up to and the fact that he was keeping Berton in the dark worried her. Abraham was talking to someone, but who? She hadn't been able to get anything out of Gloria, who'd tearfully told her that Dominique was mad at her and then explained the reason.

Carla listened without care. Gloria had been able to turn her tears off and on since she was a child, but only Dominique hadn't been able to figure that out. Dominique. Poor thing didn't even realize she was just a chess piece in a game. But Carla would make sure they won. One day she and Dominique would own everything, but not yet. She shifted her gaze to the hotel window where a dying sun swept across the city.

"What's he nervous about?" she asked Berton as he tucked in his shirt.

"The lawsuit, that's the first thing on his mind."

"Has he heard from Dominique?"

"No, I don't think he expects to."

Of course he does, he's up to something. "What has he said about her?"

Berton sat on the bed and put on his shoes. "Said?"

"He may be giving her space, but he's still keeping an eye on her."

"He hasn't said anything to me."

Carla sighed. Yes, she'd have to move on soon. He was useless if he couldn't supply her with the information she wanted.

BERTON RODE the hotel elevator to the lobby floor, stifling a yawn. God she was a bore. He was getting tired of pretending to be her lapdog, but it got him close to the action. A woman like Carla was a king maker and he planned to be the next one on the throne, but she didn't need to know that. He'd let her think that she was using him, as well as let Cartwright think he would sit idly by and believe his promises. He was nobody's donkey, but the Cartwrights would find that out.

Man, he'd thought his family was messed up, but the Cartwrights made dysfunction look like a compliment. He'd targeted Dominique because she was a good strategy, but when Cartwright approached him with his scheme, he knew there was something more and then Carla had grabbed his ass at a company party, making her intentions known. Dominique had no idea she was just a piece in her parents' weird game.

But he didn't feel sorry for her. She was as cold as ice. He'd gotten freezer burn just trying to get a leg over. Kevin Jackson would find that out. It'd been easy keeping the affair secret; Carla was clearly a pro and had likely taken Dominique's other boyfriends to bed, although he didn't understand what pleasure she got out of doing it. She was fiercely loyal to her daughter in other respects, always talking her up and saying how great she'd be as president, but that was where the devotion ended. She was a cool, calculating woman. He'd enjoy her a lot more if she didn't talk so damn much or ask so many questions, but at least it was a way to keep an eye on her.

She'd get rid of him soon, but he'd come up with information that would make her interested again. He knew how to pull her strings.

CHAPTER TWENTY-FIVE

*H*e was in pain. No one else could see it from the smile on Kevin's face, but Dominique had become attuned to him. It was the way he leaned against the wall, the way he flexed his hand. She almost regretted allowing him one last party, but she knew stopping him would be impossible. Plus, he'd told her that a party at his house was one of the last things he'd remembered before the accident. A party Cassie and her husband had come to, but they hadn't stayed.

Dominique could understand why they hadn't.

She didn't even know why she'd accepted Kevin's offer to come. She knew it had been a challenge she should have ignored. Partying wasn't her thing and she felt as out of place as a giraffe among flamingos. Most of the guests were women—the ratio seemed to be three to one—and she didn't do chit-chat well. She'd had plans to make a quick exit when she'd spotted Kevin in the hallway with a woman pressed so close to him, if she pressed her body any closer, she'd be behind him. Seeing him in action was always amusing because he handled women well. He'd end conversations without being rude or insulting, flatter without sounding glib or insincere. He had his choice of women, who were putty in his hands. She wondered why he didn't disappear upstairs with one of them. Was it his leg?

She didn't care. What he did was none of her business. She watched the woman run a bright pink fingernail along his jaw.

She realized that seeing him with other women didn't make her feel jealous. He never inspired that in her. He never made her feel ignored or discarded. She could see why he had so many female friends.

Kevin was easy to love. And loving him wouldn't feel like a risk. A woman would be cared for and treasured and not mind that she'd just be one of the many who adored him and wanted him to be happy. Kevin didn't need her. He didn't need anyone. He had all that he needed. Looks, money, attention.

She wanted to walk out the door.

If only it hadn't been for his damn mouth—the way it curved slightly down when he was hurting—she'd be in her bedroom, out of her dress and heels and sitting on her couch with a nice roll of hob nobs, looking through the report from the investigator she'd hired to watch Cassie's family. She wanted to make sure her father wasn't having anyone follow Drake or the kids. So far it seemed his only interest was Kevin. She hadn't told Kevin what she'd learned about him getting into the wrong car or the bugged necklace. She wanted to find out more first. Their search for a fourth passenger had come to a dead end and her father wasn't talking. She and Kevin had spoken to the technician on call that day who'd given Kevin the car, but he didn't remember anyone being with them. She wanted to go home and come up with her next strategy.

Unfortunately, his mouth bothered her.

Dominique walked up to him and whispered in his ear,

"Don't fight me on this," then collapsed against him and said, "Damn, I think I twisted my ankle." She took off her shoe and winced. "Stupid heels. Could you help me to the couch?" She turned to the woman he'd been flirting with. "Sorry about this."

"Not as sorry as you will be." She looped a possessive arm through Kevin's. "I was here first."

Dominique sighed, she was not in the mood to fight over him. "You can follow us."

"He's not going anywhere." The woman tightened her hold and Dominique saw Kevin wince.

This wasn't going to be easy. She looked like the type of woman who was in the mood for a fight, so Dominique knew a belligerent attitude would make things worse. She would go on the offensive. She widened her eyes as if in shock. "Wait. Do you think?" She rested a hand on her chest. "It's nothing like that between us. I'm his cousin."

"His cousin?"

"No," Kevin said.

"Yes," Dominique quickly corrected sending him a daggered look. He stared back without flinching.

"Which one is it?" Pink Nails demanded.

"We're distant cousins."

"Very distant," Kevin muttered.

"And my foot really is killing me. I'm not used to these kinds of parties."

Pink Nails measured her up and down. "Is that why you're dressed like you're going to a funeral or something?"

Dominique kept her smile although the woman had insulted one of her best dresses. "Yes. So could you just give us a couple minutes?"

She looked at Dominique, then Kevin.

Kevin winked at the woman. "We'll finish our discussion later."

Pink Nails pursed her lips. "Promise?"

He smiled and that was all the assurance she needed. She let his arm go, brushed her lips against his cheek, then sauntered away. Dominique looped her arm through his. "What is wrong with you?" she asked as they walked towards the lounge. He rested heavily against her and she fought not to buckle under his weight. "You nearly ruined it."

"I don't like pretending we're related."

It hurt that he disliked her so much, but she kept her voice nonchalant. "I'll think of something else next time. No, wait... there won't be a next time."

"I don't care as long as you promise to burn that dress after tonight."

Dominique looked down at herself. "What's wrong with it?"

"Too many things for me to list. It's so bad it's actually making my eyes water."

She thought she looked lovely. Her mother said it was her killer dress. What was so awful about it? And why did he care anyway? Why did she? "It's my best dress. My mother bought it for me."

"You mean your grandmother."

"No," she said through clenched teeth. "My mother. My very stylish, beautiful mother."

"Everyone makes mistakes sometimes." He lowered his arm and whacked her on the bottom. "Don't frown, cousin," he said in a low voice, smiling at her look of stunned outrage. "You can be annoyed with me. Even angry, but don't frown. It makes me look bad. Women are always happy in my presence."

Dominique's voice returned to her. "You are a—"

Kevin tapped the corner of her mouth. "If you don't smile, I'll kiss you."

Dominique plastered a smile on her face. "You still are—"

He patted her hand that was resting on his arm. "Thank you, cousin. I'll tell Aunty to send you another dress. The cut and lines are all wrong in this one. Your figure disappears and the color." He squeezed his eyes shut. "If I could strip you down, I would."

"I'm sure you would like to try," Dominique said in a grim tone.

"To *redress* you," he clarified. "Although the other idea is tempting," he said, his low voice turning to velvet.

A delicious shudder heated her body. They were surrounded by people, but he made her feel as if they were alone. The voices around them became a faint hum, the low lights and music fell away. He filled every crevice of her mind, gripping her heart with a longing she desperately wanted to forget. They didn't have a chance. He didn't like her. She'd betrayed him. It could never work. She didn't want to remember what his lips tasted like, the feel of his arms around her, the sight of him naked. She didn't want to care about the soft whisper his shirt made brushing against her sleeve.

She frantically scanned the room and spotted a place to sit. It didn't look comfortable, appearing like an expensive artistic design made for style over function, but she hoped they'd reach it before someone else did.

"What's the sudden rush?" Kevin said, when she sped up.

Dominique kept her eye on the goal. She was going to get him in that chair and then disappear. "I know you're hurting, just bear with me."

"I'm trying."

"I wonder if I should get you a cane."

"Buy me one and you're fired."

"Oh, I guess bruises are the price I pay for this job."

Kevin looked instantly chagrined. He loosened his grip. "Damn, sorry. I didn't realize I—"

"You're pushing your body past its limit," she said, for the first time wishing his house wasn't so big. Her intended object felt miles away.

"I just need to sit down."

"Why didn't you tell her that?" Dominique asked, more frustrated by the distance of the seat than with him. "She'd lie down next to you if you wanted her to."

"Jealous?"

"What?" She sounded more bitter than she wanted to. "Of something that could never be?"

Kevin opened his mouth to respond, but two attractive women in form-fitting dresses interrupted him. "Oh Kevin, we—"

"Sorry," Dominique said, faking a grimace. "But he's helping me to the couch. I twisted my ankle." She exaggerated a limp and led them over to the available seat. He sank into it with visible relief, but one of the women dressed in orange took the extra space beside him.

"I really need that seat," Dominique said.

The woman looked up at Dominique in challenge. "What are you going to do, sit on me?"

It was a tempting thought. The cute little stick of a girl could be snapped in two.

Kevin patted his lap. "Wouldn't you prefer to sit on me?"

The woman eagerly did so, but instead of sitting on the one leg he directed her to, she sat on both. He briefly closed his eyes and tightened his jaw. Dominique gritted her teeth. He was trying to be Mr. Smooth and hurting himself in the process. She resisted the urge to yank the woman off of his lap. Instead, she grabbed a glass from a passing waiter and poured it in the woman's lap.

The woman jumped up outraged. "You fat bitch!"

Dominique sat down next to Kevin. "I know."

The woman glared at her, then stormed off. Her friend sent Dominique a nasty look before she followed behind her friend.

"You didn't have to do that," Kevin said.

"Stop being a martyr. Your eyes nearly rolled to the back of your head when she sat on you."

"It was from a moment of ecstasy."

Dominique couldn't stop a smile. "You were in agony."

"Same thing."

She shifted in her seat. "These chairs are as uncomfortable as I thought they would be."

"You pretend that they're not."

She turned sharply to him. Was he pretending right now? She thought of the nights when he had to pop his white pills. "Are you feeling better? Do you need a drink?" She placed the back of her hand against his neck. "At least you're not sweating."

Kevin brushed her hand away. "Stop fussing over me. You're determined to ruin my image tonight, aren't you?"

She let her hand fall to her lap and gripped it in a fist. He was right. He had an image to maintain and it wouldn't be with someone like her. She should leave him alone. That's what she wanted to do anyway. "You're right. I'm sorry. I'll—"

He tapped the corner of her mouth. "Watch that frown or I'll have to kiss you." He glanced towards the entrance of the lounge. "And I won't care who..." His words fell away. He softly swore.

She turned to see what had caught his attention and saw the skinny stick marching towards them with Pink Nails following. Both looked to be on the warpath.

Kevin held up his hands. "Ladies, I—"

"You lied to me," Pink Nails said, her gaze pinned on Dominique. "You're not his cousin, are you?"

"Yes, I am and I'm sorry about your dress," Dominique said, looking at Skinny Stick. She stood up, but remembered too late that a movement like that could be seen as aggressive. She saw the woman's gaze narrow and knew she was in trouble. She didn't even see Pink Nails raise her fist, but she felt the punch. It hit her across her face with such force that she stumbled back, tripped over her own feet and hit the ground hard.

She didn't know why she looked over at Kevin first. She saw him surge to his feet—too quickly—and cringe, but this time she wondered if it was from pain or embarrassment. *You're determined to ruin my image tonight, aren't you?* She was doing him more harm than good. She shouldn't have tried to help him; she didn't have his finesse with people. She only knew how to make enemies.

Dominique surged to her feet, wiping the blood from her nose. "Good one. You caught me by surprise," she said, then punched Pink Nails in the gut. The woman doubled over and dropped to her knees in pain. "Now let's see if you can catch me," Dominique whispered in her ear. She sent Skinny Stick a savage look. "You can have him, but stay off his lap," she said. She didn't look at Kevin, although she could feel his eyes on her. Instead she took off her shoes and ran out of the room.

CHAPTER TWENTY-SIX

"Remind me to never invite you to another party."

Dominique stared at Kevin, stunned. She'd changed into a pair of sweats and had opened her front door, for some reason expecting Ferguson to tell her what a mess she'd made. She hadn't expected Kevin.

Kevin stood there with shadows in his eyes: a mixture of pain and something she wasn't able to read yet. She looked past him at the twenty-something stairs he'd had to climb to reach her door. "What is wrong with you?" she said, although the power of her words were muffled by the icepack she held against her nose. "You should be resting."

"I'm fine now," he said, pushing past her.

"With the help of a little white pill?"

He took a seat then smiled at her. "You sound sexy even when you nag."

"I'm not nagging...wait, what?"

He patted the space beside him. "Let me see."

"What are you doing here? What about your guests?"

He sighed and stood. "Don't pretend you didn't hear what I just said."

She turned her face away. "I'm fine. It's nothing."

He wrapped his hand around her wrist. "I may have a bad leg, but I'm still stronger than you." He lowered his voice. "Want to try punching me in the gut?"

"She hit me first."

Kevin flashed a wicked grin. "I know. I saw. For a moment I imagined you mud wrestling."

"I have the advantage of size," she said in a sour voice.

His grin widened. "I know that too." He reached for her ice pack. "Now let me see."

Dominique removed the pack with exaggerated reluctance, trying to ignore the pounding of her heart.

Kevin inspected her swollen nose then nodded. "At least the bleeding stopped and your nose isn't broken."

"She caught me by surprise," Dominique said, setting the ice pack aside. "It's no big deal."

He sat on her couch. "You should have let it rest."

"She was hurting you," Dominique said, looking around her. It had never bothered her before how sparsely furnished the room was. Now she regretted that there was only a couch. She didn't want to sit beside him. She didn't dare to when she couldn't keep her heart under control.

He frowned. "I didn't hire you to be my damn bodyguard."

"I was trying to help you." She folded her arms. She'd stand. He wouldn't stay long anyway. "Why do you pretend to be okay when you're not?"

"Because that's what I do," he said, resting one arm along the back of the couch. "I make people happy."

Why did he have to look so at home? It was a casual

innocuous movement, but it felt like an invitation to join him. Dominique folded her arms tighter. "At your own expense?"

He winked. "If that's what it takes."

"That's stupid."

"At least I don't get punched in the face."

He had her there and for some reason his words and expression reminded her of her grandmother, who'd nearly fainted when as a six-year-old, Dominique had fallen face down into a mud puddle, ruining her new Easter dress. She could just imagine how ridiculous she looked getting knocked out by a woman half her size. She burst into laugh.

Kevin stared at her open mouthed. "You think this is funny?"

His surprise made her laugh harder. Tears streamed down her cheeks.

"Are you laughing at you or at me?"

She pointed to herself then gasped. "I must...have looked... like such an idiot," she said. "Oh my God." She fell onto the couch before her legs gave way and covered her face. "She knocked me down with one punch." Dominique looked up at him and wiggled her fingers. "And didn't even break a nail. It's like some warped comedy sketch."

Kevin shook his head. "You're a strange woman," he said, but she heard laughter in his voice.

She wiped her eyes and nodded. "I know. But you're right, never invite me to parties. They're always disasters for me."

"Always?"

"Always. I remember my prom..." She stopped.

Kevin leaned forward. "What?"

Dominique slid away from him. "I keep forgetting how you are. You're too easy to talk to. You don't want to hear this."

He slid over closing the gap between them. "Yes, I do. Go on."

She shook her head. "I can't focus when you're this close."

He slid back. "Better?"

"Yes." She clasped her hands together ready to share her story. "Okay, it was my prom night. I had on this beautiful dress—"

Kevin lifted a brow, doubtful. "Better than the one you had on tonight?"

"Of course. It was silver and gorgeous."

"I guess I'll have to take your word for it."

"It was. And it had a long skirt that brushed against the ground and made me look as if I were floating. I loved it. Well, it got caught in the door as I was getting out of the limo. But I didn't know it and neither did the limo driver."

"Oh no," Kevin said, guessing the outcome.

"Oh yes. I went one direction and the limo went the other, taking my skirt down the block. I wanted to die."

"What did you do?"

"I ran after the limo of course." She pressed her hands against her cheeks. "What a sight that must have been," she said with a giggle. "But I didn't know what else to do. I'm sure you can see my humiliation online somewhere."

A sly smile touched his mouth. "I may have to do a search."

"Just don't tell me about it. Ever."

"What happened?"

"I was able to catch up with the limo at a stop sign, but let's just say the evening was ruined." She looked down at her lap, amusement making room for embarrassment. "I'm really sorry I ruined your party."

"You didn't ruin anything. She'd had too much to drink."

"She wasn't drunk."

"I was trying to make you feel better."

Dominique shook her head. "Sorry, Kevin, your smooth moves won't work on me tonight."

His eyebrows shot up in surprise. "Kevin?"

She blinked realizing her faux pas. She'd never called him by his name before. "I mean, sir."

"Too late. There's no going back." His eyes glinted with humor. "Besides, I like how you say my name."

He was making fun of her, but she couldn't blame him. He had a right to laugh at her expense. "I know what happened tonight and I know what I looked like. I'm just glad I didn't stumble against something and break it."

She expected him to smile, but instead his expression grew serious. "Next time, just let me handle it."

"I told you there won't be a next time," she said, startled that the space between them had closed. She hadn't noticed him move. Now the room felt smaller than it was and she couldn't keep her gaze off of his mouth. He had a beautiful mouth when it wasn't hiding pain.

She'd lied. If she wasn't careful, his smooth moves could work. She cleared her throat. "Shouldn't you be at home? Don't you have someone waiting for you to snuggle up with?"

"Are you offering?"

"Go home, Kevin."

He groaned. "Keep saying my name like that and I won't want to leave."

She playfully shoved him. "I mean it."

"Me too. You're trouble for me."

She tapped her chest. "I'm trouble?"

"Yes. The more you reject me, the more I want you."

"So it's a challenge?"

"Stop pretending you don't feel it too." He rested his head

on the back of the couch and closed his eyes. "I shouldn't be here. I don't want to be here." He opened his eyes and lifted his head. "But I am and it's not just because you're beautiful and have more curves than a race track." He flashed a grin that made her body burn. "Although that helps." He shook his head. "No, I'm here because you're driving me crazy. I couldn't stop thinking about you after you left the party. And I wanted to. I wanted to forget you and just have a good time. But I couldn't." His heated gaze fell to her lips. "When I kissed you on the boat, I meant it. Was that part of your act, or did you feel it too?"

Dominique didn't know how to respond. Was he really saying what he was saying? Was he really looking at her with a smoldering brown gaze that made her skin hot? It felt good. Better than good, it felt wonderful to have a man desire her like this. And she wouldn't lie. She wanted him too.

"It wasn't an act," she said, then kissed him. He kissed her back with a passion that sent waves of excitement through her. His words were real. He wanted her as much as she wanted him. She unbuttoned his shirt and deepened the kiss. He covered her hands when they fell to his trousers.

"I can't."

She blinked, waking out of her dream. "What?"

He drew away from her, keeping his gaze lowered. "I can't do this."

"Because of who I am?"

"Yes...no." He gripped his hands into a fist. "I want you so bad it hurts."

"You have me," Dominique said, confused, certain she'd given him all the right signals. "I want to do this." She stopped as a thought occurred to her. "Oh...is it because we don't have condoms? Do you want to do it at your place?"

"If only that were the problem," he said with a hollow laugh. He stood and began to button his shirt. "I'm sorry, I really shouldn't have come. It's not fair to you."

"Is it because of Cassie?"

He briefly looked up at her. "You think I'd put my life on hold because of how I feel about her?" He lowered his gaze and continued to button his shirt. "I'm not that noble."

"But you haven't been with a woman since--"

"You don't know that."

"You're right, I'm just your driver. I don't know anything about you. I guess it's just me.'

He tore a button from his shirt. "It's not you," he said, taking a deep breath.

"Then why--"

"Because I can't!" He threw the button across the room. "After the accident I haven't been able to be with a woman."

CHAPTER TWENTY-SEVEN

*D*ominique stared at him, trying to process his words. What did he mean he couldn't be with a woman? She had to be delicate with him and very careful. She knew it was hard to admit and she didn't want to embarrass him. "You're not alone," she said, taking a hesitant step towards him. "A lot of men have...deal with those issues. There are medications. Are you afraid of the side effects?"

He stared at her for a long moment and then a grin toyed with the corner of his mouth. "I don't physically have a problem. I can't..." He sighed. "It's not just my leg that sometimes hurts." He sighed again, this time with more feeling. "The pills I take help me with major migraines that leave me flat on my back sometimes for days. I get them when I dance or make love. And before you say anything, I have tried everything you can think of. Nothing works."

Dominique looked at him, feeling as if someone had dumped cold water on her. That's why he'd never taken a woman home with him. His partying had all been a show. A mystery had been solved and it broke her heart. The man she wanted to be with, the man with a reputation for being with women that was legendary, couldn't perform. She felt robbed, and angry then she felt an overwhelming sadness, first for herself and then for him.

Now she understood the pain in his eyes, the shadows. The pleasure he could no longer have. A pleasure he must miss. She felt weighted down by the secret he'd shared with her. A secret he'd been hiding for months.

Kevin regretted telling her the truth as the silence stretched between them. He shouldn't have told her. She'd probably start laughing again. He was prepared for it. He'd taken a risk because he'd wanted to shake things up. He was heading down a road he hated: the friend zone. He'd made that mistake with Cassie, and he wasn't going to do it again. Let her hate him or want him, but he wasn't going to let her see him as anything less than a man.

A man. He wished he could show her how much of a man he was, but he couldn't take that chance. A couple months ago, the challenge would have been fun, but not now. He couldn't let himself be vulnerable and give her that kind of advantage.

She'd probably quit. That would be good for both of them. He'd continue his inquiries on his own. He didn't need her. He didn't want her.

You're a liar, Jackson. That's what frustrated him the most. He did want her, more than ever. Not just because she was a challenge, or because he knew there was a soft center under that hard shell, but because she could laugh at herself and he felt more like himself when he was with her. He held her gaze, seeing her surprise, and waited for her response. He silently dared her to laugh or to pity him. He wanted a reason to hate her that would keep him safe.

Safe. He'd never worried about keeping himself safe from a

woman before, but he'd never felt this way. Never been this confused. Never wanted to push someone away and hold them close. This wasn't like him. When it came to women, he was always in control; he just let them think he wasn't. But this time it wasn't a game. He was losing his edge, and he could feel it unraveling. Cassie had been his first. He wouldn't make that mistake again. He shoved his hands into his pockets and said, "Now you have the dirt you need to ruin my reputation."

"It's not funny," she said.

He paused, surprised to hear tears in her voice. Or was that laughter? He couldn't be sure. He didn't want to care. He turned to the door. "I should go."

She raced ahead of him and plastered herself against the door like an overzealous coed at a 'Save the Earth' rally. "No!"

He bit his lip and swore. If he wasn't careful she was going to make him laugh. He cleared his throat and narrowed his eyes, hoping he didn't look amused. "What are you doing?"

She widened her eyes and waved her arms. "Do I need to be any more obvious?"

He spun away and fell back on the couch. He lay on his back and covered his eyes. "Yes, you're definitely driving me crazy."

Dominique knelt beside his head. "There are other ways we can be together."

He sent her a pointed look. "Do you like being on your knees?" he asked nodding towards her present position.

She looked thoughtful. "If it will help. Is that all you can do?"

He stared at her amazed. "I haven't tried," he admitted, then he sat up and shook his head. "No, wait. We're not having this conversation."

"We don't have to do anything tonight, I just want you to know that we have options."

"We're not talking about this. Now get up. I can't stand seeing you on your knees."

Dominique shifted until she was positioned between his legs. She gazed up at him and fluttered her lashes. "Are you sure?"

Kevin crossed his legs. Just the thought made him hard. "I'm sure that you're trouble."

She rested her chin on his knee. "I won't tell anyone." She lowered her gaze to his crotch, her look as powerful as a caress. "But I won't pretend that I'm not disappointed."

He jumped up, causing Dominique to fall to the side. "That's it. I'm gone."

"Please don't go." She scrambled to her feet. "I want to be with you."

His tone hardened. "You've made that very clear even though you know I can't—"

She quickly shook her head. "No, I mean, I like being with you," she said, looking suddenly shy. "Just as we are. Like this. Together." She smiled. "You're not only good for one thing."

Kevin hesitated, unsure of what to make of her words. What did she mean she liked being with him like this? This was new territory; he'd never been abstinent with a woman he wanted. He felt his heart go cold as a thought came to him. "We're *not* going to be friends."

"What?"

"I don't want to be your friend," he said slowly, punctuating every word.

"I don't want to be your friend either."

He felt his tension ebb.

She brushed her lips against his. "But is it okay if I kiss you?"

He nodded, afraid to speak.

She slid her hand down his chest. "And touch you?"

He nodded again.

She wrapped her arms around him. "And hold you?"

"Hmm," he said, feeling his body respond. It was sweet agony.

"Relax, Kevin, and you'll enjoy this."

"This is new for me," he said, feeling awkward. "I don't know what to do."

"You can start by putting your arms around me too."

He groaned. "Not unless we're both naked standing under a cold shower."

Her face fell. "You're not enjoying this?"

He smiled down at her. "It's like asking a hungry man to enjoy a meal the size of a thimble."

"Oh." She let her hands fall.

"It's okay." He lifted her arms and fashioned them around his waist. "I can get used to it. It will take practice."

Her smile returned. "I like practicing."

"Until you get bored."

"I won't get bored," she said, giving him a light squeeze and resting her head on his chest. "I like being with you."

She meant it. That was what amazed him the most. She didn't need him to perform either in bed or out.

"We can cuddle in front of the TV with some munchies," she said.

"I've never cuddled with a woman in my life."

She looked up at him, surprised, then stepped away from him. "You've never tenderly held a woman in your arms?" She hugged herself to demonstrate.

"Of course I've done that, but I don't call that cuddling."

She let her arms fall to her side. "Then what do you call it?"

"Foreplay." He held up his hands. "Don't touch me any more tonight. I've had all the practice I can stand."

"Okay."

He took a deep breath. "If you promise not to touch me, I'll stay."

Dominique scratched her head. "I don't know if I can." Her gaze dropped to his shirt where it was missing a button.

"Dominique," he said in warning.

She held her hands together and beamed at him. "Just kidding. I'll go make some popcorn." She headed for the kitchen. "Don't worry, you're safe from me."

Kevin watched her, realizing she had no idea how wrong she was.

CHAPTER TWENTY-EIGHT

Safety zones and danger zones. That's what their relationship involved and Kevin was determined to get the hang of it. Her place and his bedroom were definitely danger zones. As was his private theater. They tried not to be alone as much as possible. Dominique helped distract him by focusing on trying to figure out the possible fourth passenger. She'd also told him about the investigator she'd hired to watch Cassie's family.

One afternoon, as they sat in his entertainment lounge, he caught Dominique searching through some images on her phone that the investigator had sent her. "Let me see that," he said.

He looked through the pictures and stopped when he saw one of the pictures showing Henson's nanny with Marcus at the playground. "I've seen this dress. Cassie was wearing it the night of the party."

"A dress similar to it?"

He shook his head. "No, not similar. Exactly."

"Well, it can't be the same dress because they're different in size."

He frowned. "Even the shoes are the same."

"Well, maybe it's a popular look. I can't tell you much about women's fashions."

I can and it's not popular, he thought. Kevin shrugged, wanting to shed his sense of unease. It was a coincidence. "Hmmm. You're probably right." He turned on the TV, then looked at Dominique to ask her what she wanted to watch, but saw her eyes fixed on the screen.

"Reginald Avery has gone missing," the news anchor said.

Kevin turned. But he didn't hear the rest of the report. The face was all that mattered. He knew that face from somewhere. "I think I saw him that day. The day of the accident. Maybe he was outside the building or one of the sales managers."

"You couldn't have met him there."

"Why not?"

"Because he's one of my father's biggest rivals."

CHAPTER TWENTY-NINE

Speak and your mom dies. That's what the man told him. He couldn't talk no matter what. He had to save Mommy.

"You have to speak," Ms. Ruth scolded Marcus as she tucked him into bed. "Do you want to keep making your Dad sad? It's your fault if he is." She pinned him with a stare. "You're being selfish and mean. Do you like being mean?"

Marcus shook his head, gripping Toro tight. He wished Toro wasn't a stuffed dinosaur but real. Real enough to scare all the monsters away.

Ms. Ruth smoothed out the sides of the sheet. "If you really loved your dad, you would say something."

She was angry with him, but he didn't know what to do. He didn't want his Mommy to die; he was scared. He didn't want his Daddy sad. His Daddy was so sad. Was that because of him? Because he was sad too? He wanted to be good. He hadn't said anything, so why hadn't Mommy come home yet? How long did he have to be quiet?

"You're a big boy now," Ms. Ruth said, tucking the sheets

tight against his neck. He hated when she did that, but he didn't want to get into more trouble. "Say something." She frowned when he continued to stare at her. "You can't keep this up. It's not hard, just say one word. Can you do that?"

Marcus closed his eyes, wanting her to go away. Wanting her to leave him alone. Wanting his mom to be the one tucking him in. *Mommy, come home please. I'll be good forever, I promise.* He heard Ms. Ruth's footsteps head for the door and then the sound of the light clicking off. He opened his eyes to the darkness, fighting against tears. Ms. Ruth was right. He was a big boy now and he'd save his mom by doing what the man told him to.

DRAKE STRETCHED out on the couch, a single lamp the only light in the room. The last couple of months he'd spent more time on the couch than in his bedroom. He still hadn't gotten used to sleeping alone. He never wanted to get used to it. Every day he told himself that they were closer to Cassie coming home.

He turned on the TV and flipped through a series of cooking channels to watch. Food and cooking always helped him relax. That was one thing that connected them. He'd already imagined the first meal Cassie would ask him to make. He pictured her sitting at the table while he cooked. And at times, he imagined her in the kitchen, making their favorite Jamaican dish, ackee and saltfish. Cutting up a banana for Ericka to eat. Showing Marcus how to fold an egg into cookie dough, and helping him make a smiley face on his pancakes with strawberries and blueberries.

Marcus. Drake sighed at the thought of his son. He'd come

home too late to see him before he was put to bed. Regret and exhaustion made his arms and legs feel like lead. He was about to drift off to sleep when he felt a small hand on his arm. He blinked and sat up when he saw Marcus. "What are you doing up?" He rubbed his eyes. "You can't sleep?"

Marcus shook his head.

"Want some milk?"

He shook his head again, then took Drake's hand and tugged on it. Drake stood and let his son lead him to the kitchen.

"Do you want a snack?" Drake asked him.

Marcus shook his head again, then pointed to the stove then the pots.

Drake shook his head. "I don't know what you want."

Marcus pointed again with more animation.

"Honey, what do you want? You want me to cook?"

He nodded.

"What do you want me to cook?"

He shrugged.

Drake knelt in front of him. "Can't you tell me? Don't you want to tell me?"

His gaze fell.

"Try."

He shook his head.

"I can't cook if you won't let me know what you want."

Marcus pointed to the stove again, firm.

"What are you trying to say?" Drake snapped, losing his patience.

Marcus's lower lip trembled and his eyes filled with tears.

"No, don't cry. I just..." He drew him into his arms and hugged him. "It's okay."

But Marcus cried as if his little heart would break and

Drake didn't know how to comfort him. "I know you miss Mom. Did you have a nightmare?" He stroked his back. "It's going to be okay." He stood with Marcus in his arms. "I know, let's make some cocoa and you can keep me company. Would you like that?"

Marcus nodded, then kissed him on the cheek.

"I love you too," Drake said, setting his son down. He grabbed two cups, wishing he didn't feel so inadequate. He wished he knew how to break his son's silence without making him cry.

CHAPTER THIRTY

$\mathcal{E}$ric returned home to the sound of the smoke alarm and the acrid smell of something burning. He set his things down in the foyer and raced into the kitchen where he saw his son crying in his high chair, dirty dishes stacked in the sink, and something charred sitting on top of the open stove. He also noticed another mysterious dish on the counter. Eric closed the stove and picked Geoffrey up to soothe him. "Your mother made a right mess, didn't she?"

Adriana came around the corner, smoothing down a bandage on her forearm.

"What did you do?"

"A slight burn. Don't worry, I took care of it."

Eric glanced at the blackened mess on the stove, then poked the mysterious mash on the counter. It moved, and he didn't think it was supposed to do that. He looked at Adriana. "Should I ask?"

Adriana frowned and grabbed a fork. "Maybe it tastes better than it looks."

Eric snatched it from her. "I'm not eating that and neither is anyone else."

"What else are we going to do about dinner?"

He sighed. "You're determined to have a family meal, aren't you?"

"Yes."

"What is that awful smell?" Nina asked, coming into the kitchen after arriving home from summer camp.

"Your Mom won't tell me."

"It was supposed to be dinner."

Nina frowned. "But you never cook dinner."

"I cook sometimes."

"A frozen dinner isn't cooking."

Adriana folded her arms amused by her daughters disdain. "It's still food."

"But—"

"She was trying to replicate the Sunday dinners we have at Uncle Drake's," Eric clarified.

Adriana made a face at him. "Replicate? Do you have to talk that way?"

Nina smiled, clasping her hands at the thought of the family being together. "Oh yeah, those are so much fun. Aunty Cassie always..." She let her words fall away.

Adriana tore off her apron in defeat. "I know I can't compare to her. I shouldn't have tried."

"Perhaps we could serve bread and tea," Eric said, setting Geoffrey back in his high chair.

Adriana managed a watery smile. "Cassie would laugh at this." She shook her head. "Oh, what would I do without her?"

"I think Sunday dinner would be great," Nina said.

Eric shook his head. "I'm not sure, Drake..." he stopped

when he saw the hope on their faces. "Okay," he said, holding his hands up in surrender. "If everyone wants to come we'll hire a caterer."

CHAPTER THIRTY-ONE

To Eric's surprise, Drake readily agreed to the idea and suggested they have the dinner at his house as always. He even offered to prepare the meal, brushing Eric and Adriana's protestations aside. When everyone arrived, an elaborately set table greeted them, along with the sight of chicken cashew with citrus rice and scalloped tomatoes, which they all ate with relish. They later enjoyed a succulent bread pudding with lemon sauce for dessert.

After an initial awkward conversation, they soon fell into their old routine, Eric sharing Adriana's disaster in the kitchen and Clay entertaining them with a tale of a crazy client he'd had to help. Nina looked at the adults, her heart glad. She'd been nervous about tonight and remembered shyly going into the kitchen where Uncle Drake was cooking and handing him herbs from her garden. She'd done this before, but she wasn't sure if he'd want them anymore. She hadn't even known what he was making for dinner, or if they would help, but she wanted to give him something. She wanted everything to be the same like before. So when she called out his name, her voice cracked a little.

He looked down at her. She held out the container.

Drake took it and smiled, lightly touching her cheek. "Thanks love, it's just what I need."

"You haven't even opened it yet," she said, but she couldn't help smiling back at him. When Uncle Drake smiled, his whole face changed and it made her happy.

"But I know it will be perfect. Go wash up and you'll see."

And she did. She could taste the basil on the chicken and it was wonderful. Aunty Cassie had to come back to this. She didn't want any of it to change. She felt a little guilty feeling so happy when her cousin Marcus didn't look happy at all. His nanny, Ms. Ruth, had been given the night off, so when they were excused from the table and went into the kid's playroom, they were alone.

"It's okay to whisper," Nina said as she and Marcus sat on the ground coloring. "Whispering isn't the same as talking."

Marcus continued to color a picture of a family having a picnic, adding purple to the green grass then whispered, "She says I'm bad."

Nina felt her heart stop then begin to race. "Who?"

"Ms. Ruth."

"Why?"

He grabbed another crayon to color in the sun and his voice filled with tears. "She says I make Daddy sad because I don't talk."

"Why won't you talk?"

Marcus shook his head and colored harder.

"You can tell me."

Marcus stopped coloring and broke his crayon in half. He grabbed two more and broke them too.

"Didn't your mom teach you that secrets are bad?" Nina quickly waved her hands and shook her head when his tears started to fall. They splashed on his picture. "No, wait, I didn't mean it like that. You're not in trouble and you're not bad. It's just...we all really like when you talk. Don't you want to?"

"Yes," he whispered, then fell forward and cried on his arms.

Nina patted his back, anxiously glancing at the doorway. She didn't want to get into trouble for making him cry. She didn't mean to. "It's okay. I'm sorry. You don't make Uncle Drake sad, okay? He's happy that...that you're so strong and brave. He told me so."

Marcus lifted his tear-stained face. "Really?"

"Yes," she said, hoping he would believe her lie. "When I was in the kitchen with him, he said so. We're all so glad you're so much better than before. So Ms. Ruth's wrong. You're not bad."

ERIC GLANCED at Nina through the rearview mirror as they drove home. "You've hardly said anything. What's wrong?"

"Didn't you enjoy yourself?" Adriana asked.

"I did," Nina said. "It was fun."

"Then what is it?" Eric asked when she grew silent again.

She scratched her head. "I don't know."

"You look very serious," he said.

She bit her lip. "I got Marcus to talk to me."

Adriana turned in her seat to stare at her daughter, amazed. "That's wonderful." She looked at her husband. "Eric, we should go back and let Drake know and—"

"No, no Mom...it wasn't like that," Nina said in a rush.

"What do you mean?"

"I didn't really get him to talk, it was more like a whisper. I told him that whispering was different."

"What did he say?" Eric asked before Adriana could respond.

"You should turn the car around," Adriana said. "So we can—"

Eric shook his head. "I'm not turning the car around." He glanced at Nina's reflection. "What did he say, Nina?"

"That's the funny part. He said Ms. Ruth said he was making Uncle Drake sad. And I think he wants to talk, but he's afraid to."

Adriana frowned. "She shouldn't have told him that. I'll have to tell Drake."

"No, don't," Eric said.

"Why not?"

"Because if he confronts her and there's a conflict, Marcus might think it's his fault and stop even whispering. We have to handle this carefully."

"But if she's telling him lies that make him feel bad—"

Eric sighed. "I know. I don't like that either."

"We have to do something," Adriana said.

"Agreed."

"Let me talk to her first. Maybe he misunderstood her," Adriana said.

"Marcus isn't one to lie."

"I didn't say lie, did I?"

Eric playfully tugged on her hair. "No, I'm sorry." He looked at Nina and smiled. "Well done. I'm glad you told us."

She grinned, sitting taller in her seat.

"You're sure you don't want to tell Drake about this?" Adriana said.

"I'm sure," Eric said in a grim tone. He had to handle the situation delicately. "But I can think of someone else who should know."

CHAPTER THIRTY-TWO

"You have to tell Drake," Jackie said when Eric told her and Clay about Marcus. The three sat in a DC café at the end of the afternoon rush.

"About Ruth?" Eric said, stirring a fourth spoonful of sugar into his coffee.

"No, about Marcus talking. At least give him some hope that his son is improving. He needs it."

"Kevin should know too," Clay said.

They both looked at him.

He shrugged. "It's true. It's not just Drake who's suffering. It'll ease his mind."

"Maybe an uneasy mind is what he needs," Eric said in a bitter tone.

"I'm not defending the bloke, I'm just saying it might help."

"He's right," Jackie said. "Maybe Marcus should see him."

"Drake won't like that," Eric said.

"If we tell him it's for Marcus's sake, he might."

Eric shook his head. "There's no way he'll say yes to that."

Jackie flashed an impish grin. "You leave Drake to me."

DOMINIQUE SAW the little boy's face light up at the sight of Kevin. She and Kevin had been in the garden, discussing the missing person's report about Reginald Avery when Ferguson announced Jackie and Marcus's arrival. Before Kevin could even get up to greet them, Marcus rushed ahead and threw himself into Kevin's arms. Kevin hugged him back, looking embarrassed and a little awkward, which surprised her. He was usually smooth about everything.

"Sorry we didn't call first," Jackie said. "But coming here was sort of a spur of the moment idea."

"Does Henson know you're here?" Kevin asked.

"Yes, and he's not happy, but we both thought it might be for the best." She looked at her nephew, who now sat on Kevin's lap with a large grin on his face. "And I think I'm right. I haven't seen him this happy in a while."

Kevin rubbed Marcus's head with affection. "It's great to see you." He set him to the side.

Marcus continued to smile.

Kevin motioned to Ferguson. "Get us some refreshments."

Jackie shook her head. "No, I'm not staying." She took a step back.

Kevin stood with mounting unease. "But you both just got here."

"I'll come back to get him in an hour."

"Come back?"

Jackie laughed at the shock on his face. "I thought maybe you two could spend time together. He might open up to you."

"But I don't know what—"

"Make it two hours," Dominique said, ignoring Kevin's panicked look.

"Two hours?" His voice cracked. "I don't know what to do with a—"

"Are you sure?" Jackie asked.

"Yes, trust me," Dominique assured her.

Jackie laughed again. "I do." She wiggled her fingers at the stunned man standing behind Dominique. "Goodbye, Kevin."

He blinked as if coming out of a stupor. "But—"

"Relax," Dominique said affectionately, patting his cheek. "We'll be fine."

THEY WERE BETTER THAN FINE. Once she'd helped Kevin get over his reticence, they had fun. They played hide and seek, a video game, read a story from one of the picture books Marcus had brought, and laughed at a cartoon until he was ready for a nap.

"That wasn't too hard was it?" Dominique said as they sat in the living room. She nodded to the little boy whose head rested on Kevin's lap.

"No," he admitted, surprised.

"He really likes you."

"That must keep his father up at night."

"You sound pleased."

"Annoying Henson is a hobby of mine."

"I'm glad you don't take it out on his son. He is such a cutie and he adores you."

Kevin frowned down at the boy. "I don't know why."

"You're very likeable."

He nodded, accepting the compliment as obvious. "Of

course, he's got his mother's good taste." *Good taste.* He remembered saying that to Marcus that day. Kevin had worn the macaroni bracelet Marcus had made for him. He remembered the smile on the boy's face when he showed him. He remembered the feel of the wind, glancing at the bracelet as he switched gears. The feel of the road. Laughter. They'd been so happy.

The missing man. He'd seen him by the car. But he shouldn't have been there. The image changed and he saw the bracelet broken and scattered on the ground covered in blood. Whose blood? His? Cassie's?

"What is it?" Dominique asked in a sharp tone.

He blinked, the memory fading. "What? Why?"

"You had a faraway look. Did you remember something?"

I think so. "No. Nothing that can help us."

"Why were you so awkward with him when he came?"

"I guess I don't know what to do with boys. I'm not..." He searched for words.

"One of the guys?" she finished.

"Yea, something like that. I always got along better with girls and they with me."

"Is that why you don't have any male friends?"

"Probably. I get bored with beer and car talk and business and sports events."

"Not all men are into that."

"I know. Thanks for today. I've never spent time with him like this and it was fun."

"You can show him what interests you. Things that are age appropriate," she quickly added when he started to grin.

"I won't introduce him to the club scene until he's at least sixteen."

"I take it back. Stay away from him. I'd hate to see what you'd turn him into in a couple of years."

"A man who appreciates all things beautiful."

The doorbell rang. Dominique stood up. "That's probably Jackie. I'll go get his things." She left.

Kevin nudged Marcus awake. "Come on. Your aunt's here to take you home."

Marcus blinked his eyes then sat up. When he saw that they were alone he said, "Nina said it was okay if I whispered."

Kevin leaned in close, surprised he was talking. "Why do you have to whisper?"

"Because the man said if I talked, Mommy would die."

CHAPTER THIRTY-THREE

He was waiting for a reward. Ain't no way he was saying nothing without some financial compensation. Yeah, that was the word them big-ass lawyers always used on the TV. He wasn't no dummy. He knew what he saw was worth something, but it was taking the damn police a long time to figure it out. They'd only casually asked about information, but that was months ago and they hadn't added no reward to it. Did they really think he was going give up the goods without getting something in return?

Lyle Huntley walked to his kitchen and swore when he stepped on one of his kid's Legos. Damn things hurt like hell. How many times did he have to tell them to clean up after theyselves? Not that it was their fault, their mother acted like their new trailer was her palace or something. She never cooked or cleaned like a proper woman, just sat her fat ass on the couch barking out orders as if she ran the place. He didn't know why he stayed. His mother had warned him she was no good—maybe that was why he stayed, to prove her wrong. But after seven years and three kids—he wasn't even sure the last one was his—he was getting antsy.

Money would be a way out. His ticket to freedom was at hand and he wasn't giving it away to nobody. But it sure was taking longer than he thought it would. He wanted to tell somebody so bad he nearly spilled it at the bar after one too many drinks, but fortunately he stopped himself. He knew if he spoke, someone else could go to the police before him and take all the glory. Nah, he couldn't have that.

But maybe he had to do this another way. Police gave up too easy, but the family might be willing to pay and he knew they had money. They may be more interested in giving him a reward.

CHAPTER THIRTY-FOUR

*H*e *had eyes that knew too much*, Dominique thought when she found Clay standing in the hallway.

A cool smile touched his lips at the look of her surprise. "Jackie had an errand to run."

Way too much. She'd sensed it when she'd first seen him at the hospital and later at his house, but in the dying light of the evening, she saw it even more. He was a man who'd seen a lot in his life, most of it bad. She had to play it cool. "Well, Marcus is almost ready."

"No rush. I wanted to talk to you."

That was what she was afraid of. "Me?"

"Does Kevin know about you?"

"I don't—"

"I may look like a right git to you, but I assure you I'm not. So there's no need to play games with me, Ms. Cartwright."

"Kevin knows."

"How much?"

"Do you expect me to play my hand without showing yours?"

He folded his arms. "You think I'm hiding something?"

"I know you are."

"Why? Because you're hiding something bigger?"

Before she could respond, Kevin came into the hallway holding Marcus. "Clay, good. There's something you need to hear."

Now that he could whisper, Marcus told them about the man, but wasn't able to describe the man in any detail. When they'd shown him a picture of Reginald Avery, he shook his head. They also asked if the scary man had been in the back seat with him and he said no. Not wanting to overwhelm him with questions, they let him go play a video game with Ferguson.

"I think it's about time we start working together," Clay said. "No more secrets. I'll tell you what I know." He pointed to Dominique. "I know she's not your driver. That she's the daughter of the owner of Cartwright Cars and her father, or someone with money, doesn't want the accident solved." He briefed them on what his friend, Nicolas, had told him then nodded to Dominique. "Your turn."

"It wasn't an accident," Dominique said. "Cassie wasn't a target, it was a mistake."

"A mistake?" Kevin said stunned.

"Yes, you...you got the wrong car," she said, repeating what her father had told her.

"When did you find this out?"

She hesitated, then gathered her courage. It was time to tell the truth. "After...I learned that Cassie had been shot, I went to my father demanding answers."

Kevin folded his arms and sent her a hard look. "And you didn't tell me this because...?"

"I wanted to find out more."

"You wanted to protect your father," Kevin said.

"That's not it."

Kevin shook his head. "Every time I start to trust you, you give me a reason not to."

"It was you I was trying to protect, not him."

"How noble."

Clay gave a delicate cough. "Can we have this lover's quarrel later?"

They both glared at him.

"He actually had my necklace bugged," Dominique said, eager to prove her point. "Trust me, we're on the same side."

"At least we have one thing cleared up," Clay said. "Based on what Marcus remembers, there wasn't a fourth passenger. You didn't pick up anyone."

"Then how did Cassie get shot?"

"It could have come from the outside."

"The police didn't find any bullet holes," Kevin said.

"But after what Clay's friend told him they may not have been looking hard," Dominique said.

"Who was the real target?" Clay asked.

"I don't know yet," Dominique said.

"Do we really want to know?" Kevin said.

Clay and Dominique looked at him, stunned. "Of course we do," Dominique said.

Kevin shook his head. "I don't think you two are seeing the big picture here. Someone threatened a kid, and attempted to kill Cassie or myself thinking we were somebody else. Someone with money tampered with police evidence. I don't know about you, but finding out who's behind this won't help Cassie."

"You expect me to step back and do nothing?" Clay asked.

"You've done enough. We got the answer we wanted."

"No, you did. You're off the hook because you know you weren't to blame." He flashed a cold smile. "I knew you were lazy, but I didn't think you were callous. You really don't think about anyone but yourself."

Kevin rested a hand over his heart. "Should I get a box of tissues?"

Clay's face changed. "You really are a—"

Dominique held up her hands. "We're on the same side, remember?"

"No," Clay said, shaking his head. "He isn't one of us. He isn't even like us. There's no one he's loyal to. No one who depends on him. He doesn't need answers because as long as he's all right everything's fine."

"I bet you wish I was in a coma instead of Cassie," Kevin said.

"Every day," Clay replied, his tone marked with loathing.

Kevin shrugged. "You're right. I'm not like you and I make no apologies for it." His gaze darkened. "But don't forget who you're talking to. I know you have your own reasons for seeking answers that has nothing to do with family loyalty. Chasing after shadows won't make Cassie wake up."

"Neither will pretending they're not there."

"I know shadows are there," Kevin said. "They've always been there and they always will be. As long as the sun shines there will be shadows."

Clay stood. "I am not going to let someone get away with threatening my nephew."

"Are you prepared to make Jackie a widow?" Kevin shot

him a look. "You're a married man who continues to act like a single one."

"Jackie knows—"

"That she can't fight you. That you'll see this through no matter what."

"Don't tell me about my wife."

"Then stop setting out to be the martyr, the sacrificial lamb. Are you willing to make Jackie go through the fear of losing you again?"

Clay slowly sat, holding Kevin's gaze. "I uncovered that cult and took the poison because—"

"Everybody knows why you did it. You were deemed a hero. You saved others, but Cassie told me how Jackie suffered while you were in the hospital. When are you going to start thinking about her when you race into danger?"

"I always think of her," Clay said.

"Before or after?"

Clay narrowed his eyes.

Dominique leaned forward. She didn't know what they were talking about, but knew it had been something dangerous. "Let's put our personal prejudices aside and just look at the facts, shall we?"

The two men continued to stare at each other.

"We can't just walk away from this," she added. "But I admit we have to be careful."

Kevin shifted his gaze to hers. "The question is what price are you willing to pay to learn the truth?"

CHAPTER THIRTY-FIVE

"I heard Avery's gone missing."

"You sound worried," the voice on the phone said.

Abraham rubbed his hand on his lap. He sat in the living room where a six-foot indoor palm cast shadows on the marble floors. It wasn't like him to get sweaty palms. "No, just wondering."

"He's just an example of what happens when people get scared. He has nothing to do with us."

Abraham licked his lip, he didn't dare ask if they had anything to do with the disappearance. "I see."

"I hope you do. Settle with Jackson." The line disconnected.

Abraham put down the phone and wiped his forehead. He was getting tired of this.

"Worried, darling?"

He looked up and saw his wife coming from the pool, her bikini bottom covered by a towel. "No."

She took the corner of her towel and dabbed at his forehead. "You look a little hot, maybe you need to cool off."

"I'm fine."

"Or tell me what's going on." She sat on the arm of his chair. "Maybe it's your conscience that's burning you."

He rested a hand on her thigh and let it slowly inch up. "You keep making that mistake."

"Mistake?"

He watched his hand disappear further beneath the towel. "Thinking I have one."

"I know you do, especially when it comes to Dominique. Did you lose your hold on her?"

He paused and met her gaze. "Don't sound so smug. I don't believe you've heard from her in a while."

"You don't know that."

"Why isn't she home yet?"

"She's making plans."

He slid his hand further. "You don't know her plans."

"Neither do you." She crossed her legs, trapping his hand in between her thighs. "Do you want me to find out?"

"What do you want in return?"

"Make sure she doesn't get hurt."

He wiggled his fingers. "Is that all?"

She bent forward, pressing his hand closer to her warm center. "For now."

CHAPTER THIRTY-SIX

*E*ric walked into his brother's main office and swore. Although the window was open, the smell of cigarettes hung in the air. Drake stood by the window, taking a long drag. The fact that his brother was no longer hiding his habit wasn't a good sign.

"I know you don't like Marcus spending time with Jackson, but it doesn't mean you have to smoke like a chimney."

"Her parents came to see me," Drake said.

Eric opened another window. Since they didn't share this office, he couldn't complain. The room was well ventilated. "About what?" It wasn't like Cassie's parents to have much to do with them.

Drake kept his gaze focused outside the window. "They're thinking of fighting me."

Eric took a seat. "Fighting you for what?"

"About whether Cassie stays in the hospital or is taken to a nursing home."

Eric stilled. "What do you want to do?"

"I'm doing it. I'm not moving her."

"Is that what Cassie would want?"

He spun around. "Did you talk to her mother or something?"

"No, I just—"

He stubbed out his cigarette in the blackened ashtray on his desk. "It's too soon."

"You'll have to face it."

"I'm facing it."

"This is not the life they want for their daughter, but her mother was always about appearances so I don't take her words too seriously. I wonder if she's more concerned about her reputation than Cassie's life."

Eric took off his glasses and cleaned them with a cloth. "I doubt it's that simple. Did Cassie ever talk about a moment like this?"

Drake reached for another cigarette. Eric snatched it away. Drake glared at him. "Don't you lecture me now."

Eric met his brother's unflinching stare, unafraid. "I asked you a question. Did she ever talk about being in a coma?"

"Yes."

"And what did she say?"

Drake turned back to the window.

Eric knew by his brother's silence what the answer was. Cassie wouldn't want to live like this. He stared down at the cigarette carton in his hand, feeling the weight of the painful choice that faced them.

Drake didn't tell him how every evening he listened to the sound of Cassie's hospital machines as he held her hand. He'd stopped talking to her, because for the last few days he'd been unable to do so without his voice cracking. He'd spoken to the doctors about his options. She'd already recovered from a disease of the lungs and hospitals could be dangerous for those who had to stay there too long because of infections.

He didn't tell his brother how he dreamed about her waking up. How much he wanted to see her brown eyes staring back at him.

After a long moment, Drake said, "You think I'm selfish, don't you?"

"No."

"She's alive to me, I touch her skin and it's warm, my wife is there. If I didn't think so I'd let her go."

Eric nodded, not sure if he believed him. How much was real and how much did his brother want to be real? The doctors had been worried that she hadn't recovered as quickly as they had hoped.

"I haven't had her long enough," his voice was soft, but Eric heard the anguish in his voice. "I can't lose her now," he said. "But if..."

Eric nodded again, hearing the finality of the decision Drake had to—would make. He pulled one cigarette from the carton and held it out to him, as a silent goodbye. "Let this be your last."

CHAPTER THIRTY-SEVEN

*D*ead ends. That's all they kept running into. It had been a week since Dominique and Kevin had spoken to Clay.

"You don't really mean that," she'd said to Kevin after Clay had left with Marcus.

"Mean what?"

"That we should stop. You were just trying to provoke him."

"No, I wasn't. I meant every word I said. Sometimes it's better not to know."

"I think it's always important to know the facts."

He stared at her for a long moment then rose to his feet. "I believed that once." He walked out of the room.

Dominique briefly hung her head and closed her eyes. She didn't want to press him, but he was forcing her to. She took a deep breath and followed him into the hallway. He wasn't there. She searched the house and finally found him sitting in his breakfast nook, staring out the landscape window. She pulled out a chair and sat. "What happened?"

"Life taught me a lesson," he said, watching a squirrel scurry across the lawn. He sent her a hooded glance. "Ever wondered why I never talk about my mother?"

She hadn't wanted to pry. He'd spoken a lot about his workaholic father and uncle, but never his mother. "Yes."

"I didn't know her growing up. She left the family when I was three. After my father died, my uncle raised me. My two older sisters and I went to the best boarding schools and I hated every minute of it." He sighed. "Unlike my sisters, who loved them and flourished. They were more like my father in that sense, they liked discipline, order and academics. I loved them and my uncle, but felt different. I thought I was more like my mother. I asked lots of questions about her and my uncle would tell me how beautiful and glamorous she was. How smart and witty. By age twenty-three she was a goddess in my mind and although she'd abandoned us I wanted to know her.

"My uncle warned me. My sisters did too. They told me that there was more to the story than Uncle wanted us to know. They said I should leave it alone. But I wouldn't. I wanted to find her and get to know her. I felt as if a part of me was missing without her being in my life. So I searched and I finally found her." He bit his lip and returned his gaze to the window. "I convinced one of my sisters to go see her with me. I was so nervous. I don't think I slept that night.

"When I met her...She was everything my uncle said she was. Beautiful, witty and she hated me. No, I'm not exaggerating. She barely looked at me the entire time while she beamed at my sister. She looked at me with a disgust in her gaze. I later learned why." He swallowed. "If I hadn't come along she would have stayed with my father. She hated boys. She tried to smother me when I was six months old."

"Then she's mentally ill," Dominique said horrified by the

story. "And it's not your fault she left. She used you as an excuse. She's manipulative and rotten."

"She's Irene Hayward."

"*The* Irene Hayward?" Dominique said, referring to the noted international black philanthropist beloved by millions.

Kevin nodded. "Yes. And my uncle and sisters were right. It would have been better not knowing."

Dominique reached over and gripped his hand. "But didn't the wondering hurt too?"

He shook his head. "Not this much."

Dominique sighed. "I can't let it go, but I won't force you to go down this road with me."

"Are you truly ready to face who your father is? Who he possibly could be?"

Dominique took a deep breath. "Yes."

But now, as she sat with Kevin in an Italian restaurant, she felt her determination waning. What if she never found out the truth? What if her father could outwit her? She knew it strained their relationship, although Kevin wouldn't admit it. So to take his mind off things, she'd decided to teach him the pleasures of 'outercourse.' He took to it faster than she could have imagined and showed his pleasure by giving her a beautiful bracelet he wouldn't let her refuse.

She looked at that bracelet now, remembering his words, *Whenever you look at this, think of me.* His words were meant to comfort her, but she couldn't help but think of her sister's betrayal.

"Kevin?" a female voice asked.

They both looked up and saw a striking black woman wearing a chic black and white ensemble approaching the table. She kissed Kevin on the cheek. "It's been too long."

"You're looking fabulous as always," he said, pulling out an extra chair.

The woman sat down and winked at him. "Of course."

His cell phone rang. He looked at it and frowned.

"Business meeting?" Dominique guessed.

He grinned at her insight. "Yes, and they want to talk. Excuse me," he said, then left.

The woman followed him with her eyes and gave a low moan of appreciation. "He's just as gorgeous from behind. " She looked at Dominique. "Was I interrupting anything?"

Dominique waved her hand. "No, we were just—"

The woman's eyes widened and she grabbed Dominique's wrist. "Wait. Oh my God. How did you get one?" she said looking at the bracelet as if she were a bear and the bracelet a hive full of honey.

"Kevin gave it to me."

The woman stared at her. "Kevin bought you a Sandstone?" Her voice fell away and she abruptly let Dominique's wrist go. "He told me he never spends more than five thousand on a woman, cheap bastard," she said with affection. "He makes money like Midas. Everything he touches turns to gold. Bet you didn't know that he co-owns an organic makeup company and helped his sister turn it into an international powerhouse. Don't worry, you wouldn't know, I do because a friend of mind is a friend of hers."

Dominique didn't know how to respond. She hadn't known the bracelet was a Sandstone, but recognized the name of the world-renowned jewelry designer. Her mother loved his unique designs and they started at a price point twenty times what she thought it had been.

The woman leaned forward. "How did you do it?"

"Do it?"

"Get him to spend this much? Did you get a place too? I have a girlfriend who got a gorgeous little condo from one guy."

"No, we're—"

The woman's eyes widened. "We're? You're a couple? You two are...together?"

"Well we..."

"You are!" Her face split into a wide grin. "You lucky woman. He's one of the best lovers I've ever had. You must be holding onto him tight."

Dominique just smiled.

"Does he still do that thing?"

Dominique frowned. "Thing?"

She wiggled her forefinger. "You know that 'thing' that makes you go to the moon and back."

To Dominique's relief, Kevin returned to the table. "What are you two talking about? I hope it's about me."

"Of course," the woman said. "But she's keeping me in suspense." The woman pressed two fingers on her lips. "Even though there are few secrets between us, right?" she said pressing those same fingers to his mouth.

"Hmm."

She lifted a brow at Dominique. "I don't know why you're being so coy, a night with Kevin is something to sing about."

"I don't sing," Dominique said, feeling Kevin tense beside her.

"Honey, I don't sing either, but one night with him and I was—"

"It was great seeing you," Kevin said, "but we have to go." He motioned to the waiter.

"Pity. We'll talk later." She kissed Kevin, then winked at Dominique. "Happy memories."

Once she was out of hearing, Dominique held up her wrist. "Twenty-two thousand?"

He shrugged, sending the waiter away with an apology. "It was either that or a cheap car. I thought this was better." He lowered his voice to a husky whisper. "I have a budget."

"We haven't even been dating that long. You can't spend money like that this early in a relationship. You should have told me that you were buying me this."

"Would it have made a difference?"

"Yes."

"Why? It's a damn consolation prize."

She frowned. "What do you mean?"

Kevin glanced at the door where the woman had exited then shook his head . "I can't do this."

"Her words don't bother me," she said, noticing the tightness of his jaw and guessing his train of thought.

"They bother me. I'm being unfair to you. Selfish."

"No, you're not. I like being with you. How many times do I have to tell you that?"

He pinned her with a dark glance. "It's not enough."

"Of course it is."

He folded his arms on the table. "She's not the only one." He held her gaze. "Are you sure you can take my past?"

"Not if you keep reminding me."

His gaze heated. "If you only knew what I really wanted to do with you."

She kicked him under the table, feeling her face burn. "Stop it."

He ignored her. "But I can't even slee—"

She covered his mouth with her hand and looked around. "Be quiet, do you want someone to overhear you?"

He removed her hand. "Maybe public humiliation would hurt less. Don't pretend what she said didn't bother you."

"I'm fine."

"There are women out there who know a lot more about me than you do."

Dominique shoved back her chair. "If you're going to keep rubbing it in, I'm leaving."

"I'm not rubbing it in, I'm making you face who I am. I know you're curious how it would be with me."

"Yes, but I don't need that from you. I actually like that we just...get to know each other. That we get to talk. Does that make me weird? A freak? Because I like being in your presence. It is enough. You don't have to do anything to make me like you more."

He nodded at her impassioned speech. "Okay, I understand. Unfortunately, I want to do more." His voice deepened to a growl as his gaze caressed her body. "A lot more."

Dominique toyed with the buttons of her blouse, feeling suddenly warm. "I'm happy as it is."

He rested his hand on his fist and looked away. "I'm trying to believe you."

"Or maybe I'm not enough."

He turned to her. "What?"

"Be honest. If you...were your old self we wouldn't be together. We'd have one fun night and nothing else. Maybe that's what's frustrating you. The thought of being tied down."

Kevin looked at her for a long moment. She understood him better than he thought. She was right. If he'd been the man he'd been months before they wouldn't be here like this. But he'd grown tired of the conquests; he'd been intimate with many women, but never like this.

He'd never been this naked with a woman before. That's

what bothered him: he felt exposed, vulnerable. He saw her deep brown eyes and saw the hesitation there, as if she expected him to hurt her. He squeezed her hand. "That's not it. I'm frustrated for a very basic primitive reason. Ever hear of lust?"

"I'm not saying I don't want it too, but I'm willing to wait until you're better." She rested a hand on his thigh. "I really did enjoy the time we spent together the other night."

He couldn't help a smile, remembering the moment. It was a first for him, he'd never been intimate with a woman that way —uncovering ways to use his hands and mouth that he'd never thought possible, but he quickly mastered it. "I aim to please."

"Didn't I please you too?" she teased.

Kevin rested his chin in his hand and looked up at the ceiling.

"You have to think about it?" she said, stunned.

"I'm not thinking, I'm reliving." He closed his eyes and moaned. "Yes, I liked when you did that...oh yes, and that was even better."

She laughed.

Kevin opened his eyes and grinned. He loved the sound of her laughter. And that wasn't the only thing he loved.

His grin faded. No, he wasn't supposed to fall in love with her. They were just having fun. It wasn't serious. She wasn't taking him seriously, but no woman did. If he wasn't careful he'd get his heart broken again. Cassie hadn't taken him seriously either. He'd thought Dominique was different, but she saw him the same way. Just the fun-loving guy to fill up the time until she found the man she wanted to settle down with.

He was never that man. He'd never minded being referred to as a playboy before. But now it bothered him. He wanted to be seen as a catch. He wanted Dominique to miss him. To not just worry about him, but to really care about him. He wanted her to love him, not in the way most women did, they told him they loved him all the time, but it wasn't romantic or long lasting.

This wasn't a real relationship. Part of it was pity. When a man she could really be with came along, she'd leave him. If not that, she'd find out what her father was hiding and then disappear. She wouldn't turn to him. She'd blame him, even if she didn't want to. She'd blame him because his accident had forced her to uncover the truth, whatever it was.

He should break it off with her. But he wouldn't. He was going to keep her close a little while longer. He'd make up for his lack with trips and jewelry and whatever else he could offer. He wasn't a saint. He could be a greedy bastard and that's what he would be. Then he got another phone call that shattered his heart.

CHAPTER THIRTY-EIGHT

Dominique never thought she'd find solace at a funeral. She'd gone to support Kevin and to get away from her mother, who'd unexpectedly arrived on her doorstep.

"You can't be serious," Carla said, looking around Dominique's apartment in disdain. "Dear God, my toilet's bigger than this room."

"I like it here."

"Your tantrum has lasted long enough." Carla sat on the edge of the couch as if she were afraid it would collapse. "It's time you get serious about your future."

"Did Dad tell you what happened?"

"That little incident has nothing to do with us."

"Little incident?" Dominique nearly choked on her words. "That little incident left a woman in a coma, a child—"

"I know, I know and it's sad," Carla said with a dismissive wave of her wrist. "But what can you do about it?"

"I'm staying. I like it here."

"Is it him? I've heard rumors he's a fabulous lover, but if you need—"

"Mom, I don't want to argue with you. Please go."

"You're being ridiculous and only hurting yourself."

"I—"

"Are you staying because of him or because of your father?"

"Does it matter?"

"Of course it matters. A woman must be very strategic when it comes to alliances, you know that better than anyone. Kevin Jackson is not the kind of man you give—no, waste—your loyalty on. I don't care about his sweet lies and firm ass. Men like him are a dime a dozen. They'll never be true in the ways that count for women like us."

"Like us?"

"We need men of ambition. It's the only way to control them."

"I don't want to control anyone."

"I know you're not a fool, so stop acting like one." She glared at Dominique. "You haven't fallen for him, have you?"

"Of course not."

But that had been a lie. She hadn't wanted to, but she'd fallen for him hard. And it was foolish and it was ridiculous, but she didn't care. Elizabeth had shown her how fleeting life could be. It seemed like only yesterday she'd seen her at the university giggling with Kevin, kissing him on the cheek. Now she was gone. Not from cancer, but from heart failure. An unexpected complication that took her away.

Kevin didn't say anything as she drove him home or when she helped him to his room. She'd seen him grimace as he'd exited the car and knew he'd stood by the gravesite too long.

He leaned heavily against her. Afraid that he would

collapse, she led him to his bed. The early evening sun painted the room in a pink and purple haze. She gently released him, expecting him to fall onto the bed. Instead he tightened his grip around her shoulder and pulled her down with him. He wrapped his leg around her and whispered, "Stay with me. I hurt so bad."

"Then you need to rest." She struggled to sit up.

He tightened his hold. "No, I need you. I need you to feel alive. I should have died in that crash. Cassie shouldn't be in a coma and if she dies..."

"Don't think about that right now. You weren't the target and—"

"That's not what I mean. I don't feel alive. I feel dead inside. I want to be with you tonight. Completely. I don't want to hold back."

She bit her lip, for a moment she wondered if she was just a stand in. Did he imagine he was holding Cassie this way? Had Elizabeth's passing left him with longing and regret? They were the same build. Was it just a transference? She wanted to push him away and tell him that she wasn't Cassie, that she never could be, but she didn't move and instead let him hold her as tears touched her eyes.

Never waste your tears on a man, her mother had told her. But it hurt. It hurt because she'd felt fine with Kevin caring for all the other women, but Cassie was different. He loved her. She'd gotten greedy. She didn't want to be just another one of his women. She wanted to be special.

"I'm not her," she said in a flat voice.

Kevin searched her face. "What? Who?"

"Cassie." When he continued to stare at her she said, "I know how guilty you feel and—"

He smothered the rest of her words with a kiss like no

other. It was raw, real and filled with hunger. "Don't deny me this," he whispered against her lips.

And her body whispered the same, urging her surrender and she murmured her consent. Their clothes fell away and she stared at his naked form in rapturous awe. He was magnificent. Beautifully made. The sight of him was just as mesmerizing as the first time, except now the air was electric with anticipation. All her senses came alive when he touched her. She closed her eyes, finding protection in the sudden darkness.

She felt his lips trail kisses between her breasts to her stomach, murmuring with pleasure his breath warm against her skin. She felt his hands cup her breasts, his tongue capturing a nipple in his mouth.

When his body covered hers, she felt the soft give of the bed beneath her, a swift excitement when he caressed her inner thighs with his mouth and spread her legs. Her body felt heavy with a longing that demanded release. She arched into him, holding onto his broad shoulders, feeling the hard presence of him against her thigh as she welcomed the thrill of discovery.

Then he stopped. He didn't move. All she could hear was his breathing and her pounding heart.

Dominique opened her eyes, alarmed, and saw him leaning over her, his arms resting on either side. "What?" she asked.

A wicked grin touched his mouth. "That's better. I like when you look at me," he said then covered her mouth with his and entered her in one fluid motion.

It was swift and hard and hurt like hell.

She stiffened, holding her body tight, barely breathing, determined to pretend that the pain wasn't there. *If she made a sound he would know.*

"Dominique?" Kevin said in a deep voice, his lips close to her ear.

"Yes?" *Breathe through the pain, just breathe. Maybe he won't notice.*

"You forgot to tell me something."

Damn, he noticed. "No." She cleared her throat. "Just... um...I'm used to smaller men."

Kevin took a deep, steadying breath."You really had me fooled." He softly swore.

"I didn't fool you." *Don't argue or be defensive. Just do as he says. People do this all the time. And women love this. They love him.* "I want this, please."

"Why didn't you say anything? All those times we—"

"I know, I know. I told you I'm not...normal."

"You're normal, but I wish you'd told me you've never done this before."

Embarrassment made her cheeks burn, tears stung her eyes, but she kept them from falling and boldly met his stare. Why did he have to talk? Why did he have to make it an issue? Weren't men the ones who liked to 'hit it' and then forget? Did he have to make her feel so ashamed? "I have. Just not with someone so..."

He lifted an eyebrow, doubtful. "Big?"

"Yes," she said, wishing he would look away and didn't study her with such intensity. "All the other men I've been with—"

"The invisible men."

"Were smaller," she finished. "You should be flattered." She looked away no longer able to hold his gaze.

"I was flattered the moment I saw you naked." He kissed her forehead. "But since I'm your first...big man," he said stressing the word. "I'll be gentle." He cupped her chin and forced her to look at him. "Don't turn away and don't close your eyes." He kissed her neck. "Do you trust me?"

With all my heart. "Yes."

He slid inside her again and it hurt a little less, sending a tiny fissure of pleasure through her.

"How much?"

Dominique fought the urge to close her eyes, to disappear in darkness again. This wasn't how she'd imagined it. Why did he always ask so many questions? "A lot."

He thrust forward a third time and she braced herself for a pain that didn't come. Instead an exquisite, overwhelming pleasure shimmered through her body. And it happened again and again and again. Until she had to close her eyes as she felt her body carried to a height of ecstasy that knew no limit.

And then it happened: An awakening. A moment when her body no longer felt like her own, no longer belonged to her. Her body became his and his body became hers. Kevin wasn't just inside her, he consumed her, engulfed her and she delighted in being swallowed up in a fever of emotions so over-whelming for a moment she couldn't breathe, she couldn't gasp, she couldn't scream or cry out. She reached a height of pleasure so potent she felt as if her soul would rip from her body and expand the globe.

Pleasure sweet, hot, delicious pleasure with a man patient enough to let her find it. She wasn't odd, she wasn't strange. This man who loved women made her feel like one for the first time. Not a husk of one or a masquerade, but complete. He'd embraced her fears and her strength and she held him close, realizing the treasure he was to her. He understood her like no other man had ever tried to. And she understood him.

In that moment, their labels fell away. It wasn't about being a man or a woman or two bodies connecting, it was their spirit. She knew him in spirit as if they were twin souls who'd finally found each other.

She let herself explore him with no inhibition. With her eyes and her mouth and her hands. He was so beautiful to her. This moment she'd remember forever, she wouldn't be greedy. She didn't think it would ever happen again. He was the man of fun and no commitments, but he'd given her a gift she'd never forget.

CHAPTER THIRTY-NINE

The monster caught him unawares. He hadn't planned to fall asleep and be by her side until morning. Morning was dangerous. Morning meant bright lights, a cruel enemy to a migraine. Kevin slowly opened his eyes, but the touch of brightness had him quickly closing them. Damn, he'd stayed too long. The monster in his head clawed for control and he could feel it winning.

He hated to leave Dominique, but he couldn't stay.

He had to escape before she saw him. He groped for his cell phone and texted Ferguson his special emergency code.

Minutes later he was safe in his other room after losing his dinner and lunch. He lay as still as possible in the dark room with a wet cloth on his forehead, fighting the roiling waves of nausea and the crushing pressure in his head. He was going to pay for it. For his lust. For his arrogance. For his ego. He wanted her to see him in a different light. Bitterness mingled with rage. He wanted to be at Dominique's side. Needed her. Needed her to know that he was a man she could depend on.

Women play with boys, but they marry men. Henson's

words continued to haunt him. He *was* a man, dammit. If only given the chance, he could have proven it to her. He would have shown her what waking up in his arms was like, he'd help her change, share a shower, feed her breakfast in bed, but that option had been stolen from him.

Soon the monster gave him no time to think. Between lying on his back or bending over a bucket, time melted into nothing. He survived in his private hell.

He didn't know when she entered his room. He hadn't heard her footsteps, hadn't heard the door open or the chair move, but felt her hand on his arm. What was she doing there? She was never supposed to see him like this. Ferguson should have stopped her. When he was better, he'd wring Ferguson's neck. Nausea rose in him, but he fought it. He wouldn't be sick in front of her.

"I didn't realize it was this bad," she said softly.

Don't be sick. You can't be sick.

"Do you need anything?"

He couldn't fight it. He bent over the bucket and lost the rest of his meal. "Get out," he managed in a hoarse whisper. He remembered with heated embarrassment the first time it had happened with a woman he'd been seeing casually. He vividly recalled the disgust on her face, but fortunately she'd just thought he'd had too much to drink. After the third time he knew there was a problem, but she didn't care to stay and hear the reason. She found someone else.

Dominique would too.

He waited to hear her footsteps, but she didn't move. He couldn't make her go and part of him didn't want to. He wanted her to stay, and he liked having her by his side.

"Do you need anything?" she asked again.

"No," he said, barely mouthing the word.

He heard pages turn and then she began to read. Ferguson must have told her because that was usually something he would do. She read softly to him and although he couldn't focus on her words, her voice soothed him. Her presence soothed him, although it didn't take the pain away. The voice he'd at first thought so sexy now lulled him into a state of rest. It was an elixir. The duration of his migraine didn't seem different, but the severity seemed less...because of her.

By the following night he was able to sit up, but he didn't leave the dark solitude of the bedroom. A different kind of pain entered his soul. One of self-loathing. How could she see him as a man when she'd helped him as if he were a helpless child? He couldn't claim her. Any man could come—a man like Henson—and take her away. He didn't want to need her so much, but he did. He needed her cool rational mind; she kept him grounded. He helped her be free. She'd been free in his arms, he'd felt it, knew it. He'd been her first. He wanted to be her first and last.

But that wasn't in the cards for a man like him.

He heard the door open before he saw a shaft of light. He turned and saw a female figure silhouetted in the doorway.

"I'm glad to see you looking better," Dominique said, coming into the room. "I've got good news and better news for you."

He didn't know how to take her tone. How could she talk to him as if he hadn't disgraced himself in front of her? But he was used to pretending things didn't matter so he did so now. "You can turn on the light if you want to," he said, his voice raw and dry from lack of use.

"No, that's okay." He felt the bed give as she sat down beside him and his pulse quickened as he inhaled the fruity scent of her lotion. He gripped his hands together, resisting the urge to touch her. "What's the good news?"

"I contacted a top specialist who's willing to see you about your migraines."

"You told someone about me?"

"Kevin, I can't stand around and watch you suffer like this."

"But I told you I've seen—"

"I know you've seen other doctors, but just give this a chance. I'm not willing to give up on you, so don't give up on yourself. I've researched his background and he's been able help many patients. Especially those who've suffered head trauma."

Kevin sighed, although a small light of hope filled his chest. "What's the better news?"

"Cassie's awake."

CHAPTER FORTY

She wailed.

Ruth sat alone in her room, a pillow pressed to her mouth, so that her sobs could not be heard, and screamed her fury, her rage and despair.

Cassie was alive! How dare she live! She was supposed to die. She wasn't supposed to recover. There wasn't even signs of her brain trauma, although she couldn't remember the accident, but other than that she was back to normal. She'd be coming home and would be the mistress of the house again and Ruth would be forced back into the shadows. Cassie would take back the family that Ruth had claimed as hers. They were hers. They would have fallen apart without her. They needed her. This wasn't right.

Drake had come home looking more handsome than she'd ever seen him and told her to get the children ready to take to the hospital.

"Are you sure that's wise?"

"She's awake and I know she wants to see them." She'd

never seen such joy on his face, such love shining in his eyes. It made her stomach turn.

Ruth hadn't gone with them. She didn't remember what lie she'd told him, but it had worked and the house was now empty and she was alone. Alone all over again.

How could God do this to her? How could he turn his back on her like this?

Cassie was supposed to die so that she could have a chance at a life she deserved. With a man she deserved. Drake cared for her. She'd just needed more time for him to know it.

Time.

She still had a chance. God always had someone do something for a miracle to happen. This was just a test of her faith. God was testing to see if she was strong enough to follow him. Would she sit idly by or take action? *Faith without works is dead*, she remembered that Bible verse.

Works. She had to do something. Cassie wasn't fully healed yet; she'd still need some time to recover. No one would be surprised if she took a sudden turn for the worse, right? She would do something and then her prayers would be fully answered and glory would be hers.

CHAPTER FORTY-ONE

*I*t took Lyle Huntley two seconds to realize he'd made a mistake. He'd talked too big to the wrong person. He'd gone to the bar for some liquid courage and had gotten too much. He should have called the family with his information. He should have told the police. He shouldn't have been so greedy and tried to blackmail Cartwright. But it was too late to change anything now.

If you want to live to see your baby walk, you'd better forget what you just said, he remembered the warning.

Yeah, he'd forget it all right. He'd forget everything.

"Where are you going?"

He glanced at his old lady, a woman he'd thought pretty once, as she held one of their crying rug rats on her hip. The kid had snot running from his nose; she didn't even notice. "Just outta town," he said.

"Where?"

He continued to pack. "Just some place. If anyone comes looking for me—"

"You in trouble with the police again?"

He zipped up his bag. "Just don't tell nobody nothing."

She blocked his exit. "When will you be back?"

"I don't know."

"I'm not going to be left alone with all these kids. You're not leaving without me."

"I'll be back, woman," he said, raising his voice over his kid's cries.

She raised hers too. "Don't you be lying to me."

"I'm not lying."

"I can drop the kids at my mom's and we can disappear together."

It was a thought, but her mother talked too much and he didn't have time to pack her up and all the kids. No, he was better on his own. Fresh start and all that.

"I said I'll be back." He pushed past her and left the bedroom, the defiant move feeling liberating. Yeah, he was free of all this. He was gonna get a new life.

He headed for the front door, kicking a toy truck out of the way. A bullet whizzed past his ear. He spun around and stared at his wife, then dropped his gaze to the gun she had pointed at his leg.

A gun her father had taught her to use for her fifteenth birthday. He could tell by her cool gaze that she'd missed on purpose. She wouldn't miss the second time. "I said, you're not leaving without me."

CHAPTER FORTY-TWO

*K*evin stared up at the large abstract mural that movers had hung in his entertainment lounge. Elizabeth's artwork had finally found the right place. Initially her husband, Jed, had wanted to just give it to him, but Kevin refused and instead offered to help show him how to properly handle Elizabeth's collection. Kevin knew the widower didn't know how much money he was sitting on. He'd help make sure that Elizabeth's family and her work did well.

Kevin kept his eyes on the bright colors in the mural and sat on the couch, sinking into its plush cushions. Dominique had helped him buy it, determined that he could find furniture that was designer quality *and* comfortable at the same time. She'd succeeded. As he looked at the yellow and orange swirls he thought about the cooling autumn temperatures outside and the colors tingeing the edges of the leaves. He usually didn't stay at his Maryland home past summer, but now he had a reason to. It had been a month since his surgery and he was doing well. Following a full examination, the specialist

Dominique had found discovered the problem others had missed. There had been a tiny fragment of bone that had become dislodged from the accident, pinching a critical nerve, causing him to experience debilitating migraines after dancing or having sex.

He'd also gone to another doctor to help realign his spine, which eased most of the pain in his leg. He was getting his life back, but for some reason that made him feel uneasy.

"Dominique sent you a delivery," Ferguson said, coming into the room with a box. He set it in front of Kevin and pulled out a pocketknife. "May I?"

"Go ahead."

Ferguson opened the box and pulled out two circular pillows and a note. "The couch needs pillows," he read.

Kevin couldn't help a smile. They'd argued about that. He felt pillows were superfluous, but she felt they were a staple. He put a pillow behind his back. He'd let her win this time.

"They look good," Ferguson said, placing the second pillow at the other end of the couch. "She's got an eye nearly as good as you. You're a lucky man. Aren't you glad I told you to keep her?"

Kevin's eyebrows shot up. "You told me to keep her?"

"Yes, I knew when I saw her that she was good for you."

Kevin folded his arms, watching Ferguson close the top of the now empty box. "Is that right?"

Ferguson nodded, briefly taking off his glasses to wipe his eyes before replacing them. "She fits in around here. You should have seen how late she stayed up after your last attack. Hours on her laptop doing research and after your surgery she made sure you got the best of care."

Kevin gestured to an empty seat. "Relax, I forgive you."

Ferguson gripped his hands together, looking unsure. "Really?"

"You know I never hold a grudge."

Ferguson sat down, relieved. "When is she going to move in?"

Kevin felt his benevolent mood dim. "She doesn't want to move in yet."

"And that worries you."

He sighed, annoyed. Ferguson was right. Dominique wouldn't move in and she hadn't slept with him again. Even after the surgery.

"Let's wait another week," she'd told him the other day when she'd halted his advances. They'd come back from dinner, shared a drink on his patio, enjoyed the warm evening, and he'd kissed her, eager to extend the night.

He took a step back and sighed. "You said that last week."

"It's good to be cautious," she said, taking their two wine glasses to the kitchen. "You still need to give your body time to heal. Take it in steps. Have you gone to a club recently? Or a party?"

"No."

"Why not?"

He couldn't help a smile. "Because I've been with you."

"Oh, right," she said sheepishly. She set the glasses in the sink. "Well, don't let me stop you. If you want to go, that's fine with me."

He stared at her stunned and hopeful. "You'd go to a club with me?"

She shook her head. "No, but you could go to find out if—"

"I already know I'm fine."

She rested her hip against the counter. "When are you going to see Cassie?"

He stiffened, not understanding the change in topic. "Why are you bringing her up?"

"Why are you avoiding the question?"

He glanced around the kitchen, his thoughts racing. He hadn't seen Cassie since she'd been released from the hospital. He'd used his doctor visits, pre-operative preparations, surgery and then his post operative recovery as a reason not to see her. "I'll see her soon."

"Are you sure you're over her?"

He met Dominique's gaze. "Is that why you won't sleep with me again?"

"No."

He took a step towards her. "Do you think she's a ghost between us?"

"Is she?"

He took another step closer. "No."

"I know there's still a lot to figure out, but no one can blame you for the accident anymore and the lawsuit has been settled."

He closed the distance between them and tenderly touched her cheek. "I know that," he said, although he'd been surprised Cartwright Cars had done so. It was clear they didn't want anything more to do with him.

"The truth is that you haven't been yourself since your surgery."

His hand fell. "I haven't?"

"No. You're not the Kevin people know. Or the one I first met. You don't go to parties or clubs like you used to. You don't even throw your own parties or talk about them. You spend most of your time with me. And while I enjoy it, I know that's not who you are."

Kevin stared at her for a long moment, not sure how to process what she was saying. He felt both stunned and dismayed. He'd changed and he hadn't even realized it. But oddly that didn't bother him.

What bothered him was that Dominique still saw him as a party boy. She expected him to chase his worries away with a drink and women as he had in the past. But that wasn't who he was anymore. *Do you know why I haven't gone to a party for awhile?* He wanted to tell her. *Because I don't want to. Because they bore me now. Because I'd rather spend time with you. Because I like being me. I like not having to make people laugh and feel good all the time.*

He thought about the conversation they'd had that night as he stared up at Elizabeth's painting. Maybe there were other reasons Dominique wanted her own space, why she didn't want to sleep with him again. Perhaps she didn't like the new Kevin and found the old one more exciting. He couldn't blame her, since the last several weeks she'd been something of a nursemaid.

He'd never given her the opportunity to know what it was like to be on his arm at a gala. To mingle at a gallery and walk him around like a trophy? Other women had, and maybe Dominique wanted that too.

Or maybe he was trying to hold onto something that wasn't meant to be.

"You once told me that she needs you," Ferguson said as if reading his thoughts.

Kevin plastered on a smile, not liking to be in a low mood for too long. "I'm not sure I know women as much as I thought."

"Dominique isn't like other women."

"I know."

"She's good for you, but you're also good for her."

Kevin started to smile for real, catching the mischievous glint in Ferguson's eyes. "What are you suggesting?"

He pulled out an invitation from his inside jacket pocket. "That you raise the stakes."

CHAPTER FORTY-THREE

"But I told you I don't do parties," Dominique said with a note of panic. She stared down at the elegant wedding invitation Kevin had waved in front of her. She'd expected their relationship to take a new direction, but she hadn't expected this. Although Clay had warned her.

She'd been meeting with him secretly since she knew that Kevin didn't want to investigate the accident any further. They hadn't gotten far. She'd learned that her father's rival, Reginald Avery, had turned up in Mexico—alive and living with his daughter. The police had no interest in an accident that had been settled. But she was patient and that was something she and Clay shared.

"Be careful of Jackson," Clay said. They both sat in his office at Hodder Investigation, trying to ignore the man screaming obscenities at his girlfriend in the parking lot.

"Careful?" Dominique said.

The girlfriend started shouting at the man. Her language was even more colorful.

"He's not—" Clay paused when they both heard a slap.

The woman screamed and shouted at the man. Clay slowly rose to his feet. "Excuse me," he said, then left.

Moments later the voices became silent and Clay returned to his office. "Sorry about that."

Dominique glanced out the window. "What did you say to them?"

He sent her a significant look. "Usually when I show up, I don't have to say anything."

She grinned. "I wish I could do that."

"I'm sure you can. Now about Kevin."

"Are you warning me off him?"

He picked up a pen. "I know I'm older than you, but do I look like your bleeding Dad?"

No, you're nicer and better looking, she thought, but decided to keep that to herself. "No, what do you have to say?"

"I'm offering you a little advice. He's not what he seems."

A grin touched her lips. "I thought you said he's a lazy, callous—"

"But we both know that he's not. Why hasn't he seen Cassie?"

I don't know! "He's been busy recovering from the surgery," she said, although she'd never shared what the surgery had been for.

"Hmm."

"Should I tell him about us?"

Clay tapped the pen against his desk. "Not if you're going to phrase it like that."

"Oh," Dominique said chagrined, realizing the innuendo. "You're right."

"I'll talk to him eventually, don't worry about it. Just be prepared for surprises," he said.

And Kevin had now given her one. After fending him off

after dinner the other day, she'd berated herself for holding herself back, but she was nervous. Nervous that Kevin would get tired of their routine. Get tired of her. But she thought he may want to go to his other residence or talk of traveling to the islands, not this.

They sat in her apartment on a Saturday afternoon after spending time at an outdoor music fest a friend of his had helped put together. She'd enjoyed herself, but then he'd shocked her—and made most of the women swoon—when he'd jumped on stage with one of the acts and played the piano with a sensual confidence that still had her feeling warm. His hands moved over the keys with the dexterity of a true maestro. While other women could only imagine what else his hands could do, she knew.

She also knew that if she slept with him again and he decided that he didn't want to stay with her, she'd be more than broken-hearted. She wanted to be careful and make sure that he knew she wouldn't tie him down. Seeing him on the stage reminded her of his old self and she'd expected to see more of it. But not like this.

"You'll be fine," Kevin said.

She shook her head. "No, I won't."

"I need a date."

"You never need a date. You walk into a room and a woman appears by your side."

Kevin couldn't help a grin. "You're right, but I need a date for this."

"Get a stand-in." She pressed her hands together. "Just this once, I won't mind. I promise."

"I can't use a stand-in to meet my family."

Her mouth dropped open. "This is a family affair?"

"It's my cousin's wedding."

Dominique bit her lip in consideration. *His family?* This was a big step. He wanted to move their relationship forward and she didn't want to stop him. "Maybe I could just go to the reception near the end when half of the guests are so drunk no one will remember anything."

Kevin rested his arm behind her head, turning his body fully to her. "Nothing will happen."

"Did I tell you about the time—"

He dropped his arm to her shoulders. "I don't care."

"Isn't this too soon? You just had surgery—"

He placed a series of kisses along her jawbone. "And you won't let me show you that I'm okay."

"You may be okay, but I'm not."

He drew back and looked at her, his dark, observant eyes holding her still. "Why not?"

She swallowed. She shouldn't have said that. "Never mind. I didn't mean it."

"Yes, you did." He narrowed his eyes a fraction. "Is there someone else?"

"Of course not!" she said, surprised by his question and the sudden look of relief on his face. "It's just...I'm a coward. You were so sick after we..." She looked down at her hands, feeling embarrassed. "I mean I really liked..." She licked her lower lip as if remembering a delicious dessert. "It was so good you could turn me into an addict."

"Then let me be your drug," he said in a silky voice.

"But you suffered and..."

He sighed heavily. "What happened wasn't your fault."

"I know that intellectually, but in the back of my mind I'd feel like I was using you if—"

He kissed her, then breathed, "Use me. Use me like a tool. Ride me like a stallion. Take me like—"

Dominique pushed him back, a laugh escaping her. "You're incredible."

He looked down at her hand as it rested on his chest. "I know."

She snatched her hand away. "You rush into things without thinking about the consequences."

He took her hand and put it back where she'd put it. "And you think too much."

Dominique sighed. She'd have to face his family sometime and they had to move past this block. "Let's compromise."

"I'm listening."

"If you're okay after the wedding, we can be together."

Kevin shook his head. "I want you to be specific."

"Specific?" Her voice cracked.

He covered her hand with his. "I think that it's important that we understand each other."

"You know what I mean."

"I want to make sure." He held up his other hand. "And no biblical terms. I don't want to 'know you' or 'come unto you.'"

Humor lit her face. "What does a devil like you know about being biblical?"

A wicked grin touched his mouth. He lifted her hand and kissed the inside of her wrist. "More than you know."

Her skin tingled where his lips had touched her skin. She wouldn't fight him anymore. "If you're fine after the wedding, I'll sleep with you. Is that clear enough?"

"Sleep," he said, drawing out the word. "You know there's another word that begins with 's' and it's much shorter and to the point." He kissed the center of her palm. "Are you afraid to say it?"

"Yes, but I'm not afraid to do it."

He closed his eyes and rested his head back with joy. "You

know just what to say to make me happy." He sat up and looked at her. "You have a deal."

"Good," she said with a chuckle, trying to tug her hand free.

He held on. "But we do have one problem."

She paused. "What?"

"What you'll wear."

Dominique jumped to her feet. "That's not problem. I have that dress—"

Kevin released her hand and frowned. "I told you to burn it."

She looked at him, surprised. "You weren't joking?"

He stood. "No, let me show you what a real dress looks like."

KEVIN LOOKED at the array of dresses. He'd invited an upcoming designer, Sasha Crow, to bring over her latest collection to his house.

"You call this your best?" Kevin said in a bored voice when the fourth model left the room to change.

"It was short notice," Sasha said, nervously fingering a wooden pin that held up her abundance of dyed red hair. Dominique wondered if it was too much rouge or embarrassment that made the young woman's cheeks red.

Kevin blinked. "So I should have called someone else?"

Sasha looked alarmed for a moment. "Wait just a second." She whispered something to her assistant, a tall women who wore round-rimmed purple glasses. The assistant nodded and disappeared with one of the models.

"You're going to like this," Sasha assured him with a smile.

Kevin didn't return it. "Is that a promise?"

Her smile wavered but held. "I'll go see what's keeping them." She left.

Dominique leaned towards him. "Why are you giving her a hard time?"

"I'm not giving her a hard time, I'm giving her a chance."

"The dresses all look good to me."

"That's because you're style blind."

"I am not."

Kevin nodded to a selection of five dresses hanging on mannequins. "Choose a dress and I'll tell you what's wrong with it."

She pointed to a grey gown. "That."

"Made for a woman with less curves." He gestured to a red one. "That one is made for a woman with no cleavage. You always want clothes that compliment your best features."

"I was taught to hide my flaws."

"That's fine as long as you don't confuse your flaws with your assets."

Sasha returned with a model wearing a dark blue gown with crystal trim.

Kevin stood up. "Yes, much better." He turned to Dominique. "What do you think?" He held up his hand and shook his head when she opened her mouth. "Never mind, I know what you think. We'll take it."

CHAPTER FORTY-FOUR

Of course Kevin didn't tell her that the wedding would be in Scotland.

Or that the beaming bride would arrive in a carriage, driven by white horses, carrying her to a castle, where she'd walk up a winding staircase in an exquisite gown fit for a princess. There were red roses and white ribbons and when the bride and groom kissed there were cheers and tears—for various reasons.

In the reception hall, Dominique let herself get lost in the large crowd and watched women flock to Kevin. She'd been introduced to a host of family members whose names she'd forgotten, but they were welcoming and warm.

"Oh that dress is stunning," his great aunt told her as she and Kevin made their way to the reception hall. His aunt was a woman of more heft than height. If Kevin hadn't stopped and made introductions, Dominique would have walked right into her.

"Thank you," Dominique said, smiling down at the woman.

His aunt shifted her brown gaze. "Are you trying to cause trouble, Kevin? Your girlfriend could rival the bride."

"No one could rival her," Dominique said, pleased by the compliment.

His aunt pursed her lips, a suspicious look crossing her features. "I've got my eye on you. Behave yourself."

Kevin bent down and kissed her cheek. "You know I always try."

She sniffed at him, smiled at Dominique, then walked away.

"She is right," Kevin said, leaning close to Dominique. "You are causing trouble."

"No, I'm not," Dominique said as they entered the hall.

Kevin nodded at one guest and waved at another. "Everyone is staring at you," he said under his breath.

"They're staring at you," Dominique said, suddenly noticing all the glances.

"Why would they be staring at me when they already know me?"

He had a point, but she didn't want to admit it. If she thought about it she might jinx the moment and do something embarrassing.

Nearly an hour later she sat at one of the tables and watched while the guests danced. She'd begged Kevin off when he'd asked her to dance and was glad when he left her alone. She was determined to get through this day without incident and so far she was succeeding. Now she saw him tearing up the dance floor, making every dance partner feel as if she were the most desired woman in the room.

She didn't mind. There was nothing lewd about it. He treated a shy teenager with the same respect as a woman in her late eighties. And every few dances, he turned to her table to see if she was okay. She'd always smile and wave, assuring him that she was.

As she watched him, she saw the man he used to be before the accident. His mouth didn't turn down in pain, there weren't shadows in his eyes. He wouldn't need her to protect him, or need to use her arm to lean on. She felt the lost, but wouldn't focus on it. Their time together wasn't meant to last. She'd be one of his women who spoke about him with affection. He'd taught her so much: how to have fun, how to laugh, how to let go.

One of Kevin's gorgeous dance partners, with skin the color of ginger, stood in front of Dominique and held out a long, slender hand. "Hi, I'm Lena."

"Dominique."

She took a seat. "Sorry I didn't have a chance to introduce myself before."

"Well, there are a lot of people."

"But only one woman dating my little brother."

Dominique blinked. *Little brother?* The woman barely looked like she had parents—more like she'd sprung from the sea fully formed—let alone have a brother.

"I haven't known you long," Lena continued. "But I've been watching you and you're not like the rest."

"I know," Dominique said, trying to imagine the women Kevin had introduced her to. "I must be a surprise since I'm not—"

"It's so good to finally meet a woman who hasn't fallen for his act," Lena interrupted as if Dominique hadn't spoken.

"The act?"

"Don't pretend you don't know. He feels more than he lets on. Women always think he's just good for a good time. The dumb ones do anyway."

"But he does—"

"And there was this one woman who really did a number on him. To this day I don't think Cassie knows how much she hurt him. Have you met Cassie yet?"

The woman he loved. Had loved? Did love? Not really. "I haven't had a chance yet."

"You will," Lena said with a knowing smile. "He's never going to let her go. If she hadn't been so clueless, I would hate her guts. But she's really sweet, you'll like her."

Yes, everybody likes Cassie. Loves her. She probably had an adoring father and mother hidden away somewhere too. Dominique shoved down a flash of jealousy. She didn't know what being so beloved felt like. "I'm sure I will. But I—"

Lena pointed at her. "You know what you are? You're his anchor. Yes, that's the word I've been trying to think of. A guy like Kevin needs someone like you. Someone who will keep him grounded without clipping his wings. Someone safe to turn to. And—"

"Mommy?"

Dominique turned and saw a little boy about six. Lena held up a forefinger of warning. "Mommy's talking."

"But Mommy, I—"

She waved her finger. "What did I just say?"

The boy shifted awkwardly. "But I really—"

"I think he might need the toilet," Dominique said, guessing the boy's predicament.

Lena pinned her son with a shrewd look. "Where's your father?"

"I can't find him," he said, shifting again this time grabbing his front.

"Don't grab yourself in public," she snapped, rising to her feet.

"But I've got to go bad," he whimpered.

"Sorry about this," Lena said to Dominique, then took the little boy's hand. "Wonderful talking to you."

Dominique watched her talk to one of the attendants and hurry the boy to one of the exits. She sat back and thought about her words as she watched Kevin spin a woman on the dance floor.

You're his anchor. And that made sense.

"I met your sister Lena," Dominique said as she and Kevin rode the elevator to their hotel room.

He looked at her amazed. "Did she let you finish a sentence?"

Dominique covered her mouth and giggled. "Barely."

Kevin held up a forefinger and imitated his sister's tone. "I'm talking. I'm still *talking*. Did you hear what I just said?"

Dominique started to laugh. "You should have seen your poor nephew when he had to go the bathroom."

Kevin sent her a look of pity. "Did he make it?"

"I hope so," Dominique said, stepping out when the elevator reached their floor. "I was seriously considering picking up the kid and running out the door, but I was determined not to ruin the evening."

"I would have forgiven you for saving my nephew's dignity."

She stopped in front of their hotel room. "I had a great time."

"Me too." Kevin opened the door then sent her a slow, intimate smile. "And as you can see, I'm not hurting."

CHAPTER FORTY-FIVE

He was a man built for pleasure. He enjoyed it and gave it with exquisite detail.

Did he do that 'thing'? the woman in the restaurant had asked her. He did that thing and more.

"Don't wear yourself out," she managed in a breathless warning as the sleek form of his body caressed hers.

"I can never have too much of you," he said in a husky growl. "You don't know how much I want you. You're mine." He lifted his head and looked at her. His voice was calm, and his gaze steady, lit with a sensual flame of triumph. "All mine."

When his mouth covered hers, she felt the electric power of his passion. A power she hadn't felt before. He was strong. Stronger than her. It was different this time, he was different. Larger somehow. More compelling, demanding her surrender, not requesting it. His touch masterful, possessive. He consumed her, filling both her body and her mind. He claimed her and she couldn't resist the sensual onslaught. *Don't make me love you,* she wanted to say although she knew she already did.

KEVIN WOKE to a room shaded in darkness. He wondered if it was still night then saw slivers of sunlight peeking beneath the drawn drapes. Then he shifted his gaze and saw Dominique's worried face hovering over him.

"How do you feel?" she whispered.

He took her hand and rested it on his chest. "You tell me."

She laughed and playfully hit him. "You're definitely fine."

He jumped out of bed and bowed. "Thank you." He stood, grabbed a robe before opening the drapes, flooding the room with sunlight. "Okay, now it's your turn."

"My turn for what?" Dominique said blinking against the sudden glare.

"I think it's time I meet your family."

She blinked faster, not knowing what to say.

"Have you told them about me?"

Not everything. "Sort of."

"I think it's time we make that a yes, " he said, then disappeared into the bathroom. Seconds later she heard the shower.

Dominique remembered his fluid movements with wonder. He had even more energy than before. Could she keep up with him? Would she want to? Yes, she did, but worried that it wouldn't be enough.

He wouldn't cheat. The moment it wasn't working, he'd cut it off clean. She knew that.

But love was something strange to her. It wasn't something that could be won and held. It could be fleeting, it could disappear. She didn't want her love to chain him, he was someone meant to be free. And then there was Cassie...

Kevin popped his head out of the bathroom. "Aren't you going to join me?"

Dominique scrambled off of the bed. She'd think about Cassie later. For now she had Kevin.

CHAPTER FORTY-SIX

The third time Carla Cartwright touched his leg, Kevin knew she was going to be a problem. The first brush of her hand against his thigh, he'd deemed an accident, the second time when they sat down to dinner he deemed it a coincidence, but by dessert, when she squeezed his leg, he knew she was trying to make a point she didn't want him to ignore.

He'd sensed her interest, knowing it was more than maternal curiosity when they'd first met. Her gaze had soaked him up like a she was a cat and he catnip. He'd seen that look before, encouraged it most times, but not tonight. He glanced across the table at Dominique. To his relief she was completely oblivious, as was her sister Gloria. She had her mother's looks, but she was easier to read and therefore easier to manipulate. He'd quickly won her over with well-chosen flattery. If only he could say the same about their mother.

"So glad we were able to settle that incident a few months ago," Abraham said.

Kevin nodded, shifting in his seat, hoping Carla would get

the point.

"I already know how you met," Abraham continued. "I'm surprised it's lasted this long."

"Don't be," Kevin said. "I know when to hang onto something good." He took a spoonful of chocolate mousse and winked at Dominique.

"It's been a while since Dominique has had a friend to dinner," Carla said, sliding her hand towards his crotch.

He grabbed her hand, stopping her. "I see."

Gloria rolled her eyes. "There was Berton," she said, then quickly regretted it. "I mean..."

"So what do you do, Kevin?" Abraham asked.

"Do?" he asked, placing Carla's hand back on her lap.

"For work."

"I don't work."

They stared at him.

Dominique broke the silence. "Kevin's family owns—"

"I don't care what a man's family has," Abraham said. "A man must work. Unless he plans to live off others."

Kevin shot him a glance. "I don't plan to live off anyone. Never have, never will."

"Then how do you make money?"

"Why didn't you ask me that in the first place?"

"I thought you'd be clever enough to know they're one in the same."

Kevin shook his head. "No, they're not. You don't have to work to make money. I'm making it right now." He shrugged. "Making money's easy for me. My family owns several businesses and I have choice investments, the usual," he said, sounding bored.

Abraham looked at him confused. "But what do you want to achieve? What are your goals?"

"I live my life the way I want to, with who I want to," he said, sending Dominique a glance. "That's it."

Carla slid her hand in his lap again. "A man without ambition to rule the world? That sounds very intriguing."

Kevin jumped up, rattling the dishes. "Yes, well there you are. Will you, uh, could you tell me where your—"

"Down the hall and to the left," Dominique said. "I'll show you." She led him out into the hall. When they were a few feet away she said, "Is your leg bothering you?"

"No, why?"

"You keep grimacing."

He silently swore, he didn't want her to notice that. "It's nothing. A slight cramp."

"Did you like the mousse? I told my mother to use that chocolatier friend of yours and—"

He stopped and placed a light kiss on her lips, caressing her cheek. "Everything was delicious. Thank you."

She sighed in relief, then continued walking. "Just ignore my father's questions. He doesn't understand a life not devoted to enterprise. Fun is a foreign word to us."

"They don't bother me, but your mother..."

"What?"

Damn. She looked at him with her innocent brown eyes and he couldn't' say it. "May not like me."

"I don't care." She pointed to the bathroom. "There you go. Think you can find your way back?"

"Leave me some crumbs and I'll be fine."

Minutes later, he came out of the bathroom and saw Carla waiting for him. "Just making sure you're all right," she said. "You seemed a little uncomfortable."

"I don't know what you're into, but I'm not."

She stepped closer. "I always come to a special agreement

with the men in my daughter's life. I help them get what they want."

"I told you. I have what I want."

She smoothed down his jacket. "You're harder to read than the others, but I'll figure you out." She moved in closer. "Is this about power or revenge?"

He removed her hand. "I won't warn you again. Stay away from me."

She stroked his arm. "And if I don't?"

He grabbed her hand with enough force to make her wince. "I don't know what arrangement you had in the past, but you'll have to make an exception."

"I don't make exceptions."

"You can learn."

"I won't let you use Dominique."

"Only you can do that?"

She narrowed her eyes. "Careful, Kevin. You may be smarter than the rest, but you'll last only as long as you know how to follow the rules. Dominique loves her mother very much so if something were to happen or if I were to make an accusation. Who do you think she'll believe? You or me?"

"Mom? Kevin?" Dominique said, coming into the hall. "I'd wondered where you two had disappeared to."

Kevin released Carla's hand as if it had burned him.

Carla smiled at her daughter. "He'd gotten lost." She met his eyes. "I was helping him find his way."

"He's going to be trouble," Carla told her husband as she stood by the sitting room window and watched the lights of Kevin's Jaguar disappear into the night.

"How do you know?"

She turned from the window and sat facing him. "I can't figure out what he wants."

"Maybe he really likes her," Gloria said, flipping through messages on her phone.

"Don't be stupid," Carla said.

"He can't use her to hurt us," Abraham said. "Breaking her heart isn't going to be an issue."

"He seems savvier than that. If he were to marry her..."

"I'll let him know he'll get nothing."

"He doesn't need money, he has his own, but he doesn't seem ambitious."

"I don't trust a man without ambition."

"I think you two are over-thinking this," Gloria said.

Carla crossed her legs and leaned back. "And when did you come under the impression that we cared what you think?"

Gloria ignored the insult. "I think he's good for her."

"But is he good for us?" Abraham said.

"Why wouldn't he be? He's good looking and rich and makes her happy. Don't you realize that it's your fault they met in the first place?"

"Yes," Abraham stroked his chin, thoughtful. "Maybe they're doing this to annoy me."

"No," Carla said. "I know men and Kevin's not pretending."

"I don't like him." He sent Gloria a pointed look. " Get to know him better."

Gloria shook her head and stood. "No, way. I'm not hurting her again. I don't understand what the big deal is."

Abraham and Carla shared a look. "Exactly."

CHAPTER FORTY-SEVEN

*D*ominique wasn't sure if the evening had been a success or a failure. She couldn't tell anything by reading Kevin's profile as he drove her back to her place. She'd been surprised when he'd offered to drive. She'd grown used to taking the wheel, but ceded to him tonight. It would give her a chance to think. To think about what she'd seen in her mother's closet. She'd gone there to borrow a shawl and noticed her extensive handbag collection. Her mother had recently built a new shelf Dominique hadn't seen before. She looked at her mother's collection with affection until she spotted a purse that looked familiar.

A red and gold clutch with tiny green accents. The same purse she'd seen on Berton's coffee table. But it couldn't be. It was just a coincidence. Her mother wouldn't... No, it was a stupid thought. Crazy. She brushed the thought aside and lightly touched Kevin's leg.

He jumped and she yanked her hand back.

"I'm sorry," she said.

"It's not you," he said, avoiding her glance. "I just...was thinking."

"What did my mother say to you in the hall? Did she upset you?"

Kevin silently swore. He had to tell her. He wanted to tell her, but he couldn't. There was no way she'd believe him. "No."

"You can be honest with me. My father can be a mean SOB, my sister's a prima donna and my mother—"

He turned sharply to her when she stopped. "Your mother's what?" he pressed.

"Is vain and spoiled."

Kevin gritted his teeth. Her mother was a lot more than that. "Hmm."

"And you're going to be pulled over if you don't slow down."

He looked at the speedometer, he was pushing eighty. He slowed, then pulled over to the side and parked. "I wasn't driving fast that day, in case you were wondering."

"I know." She touched his hand. "What's wrong?"

He kissed her, his heart pounding. He didn't want her to be able to read him right now. He was glad for the shield of darkness so she couldn't read his face. He didn't want her to know the sickening proposal her mother had made him. He wanted to protect her. "I've been wanting to do that all evening."

"I'm glad you did."

He couldn't see her clearly in the dark car, the headlights intermittently lighting her face as they passed. "So you trust me?"

"Of course I trust you."

Kevin drew away, then started the car again, wanting to believe her, but not ready to find out how much.

Dominique tasted the sweetness of his kiss with her tongue, and something about it made her wonder about his true feelings, but she didn't want to press him, so she stared at the road ahead. She glanced up at the night sky and then down at the taillights from the cars, their red hue turning her mind again to the color of the clutch purse in her mother's closet.

CHAPTER FORTY-EIGHT

Kevin looked around the crowded bar in fascination. He'd never been in such a place before. He'd had Clay repeat the name of Eugene's twice just to make sure. Now he sat with Clay and a man named Nicolas, whose cool blue eyes chilled him. He'd mistakenly ordered a glass of white wine, until he was met with a look of such disdain that he asked for a martini instead. The bartender just blinked. Clay ordered him a beer.

Kevin shook his head. "I don't like beer. I'll have a whiskey."

The bartender looked at Clay as if for guidance. Clay nodded. They took their drinks to a free table.

"You don't do this often, do you?" Nicolas said, watching Kevin wipe crumbs from the table.

Kevin wiped his hands on a napkin. "What gave me away?"

"Never mind," Clay said and flashed a knowing grin. "I'm glad you could join us without your driver."

"I like keeping her to myself."

Nicolas leaned forward. "I've always wondered. Why have a driver when you can drive yourself?"

"I can clean my house, but I'd rather somebody else do it."

Nicolas nodded. "Makes sense, but—"

"We can have a discussion on the privileged class later," Clay cut in.

"What didn't you want Dominique to know?" Kevin asked.

"Does the name Lyle Huntley mean anything to you?"

Kevin thought for a moment then shook his head. "No."

"He was found floating in the Potomac with Cartwright Cars' business card in his pocket."

"What does that have to do with me?"

"When the police spoke to his wife, she said that he'd been a witness to the car accident, 'where that lady and kid were hurt' but that he'd hoped to get some money on the information he had. He didn't call you?"

"No."

"He spoke to someone who spooked him to run."

"And they killed him?"

"No, his wife did that," Nicolas said.

"What?"

Clay nodded. "Yes, they'd been on the run together, but one night he decided to get some side action. Let's just say the little lady didn't approve and tried to hide her crime."

"Luckily for us, she didn't know how to sink a body," Nicolas added.

"Where does this leave us?" Kevin asked.

"Right back at Cartwright, but we already knew they were at the center," Clay said.

Nicolas took a long swallow, then set his glass down. "But now we know something else. Lyle told his wife that he saw another car. It was the other car that caused the accident."

"Another car?"

"Yes, driving in the opposite direction. Lyle said it clipped you in a way that made your car spin out. It was expert, clean and fast."

"So the man who threatened Marcus might have been in the second car?"

"Yes. Fortunately, Huntley got a partial license plate and the make of the car."

"Good, we can—"

"Don't get your hopes up," Nicolas said. "The accident isn't high priority with police. They have enough to deal with."

Kevin swallowed his whiskey. "I can change that."

"No, it's better this way. Let them think no one's looking."

"Dominique should know about this."

"Are you sure she's not working for her father?"

"I'm sure."

Clay tapped the side of his beer glass. "Does she know you plan to marry her?" He smiled at Kevin's shocked expression. "Wait, you hadn't realized you were in love with her yet?"

Kevin opened his mouth, closed it, and hung his head, resigned. "Let's just say I've been trying to resist it."

"You might as well surrender."

He shook his head. "Not yet." He rubbed his chin. "How did you...why would you think...?"

"You're in love?" Clay finished. "Aside from the obvious, you haven't glanced at another woman the moment we came in here."

Kevin looked up and blinked. Clay was right, he hadn't noticed the wonderful array of woman of all shades and sizes in the room. "I told you it's my first time."

Nicolas nodded towards Kevin's napkin. "Just wave the white flag. There's no use fighting it."

Kevin frowned down at his glass. "You think I want to marry her?"

Clay leaned back and folded his arms. "I know you do."

Kevin stared at his empty whiskey glass. He wasn't going to ask him how he knew. "Maybe."

"Then what are you waiting for?"

Nicolas hit Clay in the arm. "What's wrong with you? You never rush a man down the aisle. He's got his freedom to think of."

Clay studied Kevin. "That's not what's bothering you though, is it?"

"No," Kevin admitted. " I have to solve a small problem."

"Problem?"

"Her mother wants to sleep with me."

Nicolas spewed out his beer; Clay stared at him and swore.

Kevin nodded gravely. "Yes, couldn't have said it better myself."

"Are you sure?" Nicolas asked, wiping his chin with a napkin.

"I was pretty sure after she tried to grab my crotch under the table."

The two men stared at him, then Clay finally said, "Before or after dinner?"

"During."

Nicolas squeezed his eyes shut and Clay swore again with more feeling.

"Dominique was sitting right in front of us," Kevin continued. "I've never hurt a woman in my life, but if given the chance I would have broken her mother's fingers."

"Are you sure it was her mother?" Nicolas asked. "Maybe it was an older sister or something."

"I can deal with a sister, I've done it before."

Nicolas's brows shot up. "You've had sisters? I've never had sisters. Did you do them at the same time or one after the other?"

Clay sent him a look. "What is wrong with you?"

"I was just asking."

Clay ran a hand over his head and sent Kevin a look of sympathy. "Bloody hell, I thought my mum was bad. She tried to get her leg over anything in trousers, but this is beyond me."

"I know women," Kevin said, "but I've never met a woman like this before."

"What does she want?" Clay wondered.

"It's obvious what she wants," Nicolas said with a laugh.

"Besides that."

Kevin's jaw tightened. "She thinks I'm using Dominique."

"So she's protecting her."

Nicolas leaned forward. "Be honest. Is her mother hot?"

"Very," Kevin said.

"If you knew you'd never get caught, would you sleep with her?"

"No."

"You're lying."

"I'm not lying. She's one of those women you don't want to mess with. If I went there, I'd want to wipe myself off."

Clay gave a low whistle. "That bad?"

Kevin nodded. "There is something very wrong with that family."

Clay patted him on the back. "I take it back. Don't even think about marrying her. She's got too much baggage for one man to deal with."

CHAPTER FORTY-NINE

She hated clothes shopping with her mother, but she wanted to be on neutral territory and shopping always put her mother in a good mood. She'd endured nearly two hours and hoped that it would be worth it. They now sat on the restaurant terrace of the store café. Outside, red ribbons encircled the lampposts, an early hint of the coming holiday season.

"This has been such a wonderful day," her mother said, sipping her iced latte. "We should do this more often."

"What were you doing at Berton's place?"

Her mother paused. Dominique waited for one of three reactions. Either a quick denial, a smooth excuse, or a blank expression of innocence. Her mother selected the latter. "I don't know—"

"I saw a purse in your closet that looked exactly like one I saw that night in Berton's house."

"Are you accusing me of something, dear?"

"Mom—"

"Women carry similar handbags all the time."

"This one was distinctive. You like one-of-a-kind pieces."

"Still, it—"

"Plus, I checked."

Carla shrugged. "Fine, I was there."

"Why?" Dominique took a deep breath. It wasn't the answer she wanted to hear, even though she'd suspected it.

Carla reached across the table and patted Dominique's hand in pity. "Do you really need specifics?"

Dominique clenched her teeth. "Yes."

"I did it for you."

"For me?"

"I test them."

Them? She'd asked about Berton, so why was she referring to 'them'? "You test them?"

"Yes," Carla said, pushing her latte to the side, "to see how faithful there are. Some women actually pay for this service, but I do it for free because I love you so much."

Anger lit Dominique's eyes and sharpened her tone. "You slept with my boyfriend—"

"Boyfriends," Carla said, stressing the 's'. "Yes, both of them. That pathetic one you dated after college and then Berton. Darling, your love life is woefully limited and—"

"Because you love me?" Dominique continued, her voice cracking in disbelief.

"Don't worry, darling, I didn't sleep with Berton until after you'd broken up. That night was just a meeting."

Dominique remembered the skirt on the ground. "I don't believe you."

Carla held up her hand in admission. "Okay, caught again."

Dominique stared at her mother, unable to comprehend her flippant behavior. "I don't understand."

"You didn't really care about him so don't pretend to be heartbroken."

"I'm disgusted."

Carla crossed her legs and flexed her foot to study the new high heels she'd just purchased. "I know. Men can be pigs."

"With you!"

Carla turned her ankle to study the side of her shoe. "Keep your voice down."

"Why? Afraid I'll embarrass you?"

Carla met her gaze. "Watch your tone. I'm still your mother."

"You're a..." Dominique shook her head at a loss for words. "I don't know what to call you."

Carla smoothed down the back of her hair. "Aren't you curious about Kevin?"

Her chest tightened almost painfully. No she wouldn't. She couldn't. "You went after Kevin?"

Carla grinned. "More like he came after me. I tried to keep him at a distant, but he insisted. His reputation suits him."

Dominique felt ill. She pictured them in the hallway, and remembered seeing Kevin releasing her hand. The look on his face when she saw them. Was it guilt? *He came after me.* No, that was wrong. That wasn't Kevin's style. She'd seen him, been with him for months. He didn't go after women. Women went after him. *He came after me.* Her sister had said something similar. And that had been a lie. Kevin wasn't like the men they knew. He wasn't a predator.

And even if she were wrong, her stomach constricted at the thought. Kevin wouldn't hurt her like this. He'd find someone else. *Are you sure?* her mind whispered. *Why would your mother lie?*

She didn't know. All she knew was that her heart screamed

that he wouldn't do this to her. "Do you trust me?" he'd asked her. And her heart screamed yes.

"I told you he wasn't worth it," Carla said, interpreting her daughter's silence as shocked acceptance.

Her mother didn't want them to be together. Why? Her father had wanted dirt on him. What made Kevin so dangerous to them? She stood up. "You're a liar."

"I did it because of your father," Carla said, a note of panic in her voice.

Dominique paused, then slowly sat back down. "What?"

"If I didn't take control of the men in your life, he would. He has. Many times. He wanted Berton to be caught so you'd fly into a rage. That's how he and Gloria were able to manipulate and control you. I was able to find out from Berton what he wanted, so I decided to be 'the other woman.' Don't you think it's better it was me than someone else?"

Was she really asking her this? "I still don't understand why."

"He never plans to let you go. He's made sure to ruin every relationship you've tried to have. He thinks that if you don't trust men, the only man you'll turn to is him. He'll never admit it, but he needs you more than you'll ever need him."

"And what about you? I know you're lying about Kevin."

"I'm not lying when I say he's not good for you."

Dominique grabbed her bags. "You're both crazy and I'm not listening to this anymore."

"You have to. There's something else you should know."

CHAPTER FIFTY

*H*e'd never heard her cry before.

Kevin gripped his phone, paralyzed as he listened to Dominique crying and apologizing on the other end. He'd been exhausted after a strenuous workout in his private gym, but now adrenaline surged through him. He didn't care about her apologies; he didn't even care what it meant. He just wanted to be with her. "Where are you?"

"I know about my mother..." The rest of her words dissolved into tears.

She knew? How did she know? And why was she apologizing? "Dominique, it's okay. Where are you?"

"I'm so ashamed."

Kevin took a deep breath. He couldn't get angry, although he was beginning to panic. It wasn't like her to cry, to sound so defeated. He softened his tone. "Baby, where are you? Tell me where you are." *Please,* he silently added. *Please turn to me. Let me be your man. Don't shut me out. That's what she wants.*

"I'm sorry," Dominique said once more and then disconnected.

Kevin called her back. His call went directly to voicemail. He texted her and received no reply, then called her again. Nothing. He threw his phone against the concrete wall and watched it smash.

Ferguson hurried into the room. "What happened?"

Kevin calmly draped his towel around his neck. "Get me a new phone with the same number." He caught Ferguson's glance at the damaged phone. "I hate dropped calls," he said then left the room to go shower. He had to think. Where would she be? Her father made her angry, but her mother could make her cry. What had that woman said to her? How could she have made Dominique ashamed of something that wasn't her fault?

Two hours had passed by the time Ferguson arrived with his new phone. Kevin dialed Dominique's number again. Nothing. He should have put a tracker on her phone.

Why wasn't she calling him back? Why was she handling this all alone? Where was she?

His landline rang. For a moment he didn't know what the sound was. People rarely used it to reach him. "Hello?"

"I need to talk to you."

He bit back a curse. He knew that voice. That catlike purr. "Where is Dominique?"

"That's what I need to know," Carla said.

Damn, that wasn't good. "What did you say to her?"

"I said too much and I shouldn't have. I need you to meet me."

"That's not going to happen."

"It will if you want to know more."

"More?"

"About my husband. Hurry. I'll be waiting."

"But—"

"Come around the back, the door will be open." She disconnected.

Kevin's first thought as he walked down the hall after entering through the back door of the Cartwright mansion, was that the house was too quiet. Of course it could be a trick, but Dominique was all that mattered. "Hello?"

Silence greeted him.

He pulled out his phone and dialed the number that Carla had used to call him. He heard her cell phone ringtone and followed the sound. He walked into a room on the far side of the hallway and saw Dominique kneeling on the ground.

He opened his mouth to say her name, but stopped when he saw blood and her mother's body.

CHAPTER FIFTY-ONE

"Did you touch anything?" Kevin asked in a sharp tone, searching the room for the weapon that had sliced Carla's throat.

Dominique looked up at him, bewildered. "No. She was like this when I got here."

"Did anyone see you?"

"No."

"Did you see anyone?"

"No."

He touched Carla's skin. It felt warm, maybe there was still a chance. He pressed a sheet against the wound then searched for a pulse. "Get out. You weren't here."

"I'm not leaving. I didn't do anything wrong, but you shouldn't be here."

He didn't have time to argue. He found a pulse, though faint. He reached for his phone to dial 911.

Dominique stopped him. "Go, I can take care of this."

"What?"

"If you stay, the police could arrest you," she said.

"On what grounds? Where's the weapon?"

"Why were you coming here through the back door?"

"She called me and I came. That doesn't make me a killer. Let me get help, if she has a chance of surviving we'd better take it."

"What do we tell the police?" Dominique asked, watching him dial.

Kevin held the phone up to his ear as it rang. "The truth."

ABRAHAM LEFT his wife's bedside and stared out the window. She would live. But it would be a few days before she could communicate with anyone. The police wanted to question her, but he knew she wouldn't have much to give. That was good. That would give him time.

His phone alerted him to a text.

YOUR WIFE IS JUST A WARNING

He deleted it. Warnings bored him. He wasn't going to change his mind.

He walked back over to Carla. She was the ugliest he'd ever seen her and she looked older too. He hoped the knife mark wouldn't leave a scar. It would bother her and he'd have to spend money on more scarves and chokers she didn't need. He touched her hand and squeezed it. She was exactly where she needed to be right now. No more complications.

He tucked his phone away and walked out of her hospital room, wondering what he needed to do.

"Why didn't you call me back?" Kevin asked Dominique hours later as they both sat in his living room. They police had their suspicions but not enough evidence to hold either of them. Although all the lights were on, the room still felt dark, as if the night had entered the room with them. He also felt cold, even with her sitting next to him. She was safe, but that didn't settle him. He felt anxious and on alert.

"I just needed time to think," she said.

"And you went to see your mother again?"

"Yes, like I said. After I spoke to you, I had more questions so I went there. I found her like that."

Dominique had told him about her confrontation with her mother after their shopping spree, but it didn't sound like it was enough to make her cry the way she had on the phone. The apology was for something bigger. Something more. Something she wasn't telling him. Why? He sighed. Now wasn't the time to pressure her. He'd be patient. "I'm glad you weren't there, because it could have been you. How are your sister and father taking this?"

"In stride. You wouldn't think anything was wrong. He's convinced it was a burglar."

"So he's not rattled?"

"Few things rattle him." Dominique fell silent, then said, "She was the woman who was with Berton that night."

Kevin frowned. "That night?"

"The night I found Berton cheating on me."

"It was your mother?"

Dominique flashed a sad smile. "You don't sound very surprised."

He drew her close, wishing she didn't feel so far away. "I'm sorry, but I met your mother, remember?"

To his relief, Dominique rested her head on his shoulder.

"I know," she said with a heavy sigh. "I'm too numb to feel anything right now. I'm glad she'll live, but I'm also angry with her at the same time."

"It still bothers me."

"What?"

"That story about how you caught Berton cheating. It was sloppy. There was no reason he should have gotten caught."

"You were right about that, he got caught on purpose. Mom said it was suggested by my father and she'd found out through Berton. If she hadn't been Berton's lover someone else would have been. My father did it to manipulate me. It seems he's done it before. I'm just a puppet."

Kevin paused, feeling a chill course through him. There it was again. That tone. That hollow, defeated tone. He didn't like it. It wasn't like Dominique. She was a fighter, but she sounded as if she'd given up.

"When's the last time you spoke to him?"

"My father?"

"No, Berton."

"Not since that night."

Kevin stroked her arm. "Tell him what you know."

Dominique looked up at him. "I don't know anything."

Yes, you do, but you're afraid to admit it. "He doesn't know that. Bluff. See what he reveals."

A tiny smile touched her mouth. "That might be good."

She sounded pleased with herself and that bothered him more. She was planning something more than just talking to Berton.

"I don't like secrets, Dominique," Kevin said. He felt her stiffen and knew he'd said the wrong words, but didn't care. "I don't think they're good in a relationship."

"But didn't you say that sometimes there are things someone shouldn't know?"

"There are things you may not want to find out, but once you know them keeping it to yourself can do more harm than good." He brushed his lips against her forehead. "I thought you said you trusted me."

"I do."

"By keeping secrets?" He released her. She stared at him, bereft, but he kept his distance determined not to comfort her. "Dominique, tell me what happened."

"I told you." She widened her eyes. "Do you think I killed my mother?"

"No," he said, unmoved by her outrage. "But you're hiding something. Is that how it's always going to be with us? Secrets and lies?"

She stood. "Maybe I should go."

"Is running your answer?"

"I'm not running."

"I've asked you to trust me, but you've never once asked me to trust you. Is it because you don't care?"

She looked at him with tears shinning in her eyes. "Why are you saying this to me? Especially now? I need you to—"

He surged to his feet, the sight of her tears making him angry. "Because I want the truth. I'm tired of trying to figure out who you are. Lies keep coming between us. Even how we met was a lie. Is anything between us even real?"

"Of course it is."

"Then how come it doesn't feel that way?"

Dominique stared at him for a long moment, but as if by a switch, the tears disappeared and her expression changed. It changed in a manner that made him realize he didn't know her as well as he'd thought. That somehow the Dominique he'd come to love had disappeared and been replaced by a stranger. "Maybe because it was never meant to."

It was when she turned to leave that he knew what he had to do. Kevin grabbed the side of his head and collapsed to the ground.

Dominique spun around and rushed to him. "What's wrong?" she demanded, kneeling at his side.

"I don't know," he said through clenched teeth. "It's my head."

"Tell me the pain level on a scale of one to ten."

"I can't."

"Okay, close your eyes and let me call Ferguson."

Kevin grabbed her hand before she could stand. When she turned to him alarmed, he smiled. "Just what I thought."

"What?"

"You scared me for a moment, but you still care, don't you?"

"That was all an act?"

"Go ahead and be angry with me, I had to know the truth. At least about you."

Dominique folded her arms. "That was a dirty trick."

He sat up, holding her gaze. "Don't you think I have a right to know that you love me?"

Her arms fell to her side. "Who says--"

Kevin shook his head and let his gaze fall. "Never mind, I just said it to tease you. I know you don't."

He could feel her gaze on him, could almost hear her thinking. Strategizing. He was doing the same. He had to be careful not to let his guard down so that she felt safe with him. She always opened up when she thought he was the most vulnerable. When she thought he needed her.

"My mother told me that my father has another business."

Yes, that's it. "Hmm."

"He's very protective of it." She hesitated.

Keep talking to me, don't stop.

"And it's very lucrative," she said.

It's okay, you can trust me.

"It may be illegal."

Good girl.

Kevin felt the tension in him ease. He hadn't lost her. She was still his and she trusted him. Carla hadn't won and her father wouldn't come between them. He'd defeated them both. Although Dominique kept talking, her words became a buzzing in his ear. His senses became more in tune with the quick rising and falling of her chest, the shadow of a strand of hair against her cheek, the deep huskiness of her voice, the scent of her skin.

It was the first time he'd seen her this vulnerable, reminding him of their first night together when she'd pretended she'd been with other men and it turned him on.

Kevin silently swore, flexing his hand. He was being a bastard. He should be listening to her. She was telling him about her father. This was important. Kevin took a deep breath then lifted his gaze to her mouth.

That was a mistake. Her mouth was even more distracting than the sight of chest. He watched her lips move, her beautiful, sweet, full lips.

"Kevin?"

His head shot up. "What?"

"Have you listened to a word I've said?"

He rubbed his chin, annoyed that he'd been caught. "No, I'm sorry," he said then kissed her as if they'd been separated for months. He felt the distance that had been creeping between them disappear. He drew back and smoothed down her hair. "I had to get that out of my system. I was scared."

Dominique blinked, confused. "Scared?"

"You scared me with that phone call and you scared me just now with the look you gave me. Now I'm feeling better." He stood up and held out his hand. "And I'm ready to listen."

Dominique stared at him stunned as he helped her up. "All this time I was talking, what were you thinking?"

Kevin led them over to the couch. "I'll show you later," he said, taking a seat. "Just start from the beginning." He winked at her. "I promise I'll make it up to you."

CHAPTER FIFTY-TWO

She was afraid to close her eyes. Dominique lay in the safe circle of Kevin's arms, afraid to move in case she woke him. But she couldn't close her eyes because when she did she saw the blood, her mother's neck wound. And in her thoughts her mother's words kept coming back to her.

Fortunately, they hadn't frightened Kevin. His expression didn't change when she told him about her father's second business: designing custom cars for an underground clientele. She hadn't been able to give him specifics, but she had been able to give him a name and contact her mother had provided. She'd told Dominique about code names for designs such as Trini-bound and African Sunshine, but wouldn't tell her what they meant.

Her mother had also told her about Berton. He was one of the key designers and expected to make it to VP within the organization. He'd hoped that by sleeping with her mother, while spying on her father, that he'd get there faster by playing her parents off each other.

"He's a greedy little man with big ideas, perfect for a man like your father," her mother had told her.

"Why are you telling me this now?" Dominique had asked her, still wanting to leave. She watched shoppers come and go while she felt her world spinning out of control.

"Because I lost control of him and he might be dangerous. Men always become that way when they get disappointed. I knew it was bound to happen when he stopped reporting to me what your father's been up to. But I overheard something you might find interesting."

"What?"

"Your father lied."

Dominique watched a little girl drop her candy bar on the ground then burst into tears when her mother picked it up and threw it away. "That's nothing new."

"About Kevin."

She felt her body go cold.

"What did he tell you about the accident?" her mother asked.

"Just tell me what you know."

"I'm saying this to protect you because...because he's no good for you."

"What do you know," Dominique repeated more deliberately.

"There was no mistake. Kevin and the woman he was with didn't get into the wrong car. They were chosen on purpose."

"Why?"

"Because Kevin knows something. He just hasn't told you."

"He doesn't know anything! His memory is gone. I know."

"Men lie."

"He hasn't lied to me."

"You want to believe that, but—"

Dominique stood. "I know it," she said, then left. If she hadn't left her, if she'd stayed, would her mother still have been attacked? If she'd returned home with her as she'd planned would her mother be okay? Or would they both have been attacked? She couldn't think of that now. She remembered her phone call to Kevin. Her heart breaking as she waited for him to pick up. She shouldn't have called him, and part of her didn't know why she had when there was nothing she could offer him.

But she had called him and as her tears fell he demanded to know where she was, she felt anger. Anger that her father continued to keep secrets.

She wanted answers. But seeing her mother on the floor had nearly broken her. Who could it have been? Berton? Her father? The man Marcus had seen?

When she told Kevin everything, she'd expected anger, questions, but after she'd shared all that she knew, he quietly said, "Are you okay, now?"

It was such an odd question. How could she be okay? "I still don't know what my father thinks you know, or who attacked my mother, if—"

"That was the wrong question. Do you feel better having told me?"

Oddly enough, she did. She felt frustrated, scared, angry, but she didn't feel alone. For the first time in her life she had someone to share her fears and burdens. She felt like her world was crumbling around her, but Kevin stayed. No other man had. Except her father. A man who wanted to be the only dominating force in her life.

Kevin hadn't allowed her to push him away. That had been her strategy so that he'd never know the truth. She didn't think he'd want to stay with her once he learned the truth. But he had. She still worried how long that would last.

"I'm scared that this is just the beginning," she told him. "That there are more awful secrets to uncover."

"I know there are, but it's going to come an end," he said then took her to his room and made love to her. Helping her to briefly forget a waking nightmare.

CHAPTER FIFTY-THREE

*S*he was stealing his love. Every day Ruth could feel it. Cassie was stealing Drake's love. All the attention he'd offered her was being taken away. She had to do something. She'd proven that she could be a better wife and mother. She didn't divide her time with work. She'd devote her life to them. She had devoted her life to them.

Ruth heard them laughing in the kitchen and felt her stomach clench.

She was supposed to make him laugh. She was supposed to make him smile. He was supposed to have his arms around her waist and hold her close.

His face had changed since Cassie's return. He looked so much more beautiful. *Because he loves her so much,* her mind reminded her.

No, she could make him that happy too. It was just gratitude. She'd finally felt she'd found a home, a place that needed her, a place to belong. She couldn't let Cassie kick her out.

She remembered her mother ironing her clothes, telling her to be good: *Be good and good things will happen to you.*

But she'd been wrong. She'd been good but that hadn't stopped her mother from dying, from her father remarrying and forgetting about her so that he could love his new family.

Didn't she matter? No. She'd been good, followed all the rules, worked hard and not once been rewarded. She'd prayed. This was her chance. She had to take action before Cassie stole all of Drake's love away.

CHAPTER FIFTY-FOUR

"Does Dominique know you're doing this?" Clay asked.

"Are you trying to be funny?" Kevin replied as the two men made their way to the nondescript building sequestered in a warehouse district in northern Maryland. The early December clouds hung low, threatening rain.

"I could have done this on my own. It's what I'm paid for. We have to be careful we don't know what we're dealing with yet."

"Right now we're dealing with cars. That's something I know and we're dealing with money. I have more than you do."

"It could get dangerous."

"Do you see me shaking?"

"It's not your kind of place."

"Ever walk into a room and see the woman you love kneeling beside her mother's body?" He nodded when Clay didn't answer. "I didn't think so. Relax."

"I am relaxed."

"You keep glancing around like a damn cop. You'll make them suspicious."

"And you don't think they'll be suspicious of you?"

"I speak their language. Money and cars."

"It may be about something else."

"Probably. I'm here to find out."

Clay narrowed his eyes. "You know something."

"Yes, I know that Cartwright doesn't like being awaken in the middle of the night by a man holding a gun to his crotch."

Clay stopped walking.

Kevin glanced over his shoulder at him. "Don't worry, I hired someone." He smiled. "You know I'm good at that."

Clay walked up to him. "What did you find out?"

"Enough to get an idea of who he's really afraid of, but there are still some puzzle pieces missing."

"Do you think he will—"

"He knows better than to touch me. Just follow my lead." Kevin walked up to the steel door and saw the intercom. He pressed the button.

"Who sent you?" a deep gritty voice said.

"Santa Claus," Kevin replied. The door opened. They stepped inside and saw a warehouse full of custom built cars. The man who approached them didn't resemble his voice. Kevin had expected a man at least Clay's height and build, but the man barely reached Kevin's shoulder and looked as if he hadn't eaten a meal in awhile.

"You here for the Ten Z?" he said.

Kevin nodded. The man lead them over to a silver Porsche. Dominique had given him the code for the customized cars, but he couldn't see the difference yet.

The buzzer rang again and the man said, "Hold on a minute." Then turned and answered.

The door opened, allowing the light to peek in, silhouetting the newcomers. Kevin felt Clay stiffen, then turn from the door.

Kevin sent him a look. "What's wrong with you?"

"My past just walked in."

Kevin turned and saw a gorgeous redhead in spiked heels with a behind as bouncy as bubblegum. He couldn't stop a smile. "She give you a lot of trouble?"

"Not her, him."

Kevin shifted his gaze to the man by her side. He had red hair too, but was at least two decades older, walking with a cane and a boot on his foot. "Oh, what did you do to him?"

"Helped put his uncle away."

"How long ago?"

"Doesn't matter, he'll remember."

"You'd better leave then, I'll find out what's going on."

"No need. I know what makes this business special." Clay made sure to keep his back turned and opened the car door to pull away the interior door frame. "Kilos of heroin, cocaine or prescription drugs can be stored here and easily retrieved. This is one of the best customizations I've seen. You can't tell from the outside that's it's been altered. Cartwright's smart. His business is in a great location. Being in one of the main cities would be too competitive. But the I-95 connection is ideal for them."

"Are these the designs Berton was helping them with?"

"Most likely."

The man returned to them. "Is everything in order?"

"We're still making sure," Kevin said, watching Clay move around to the trunk.

"Relax," the man said. "I included the bonus you requested."

Clay opened the trunk, lifted the false bottom, then paused. Kevin noticed and walked around to see what had caught Clay's attention.

"Don't worry she'll last another five hours like this," the man said. "You won't have any problems."

For a moment Kevin didn't breathe. He stared at the baby, swaddled tight so it wouldn't move or be damaged. It had been drugged so it wouldn't cry. There was space for four more or two toddlers. He'd heard whispers of a lucrative underground market available to women who wanted—or were forced—to give up their babies for profit, but he'd never expected to see it.

Clay replaced the false bottom as if the sight disgusted him.

The man noticed. "You're disappointed?"

"He was hoping for two," Kevin said.

"That would cost more."

"It's not his birthday yet."

The man laughed and Kevin paid in cash, ignoring Clay's frown.

"This is not a good idea," Clay said, getting into the passenger's seat. "You just paid for a baby."

"I paid for a car," Kevin corrected him, quickly backing out of the garage.

"With a baby in it. This could take you down."

"I can't leave the kid there," Kevin said, making his way through the warehouse district.

Clay couldn't help a smug grin. "Now who's trying to be a hero?"

The sound of police sirens interrupted Kevin's reply. Clay turned around and swore. "It's a sting."

Kevin pressed his foot on the gas. "It's not a sting."

"That's a cop car."

Kevin glanced in his rearview mirror. "Only one." He tightened his grip on the steering wheel. "And I can guarantee you a cop's not driving. Cartwright wouldn't risk involving police into his business. The profit is too great."

Clay looked back again. "It's a good mimic."

"The best ones are. They customize cars, remember? I'm sure they don't stick to just the interior."

"Think you can lose him?" Clay asked, holding onto the door as Kevin made a fast turn.

"Let's see."

For several miles it didn't look like he would. The car matched his many moves, disappearing several times only to reemerge again.

"What the hell does Cartwright want?" Clay asked. "Revenge?"

"That's not Cartwright."

"Then who--"

"The man behind it all. The man who started this mess."

"Berton?"

"No, he likely slit Carla's throat, but he's not big enough for this. " He made another sharp turn.

"If you keep driving like this the real police will be after us."

"That might work in our favor."

"Have you ever been pulled over by the police?"

"No."

"You don't want to."

"You're right." Kevin verged off a ramp then turned back towards the warehouse district that would keep them off the main roads so they wouldn't draw attention.

"Don't forget the baby," Clay said, when Kevin sped through a four-way intersection.

Kevin angrily shifted gears. He didn't need the reminder or the warning. He knew he couldn't afford to get into another crash. "I won't," he said. He knew he had a life to protect. Suddenly he remembered feeling that way before. He remembered the feeling of being chased, Cassie's question, 'What's going on?' and not being able to reply. The sensation gripped him, the question and helplessness. But it wouldn't be the same this time. He wouldn't lose control, he wouldn't panic. He turned into an empty lot and spun the car around.

"What are you doing?" Clay asked, watching the other car come at them.

"Playing chicken." He waited. He wasn't running anymore...never again. The cop car raced towards them but swerved to the left at the last minute.

Clay squeezed his eyes shut and rested his head back. "What the hell was that?"

"A warning. Did you see who was driving?"

"No."

"I did," Kevin said, putting the car in gear, "but we'll deal with that later. We need to get this baby to a hospital."

"What will you say?"

Kevin couldn't help a smile. "Don't worry. I have a way with nurses."

Clay shook his head. "Forget the nurses, we can drop off the baby—no questions asked."

CHAPTER FIFTY-FIVE

Drake drove home, trying to remember what he'd missed the most. The feel of Cassie laying beside him in bed, the smell of her papaya scented shampoo, or the sight of her with her glasses low on her nose as she sat at her laptop typing out her next book. He'd never take another moment for granted. The worse was over and he could breathe again. He hadn't gotten rid of his cigarettes yet, but he would. He hadn't smoked them, but knew the temptation would come.

He pulled to the side when he heard the sound of an ambulance in the distance; he saw it speed past.

He'd take them all away for a holiday. Marcus had started speaking and seemed as if he wouldn't stop. Telling them every aspect of his day.

He pulled down his street, the flashing lights piercing through the hazy pink of the setting sun. He stopped when he realized the ambulance was at his house. In his driveway.

He parked and jumped out of the car.

"Sir, please step back," the officer said.

"This is my house."

He saw Ericka and Julie with one of the police officers. When Ericka saw him, she broke free and ran to him. Drake lifted her up and looked at the officer who'd let him pass.

"What happened?"

"There was an incident."

"Where's my wife?"

He saw two EMTs carrying a woman on a stretcher, a knife protruding from her stomach. He rushed forward and saw Ruth.

"I'll be okay, darling," she said.

"What?" He recoiled at her touch.

He looked up and saw Cassie getting her hand bandaged.

"What happened?"

"She just came at me. I fought her and she ...she fell on the knife. She kept saying she had to defend her home."

He'd nearly lost her a second time. "Where's Marcus?"

"Thank goodness he's safe. I let Jackie take him shopping with her. She said she was going to go shopping with Dominique to get Kevin a special gift."

"I'll call her to tell her to keep him longer," he said, but when he dialed, to his surprise his call immediately went to voice mail.

CHAPTER FIFTY-SIX

"Thanks for this," Jackie said to Dominique as the two women and Marcus walked to Dominique's car in the mall parking lot. "I'm giving my brother and sister-in-law a break. Standing in line for a photo with Santa Claus takes a lot of work."

"I was surprised you invited me," Dominique said.

"I didn't, he did. He's funny that way. I told him he could come and he said could Ms. Dominique come too."

"A charmer in the making."

They packed into the car then Dominique saw Chester Lawson, the man who'd stolen her promotion. She turned her face, hoping he wouldn't see her. But he did and called out her name. She put her key in the ignition and waved. Chester came over to the car, forcing her to lower the driver side window.

He leaned against it and smiled. "A fun day to go holiday shopping."

"Yes."

"Glad to hear your mother is doing better."

"Thanks."

"Shame she can't identify who attacked her."

"Hmm."

"We're all wondering when you'll be back."

"I'm not coming back."

"Shame, things aren't the same without you. I'm sure you'll change your mind."

"Well, don't let me keep you."

He stood.

She turned and saw Marcus' eyes wide. "What's wrong, honey?"

"That's the man who hurt Mommy."

Before she could respond, Chester jumped into the back seat. "It's such a shame kids have such big mouths." He flashed the gun concealed under his coat. "Drive."

"Calm down. I know—"

"You don't know anything. You don't know who really runs your family's business. You don't know what Berton really wanted. You don't know anything. You don't know that Kevin stole the woman I love."

"I don't think—"

Chester stamped his foot. "He did! They want me to forget what I saw, but I didn't. I saw them together. She was showing him something on her phone and they were close. Then they were laughing. Laughing at me. I knew she was seeing someone else. She was using me and I wasn't going to be used."

He tapped his forehead with the butt of the gun. "I just wanted to talk to her. She wouldn't answer my calls, my texts, tried to shut me out. I wasn't going to be shut out that day. When I saw him get in the car with her... I knew I had to make her see me. I had to let her know she couldn't treat me that way. I wasn't going to let them get away with humiliating me. I had to get her to talk to me. I had to force their car off the road. And when I got up close to the car I just shot at the car to scare her."

Chester took a deep breath. "But he tricked me. When I wasn't looking he'd gotten into a car with another woman. He pulled the old bait and switch, making me hurt the wrong woman. Giving my woman a chance to disappear just like her father did."

"Her father?"

"Avery."

"You were dating Avery's daughter?"

"It was her idea for me to get a job at Cartwright. But I soon discovered that the rivalry was just a sham. They were thick as thieves making dirty money with the underground custom cars. I threatened to blow a hole in his operation if Cartwright didn't help me find out where she was. He knows how valuable I am."

"You're lucky he didn't kill you."

"Your father doesn't like bodies. That's his weakness and I used it. I wanted to know where Kevin was hiding my woman. We tried using a professional who'd left a bugged earring in his place after a party, but that didn't work. That's when he thought of using you. I was impressed. You were the closest to get Jackson to open up. But the bastard conveniently forgot everything after the accident. I guess he got the last laugh again, huh?"

Dominique searched her mind remembering the day she'd lost the promotion. She'd misinterpreted Chester's expression. He hadn't been uncomfortable by the tension in the room, he'd been in pain even weeks after the accident.

"That's enough talking." He pointed the gun at Jackie. "Now drive."

Dominique pretended to reach for the ignition then pressed the button for her seat and sent it flying back, knocking the gun from his hand. Jackie grabbed the gun before he got his bearings and pointed it at him. "No, you haven't finished talking," Dominique said. "The police will want to hear more."

CHAPTER FIFTY-SEVEN

"My father is involved with smuggling?" Dominique asked as she and Kevin sat in Clay and Jackie's living room.

"No, his boss," Clay said. "Margot Bobkins."

"What?" Dominique thought of the overlooked nondescript older woman who'd worked for Cartwright Cars for years.

"Yes, we saw her as she sped past us," Kevin said. "Your father confirmed it."

"She's been a known underground powerhouse for more than thirty years" Clay said. "She helped set your father and Avery up with the smuggling trade and promised that one of them would take over one day. Chester and Berton didn't make your father nervous, she did. Three things went wrong for him. First, Chester. His obsessive love really set things into motion. You were supposed to get the promotion, but your father had hoped by giving him a higher position he'd be satisfied. He wasn't."

"While waiting for the car I had ordered, I vaguely remember talking to a woman that day," Kevin said.

Jackie shook her head in pity. "When it comes to women, you just can't resist, can you?"

Kevin shrugged unapologetically. "She looked unhappy and I wanted to make her smile. I saw Avery's picture on her phone. My memory was wrong when I thought I'd seen him in person. Anyway, we chatted and I made her laugh, then left."

"But how did Cassie get shot?" Clay asked.

"Chester did that," Dominique said. "He shot through the back of the car to scare her. Then when he saw she wasn't Avery's daughter, he realized his mistake and gave Marcus the warning."

Clay looked at Kevin. "But why did *he* make them nervous?"

"They thought Avery's daughter had told him something about their other business. She disappeared after the meeting and they wanted to know where she was. It soon became clear that Kevin didn't know anything. When her father disappeared and then showed up in Mexico with her, they had their answer."

"And Margot was getting greedy," Kevin said. "Your father didn't mind using the second business to transfer drugs, but human smuggling was something else. He was getting in too deep and somehow your mother knew it. She was going to tell you about it."

"Margot stopped her?" Dominique guessed.

"Yes. They're looking for her now."

"You said there were three things. What were the other two?"

Clay grinned. "You and Kevin."

Dominique held her head. "I don't know if I can take any more surprises."

"Well, here's just one more surprise," Jackie said.

Dominique lifted her head weary. "What?"

"Cassie's invited you both over for a Henson dinner."

KEVIN WASN'T NERVOUS, but she was. She was still trying to come to terms with all the changes in her life. Her father was singing like a canary. He'd received full immunity and asked to be put into Witness Protection given the scope of the enterprise. Her mother filed for an expedited divorce and planned to move with her sister to California. Now Dominique would finally meet Cassie.

What would it be like to meet her? How would Kevin feel? How would he behave? What about the others? Dominique quickly got her answer when Drake opened the door and welcomed them inside a home expertly decorated for the holidays. He took her coat. "Sorry for this."

"For what?" she said.

He bent her backwards and kissed her fully on the mouth. "For that," he said, lifting her back up. He sent Kevin a significant look. "Even?"

Before Kevin could reply or Dominique could recover, Cassie rushed forward and gave him a hug. "So glad you both could make it." She hugged Dominique too. "Come in. Can I get you something to drink?"

Soon Dominique was wrapped in the aromatic scent of jerk chicken and red beans and rice. She saw Kevin charm Cassie, Adriana and Jackie, getting a kiss on the cheek from each. Dominique could see why Cassie was so beloved and why Kevin had fallen for her. Lena had been right. If Cassie hadn't been so clueless, you could hate her. But she was oblivious to her effect on others. She didn't see how much she shone, and that was part of her charm.

At the table the Hensons good-naturedly teased each other, filling the house with laughter to heal the pain of the past year.

"I knew there was something wrong with that woman," Eric said, bringing up the subject of Ruth. "I wish I'd done something more."

"We all do," Adriana said. "Don't blame yourself."

"She's disturbed," Jackie said. "At least she's being evaluated."

Cassie set her fork down. "She seemed so sweet. She wasn't like that before."

"Perhaps if you hadn't had the accident, she'd be okay. She really thought she could take your place."

"I actually saw her in a dress exactly like yours," Kevin said.

Clay shook his head. "Poor cow."

Cassie playfully hit him. "Don't say things like that."

His brows shot up. "Should I call her a daft bugger instead?"

Drake sighed. "To think I left her alone with our children."

"At least she didn't harm them," Eric said.

"Did she try to slip into bed with you?" Kevin asked.

Drake sent him a look. "Of course she didn't," he said in a low voice.

Kevin shrugged. "You never know."

Jackie clasped her hands together before Drake could respond. "Thank goodness she's gone."

"And we're all here together again," Adriana said.

"Yes, it was a long time coming."

Cassie looked around the table. "You know I love you all very much."

"What's with the mushy talk?" Eric said. "Are you trying to embarrass our guests?"

"I'm including them too."

Kevin grinned. "Don't worry, Cassie, I know how much you love me." He winked at her. "And you know I love you too."

"Does Dominique know how much?" Drake said.

Silence fell like a lead balloon.

Dominique was the first one to speak. "Yes and it's okay. I know I'm not—"

"Ignore him," Jackie said. "My brother has the manners of a thug."

"That's actually how they met," Adriana added. She sent Drake a hard look. "Cassie had to teach him some manners."

Eric adjusted his glasses. "Too bad you quit smoking," he said with a grin. "Bet you could use one right now."

Drake took a sip of juice, realizing his blunder. He'd been so focused on getting at Kevin, he'd neglected Dominique's feelings. "I'm sorry. I didn't mean it that way."

"Yes, you did," Kevin said.

"Let it go," Clay warned.

"Why? Since my feelings are an open secret let's talk about it."

Dominique pushed her chair back. "Perhaps I should go."

"No!" the women said in unison.

Cassie looked at Drake and Kevin. "What is wrong with you two?"

"There's nothing wrong with them," Dominique said with a sad smile. "They're just both in love with you."

Cassie blinked. "What?"

Dominique stood. "Now I really think I should go."

Kevin stood also, taking her hand. "You're not going anywhere."

"Please don't shame me in front of them," she whispered, her eyes pleading.

Kevin held onto her hand and glared at Drake. "You're wrong, Dominique. There's only one man who loves Cassie like that." He turned to her and his voice and gaze softened. "The other man loves you. That man won't pretend he didn't love somebody else, but you helped him forget her. Now his heart is absolutely and completely yours."

Dominique smiled, her heart healing from a lifetime of pain. She leaned forward and whispered, "I'd kiss you, but everyone's watching."

Kevin turned to the table. "Everyone, close your eyes."

Dominique laughed and soon he kissed her laughter away.

ABOUT THE AUTHOR

Dara Girard, an award-winning, national bestselling author of more than forty novels, from romance to suspense, loves telling stories.

Born in the US to immigrant parents, Dara enjoys pulling from her Jamaican, British, Nigerian heritage and exposure to various cultures to bring what reviewers and fans call "vivid emotional stories" to life. She is best known for her popular Henson Series, the mysterious Clifton Sisters, and the fun Black Stockings Society.

You can write her at:
contactdara@daragirard.com
or
P.O. Box 10345
Silver Spring, MD 20914
If you'd like to receive a reply, please send a self-addressed stamped envelope.

Visit her website to sign up for her newsletter and get sneak peeks, monthly updates on new releases, and special offers.

For more information visit
www.daragirard.com

NATIONAL BESTSELLING AUTHOR

DARA GIRARD

Careless Rapture

A Henson Series Novel